UNMENTIONABLES

UNMENTIONABLES

BY LAURIE LOEWENSTEIN

KAYLIE JONES BOOKS

Published by Akashic Books
©2014 Laurie Loewenstein

Back cover illustrations from *The Completeness of Spirella Service*, The Spirella Company, Inc., 1924, courtesy of Wikimedia Commons.

ISBN-13: 978-1-61775-194-3
Library of Congress Control Number: 2013938804

First printing

Kaylie Jones Books
c/o Akashic Books
PO Box 1456
New York, NY 10009
info@akashicbooks.com
www.akashicbooks.com

For Kaylie

and in memory of my parents,
Gordon J. Loewenstein and Darlos Coplan Loewenstein,
fourth-generation Midwesterners

At least we can begin with the invisibilities
and reform ourselves from within . . .
If we succeed . . . the rest will follow.

—Rational Dress Society's Gazette, *April 1888*

PART I

C HAPTER ONE
BROWN CANVAS

THE BREEZES OF MACOMB COUNTY usually journeyed from the west, blowing past and moving quickly onward, for the county was just en route, not a final destination. On this particular night, the wind gusted inexplicably from the east, rushing over fields of bluestem grasses, which bent their seed heads like so many royal subjects. A queen on progress, the currents then traveled above farmhouses barely visible behind the tasseled corn, and swept down the deeply shaded streets of Emporia, where they finally reached the great tent, inflating the canvas walls with a transforming breath from the wider world.

The farm wives had staked out choice spots under the brown canvas; an area clear of poles but not far from the open flaps where they might feel the strong breeze that relieved the oppressiveness of the muggy August evening. The ladies occupied themselves with their knitting needles or watched the crew assembling music stands. Some fretted about sons, already drafted for the European trouble and awaiting assignment to cantonments scattered across the country. They pushed back thoughts of the steaming canning vats they faced when the weeklong Chautauqua assembly of 1917 concluded. All they would have to get through another dreary winter were the memories of the soprano's gown of billowing chiffon; the lecturer's edifying words; the orchestras and quartets.

The strings of bare bulbs that swagged the pitched roof were suddenly switched on. The scattered greetings of "Howdy-do" and "Evening" grew steadily as the crowd gathered, burdened with seat cushions, palmetto fans, and white handkerchiefs. Leafing through the souvenir program, they scrutinized the head-and-shoulders photograph of the evening's speaker, a handsome woman wearing a rope of pearls. She was described as a well-known author, advocate for wholesome living, and suffragist. What exactly was this lecture—"Barriers to the Betterment of Women"—about? Some expected a call for more female colleges, others for voting rights.

Then Marian Elliot Adams, a tall and striking woman in her early thirties, swept onto the stage. She wore a rippling striped silk caftan and red Moroccan sandals. With dark eyes and dramatically curved brows, her appearance hinted at the exotic. In ringing tones, she announced, "I am here tonight to discuss the restrictive nature of women's undergarments."

Hundreds of heads snapped back. The murmurs of the crowd, the creaking of the wooden chairs, stopped abruptly. Even the bunting festooning the stage hung motionless, as if it had the breath knocked out of it.

Marian's gaze swept across the pinched faces, assessing the souls spread before her, and she concluded that they were the same people she'd been lecturing to for the past three months. There was the gaunt-cheeked elder with his chin propped on a cane; the matron with the bolster-shaped bosom; the banker type in a sack coat; the slouching clerk with dingy cuffs. Just like last night and the night before that, stretching back eighty-three straight nights—these strangers she knew so well.

She'd begun her odyssey on June 1, as she had for the last seven summers, driving a dusty Packard to villages across Ohio, Indiana, and Illinois, opening each town's weeklong series of talks and entertainments, and then moving on. In her wake followed orchestras, elocutionists, adventurers, sextets, chalk artists—whatever the Prairieland Chautauqua Agency felt would meet the standards of improvement and inspiration demanded by each hamlet's subscription committee. Marian was relieved she didn't have to stick around and watch the hodgepodge of entertainers following her. She and her fellow orators, she often said with a hint of irony, were the only ones true to the original Chautauqua ideal. During her brief respites from the road, she'd often settle in at her favorite Greenwich Village tea house and laughingly query fellow patrons, "Would you believe it? Me, an agnostic since the tender age of ten, toiling for Chautauqua?"

A half-century before, a group of Methodists had erected open-air pavilions beside the placid waters of Lake Chautauqua in western New York, as an educational retreat for Sunday school teachers. From "Mother Chautauqua," as the institution became affectionately known, reading courses for adults quickly sprang up across the country. Later, commercialized ventures known as Tent or Circuit Chautauquas, and connected to the original in name only, took up the cause of bringing edification and culture to the rural heartland. Circuit Chautauquas, organized by Prairieland and other booking agencies, moved from town to town, following an established itinerary. When traced on a map, the various circuits looked like a child's connect-the-dots drawing, linking isolated hamlets and farming communities in the Midwest, South, and West. An easterner, Marian saw the circuit as an opportunity to bring modern thinking on women's causes to Middle America's backwaters. This night, as she launched into her talk, she took comfort in knowing that more than five hundred other Chautauqua lecturers were mounting platforms in five hundred other byways.

She smiled broadly and asked, "Why is dress reform so necessary for the modern woman?"

The audience members, recovered from their initial shock, took up their palmetto fans, repositioned their legs, and settled in.

"Because clothing constitutes both a real and symbolic hindrance to women taking their rightful place in our country's civic, occupational, and educational realms. Did you know that a woman, preparing to go out in public, routinely dons twenty-five pounds of clothing? Twenty-five pounds. Imagine! And of that, almost all of it is hidden from view. And almost all of it serves no practical purpose. Beneath every dainty shirtwaist and skirt lie layer upon layer of restrictive undergarments."

She counted them off on her fingers. "Combination suit, petticoat, corset, corset cover, hose supporter, hose. These are the unmentionables that every woman struggles against. These are the invisibilities that drag down her limbs, sap her energy, prevent her from full participation in community life. Yes, we have made some strides in the last forty years. The hourglass figure, the tight lacings are, mercifully, things of the past. But more must be done."

As she spoke, Marian paced briskly across the stage,

her caftan gracefully shifting in the current. Some of the men wondered just what sort of unmentionables Mrs. Elliot Adams had on under the silk that swirled around her well-proportioned limbs. Deuce Garland, a widower of two years and publisher of the *Clarion,* was among them. He balanced a notebook on his calf, pencil resting on a blank page. In times past, he'd have written half of his article before the lecturer even stepped on stage. *Chautauqua opened in Emporia with a bang last evening when three thousand citizens of all ages gave a rousing welcome to* . . . That was what came of sixteen years publishing a small-town daily with modest ambitions and a mission of boosterism.

But two months ago, seven of the town's infants had succumbed to typhoid within three weeks. These deaths, very likely due to that age-old culprit, adulterated milk, shook Deuce to the core. As a boy, he'd lost two sisters to the same illness, and had never gotten over it. That same week he'd come upon an editorial in the *Springfield Times* calling for regular inspections of dairy operations. His first thought had been, I've got to reprint this! But then, he'd hesitated. He'd thought of his advertisers—the local shop owners, some with family ties to dairy farms. The subscribers, many who worshipped alongside those same hard-working men and women, the backbone of America. He couldn't afford to anger them. Once he'd paid off the new linotype, he'd be in a better position to weather a dip in revenue. Then he could turn the *Clarion* into what he'd imagined it might become when he'd first bought it—a daily that would change Emporia for the better. Even if he wasn't quite ready to make the big leap, he'd decided to at least take seriously every story he did print. No more boilerplate. Still, the typhoid, the unprinted editorial, hung at the back of his mind.

Deuce leaned forward to better hear each word of the speech. Marian's sonorous voice was being partially obscured by phlegmy hacking from outside the tent, from one of the houses that bordered the grassy Chautauqua grounds. Deuce's stepdaughter, Helen, seated beside him, heard it too and turned with an annoyed glance. Just nineteen, she was in the full flush of young womanhood, with solemn eyes, milky skin, and sleek wings of brown hair tucked behind her ears. He admired her in silence, self-consciously running a hand across his own hair that, despite the heavy application of pomade, had returned to its tight waves. He removed the handkerchief from a breast pocket and wiped his sticky palms. The carefully balanced notebook fell to the grass. Grunting, he bent to pick it up, then rearranged his legs, the wooden chair creaking beneath him.

Helen shot him a reproving look. Angrily flicking the program in front of her face, she turned her attention back to the stage. She'd been waiting for months for Mrs. Elliot Adams and wasn't about to let him spoil it with all this fidgeting. Who knew when she'd have another chance to hear a famous advocate for women's rights? Not in the foreseeable future, not in this pokey town. The acetate footlights bathed Marian from below, illuminating the folds of the caftan, the firm chin, the strong nose and brows, the clear eyes. Why, Mrs. Elliot Adams is the Statue of Liberty come to life, Helen thought with a grin. Come to life right here in Emporia.

Marian was saying, "How can a young woman weighed down with all these undergarments, not to mention long skirts, perform a day's work in an office, mill, or shop? How can she participate in the healthful activities of bicycling, tennis, dance, swimming? How can she fully join in the civic life of the community? She can't. Women's dress restricts their arms, their legs, *and* their opportunities."

There was some murmuring among the knitters near the open tent flaps on the far left. Without even looking, Marian knew these were farm wives.

"Now let me quickly add that what I am talking about is *public* dress. I am well aware that many of you women in the farmland perform demanding physical labor and that the reliable Mother Hubbard is quite serviceable, if not as aesthetically pleasing or designed for ease of movement as it might be. As is, for example, this garment I am wearing. This free-flowing gown is functional, healthy, and, so I have been told, flattering."

Three matrons sucked in their breath as they and the town realized that Marian's gown was not a costume but her daily wear. Many of Chautauqua's lecturers and performers dressed in a manner that amplified their message. The Dickens Man appeared in a Victorian frock coat as he enacted *Oliver Twist*, adding a shawl for poor Nancy, a cloth cap for Oliver, and a cape for wicked Bill Sykes. Each August, a Polynesian family appeared in grass skirts and feathered cloaks, mesmerizing listeners with their strange songs and tales of conversion from savagery to Christianity. Now Marian seemed to transform before their eyes, from the lofty and somewhat daring embodiment of social reformer, to the murky role of the outlandish.

The air in the tent was oppressive and thunder rumbled in the distance. Marian could feel sweat trickling between her breasts, dampening the bust supporter and her nainsook drawers. The extreme heat that gathered under the Chautauqua tents was as famous as their trademark brown canvas walls. "Going down the line," as the Chautauqua performers called it, was not for the faint of heart or physically frail. Marian had witnessed dozens of first-timers, delicate sopranos, even robust orators, collapse after twenty consecutive nights of appearances under the sweltering canvas, in tandem with twenty days of jolting travel on gritty trains or in dusty open motorcars. As she patted her brow with a folded hankie, she again gave thanks for her strong constitution. One summer, she'd followed William Jennings Bryan, the living embodiment of Circuit Chautauqua, down the line. The celebrated orator, former congressman, and secretary of state, was known as "The Great Commoner" for his populist stands on the goodness of the ordinary man. Besides his "Cross of Gold" speech, Bryan was famous for his endurance, sometimes giving three lectures a day in three different towns as his shapeless alpaca coat became increasingly sodden, hanging like wet burlap from his large frame. And she had triumphantly matched him step for step. For Marian, like Bryan, it wasn't just a matter of physical stamina but dedication to a cause. If she didn't bring the message of dress reform to Emporia, to all the other flyspecks on the circuit, how would these women ever enter the modern age? From the back row a baby launched into full-throated bawling, as piercing as a factory whistle. And that's another reason I'm meant for this, Marian thought, no husband, no children to tie me down or pull me off the road. She had divorced years ago and never looked back.

    Harsh coughing sounded faintly from beyond the

tent, competing with the howling infant. For most in the audience, accustomed to such disturbances, the sounds barely registered, but Tula Lake, who was sitting on the other side of Deuce, immediately recognized the consumptive cough of sixteen-year-old Jeannette Bellman. The Bellman family lived on the far side of the grounds. Tula turned in her seat. The tent was packed, the crowd overflowing beyond the flaps.

"Have you seen Dr. Jack? I'm worried about Jeannette," she whispered to Deuce.

Deuce glanced up from his notebook. The moons of Tula's blue irises were clouded with worry. "I heard her too."

Tula's features were still pretty but now blurred with age. Deuce, Tula, and her brother Clay had lived next door to one another for sixteen years. As Deuce turned back to the stage, Tula kept her ears focused outside the tent flaps. After a couple of minutes, the coughing fit passed. Thank goodness, Tula thought. Sitting back, she picked up the lecturer's train of thought. Still, she was only half-listening. Her eyes were on Deuce, whose dark brows contrasted so handsomely with the wavy sterling-silver hair. Just above his collar a dusting of talcum glowed white against his coppery skin. At last she turned back to the stage, giving Mrs. Elliot Adams, who seemed to be explaining how she became such a staunch advocate for dress reform, her full attention.

". . . of women's dress, undergarments in particular, is a matter not only of limitation, but also of life itself. With corsets and other bindings restricting the rib cage, it is impossible to draw in sufficient breath. My own dreadful experience with consumption taught me that. I cured myself by casting aside my corset and bringing fresh, cleansing air into my lungs day and night. For more than a year I slept outside under the stars as my lungs opened and healed."

Another growl of thunder sounded from out on the flat prairie. The audience rustled like a roost of startled sparrows but settled quickly. Marian didn't pause. She'd lectured through storms that hurled hailstones so large they ripped holes in the tent while the spectators sat without flinching. These sons and daughters of pioneers waited all year for Chautauqua week and almost nothing could dislodge them. A good heavy rain would at least cool things off. This time of the evening, halfway into the program, her toes were roasting in the footlights. She'd thought of The Great Commoner's system—chilling one hand on a block of ice before stroking his brow while beating the air with a palm fan in his other. He kept this double-handed routine up for his entire hour-long speech. Maybe I should try that, she thought.

While her mind considered this, her voice continued, "Like the young Theodore Roosevelt, I was determined to seize control of my destiny."

At this, the venerable Henry Wilson, several chairs down from Deuce, leaned across the laps of three matrons to catch the publisher's eye. "The gall; putting herself alongside TR!" he hissed. A spout of tobacco juice arced onto the ground for emphasis and the seventy-four-year-old member of three secret societies and honorary president of the Young Ragtags, a loose outfit organized around drinking and the swinging of Indian clubs, stood up and stomped out.

Deuce's eyes darted to his father-in-law, seated on the

other side of Helen. Had he heard what Wilson said? Father Knapp's attention was directed at his nails, which he was cleaning with a matchstick. The president of Western Illinois Savings and Loan didn't go in for oratory, light opera, or other cultural affectations, he'd told Deuce privately, but backed Chautauqua every year because "every up-and-coming town has to have one." Flicking the match to the ground, Father Knapp patted Helen's knee absently as if she were—and Deuce's gut clinched at this thought—one of his top-dollar springer spaniels.

Over the heads of the audience, Marian's voice rushed on. It traveled out into the night, across the Chautauqua grounds, to the ears of Jeannette Bellman, bundled in a wicker settee on the family's front porch. Hugging her knees to her chest, the girl smiled. The great oval tent glowing softly in the distance, the voice of the speaker, even the flashes of lightning illuminating the horizon, all seemed to be speaking directly to her.

Applause, signaling the end of the program, rippled out of the tent flaps, followed quickly by the cranking of one or two motor cars, as several patrons ducked out early to beat the rain.

On stage, Marian bowed deeply from the waist so that her clasped hands brushed her knees. Deuce, who had tucked his notebook under his arm to free his hands for clapping, pulled it out to make a few more notes. Beside him, Helen vigorously beat her hands together. The platform manager, a nervous fellow in brightly bleached white duck trousers, took the stairs to the stage two at a time, all the while shouting, "Let me remind you, ladies and gentlemen, that tomorrow's schedule includes an afternoon concert by the Chicago Lady Entertainers and, in the evening, a stupendous performance by the Mystic Entertainer! Many of you were wise enough to purchase subscription tickets but for those who were not, there are a few, but only a few, single tickets available!"

The crowd rose. A young man stood up and whooped, swinging himself around a tent pole. Women shook out their skirts and gathered their fans, knitting bags, and seat cushions. The men reset boaters and adjusted suspenders. Helen, who had continued clapping long after everyone else, brushed past Deuce and pushed her way to the stage. Marian was starting to descend the stairs off to one side when Helen called out excitedly, "You were marvelous!"

Marian paused. "Why, thank you."

"There are so many women that need to hear your message."

Marian smiled, stepped back onto the stage. "Yes! Exactly."

"Especially in Emporia; it's so backward!" Helen threw up her hands.

"I'm finding that in many Midwestern towns," Marian said as she strode toward Helen, her sandals clacking against her heels.

Marian was lowering into a crouch so that she could speak directly to the girl when her tunic caught on a loose nail. She yanked the hem, throwing herself off balance, and stumbled forward—headlong off the platform. Flailing wildly, her legs flew up and over. Her left ankle smacked sharply against a folding chair and her tailbone thudded against the trampled grass. She crashed in a heap at Helen's feet.

"Oh my goodness! Are you all right?" Helen cried,

dropping beside Marian, who was unnaturally still. "Mrs. Elliot Adams? Criminy!" Helen jumped up. "Papa, help!" she yelled at the familiar boater moving down the aisle among the dwindling crowd.

Several heads turned. Alvin Harp, owner of Emporia's garage, and Mrs. Flynn, the druggist's wife, rushed over, followed by Deuce and Tula. A boy in knickers materialized beside Helen.

"She fell!" Helen said.

"Someone get water!" Mrs. Flynn shouted.

"Helen, are you all . . ." Deuce began as he joined the cluster, then spotted Marian's face contorted in pain. He knelt and picked up her limp hand. She moaned, her eyelids fluttered. "Someone find Dr. Jack. You, go," he said, pointing to the knickered youth. "If he's not around, check the Bellmans'."

"Here, let's make her more comfortable," Tula said, snatching a floral cushion from a nearby seat and tucking it under Marian's head.

"Get this chair out from under her," Alvin said. "Raise that leg up some."

Deuce gently wedged his hands under Marian's thigh. Her eyelids jerked open like tightly sprung window shades and she yelped in pain. Alvin pulled aside the shattered wood.

"Hold on there," Deuce said. "The doctor's on his way."

Mrs. Flynn wrung her hands, all the while shouting, "Where's that water? We need water here!"

Grabbing a fan from an onlooker, Helen flapped it erratically above the lecturer's shiny brow. A panting youth from the crew appeared at the edge of the stage holding aloft a pitcher of water.

"What's happened?" Dr. Jack asked, stepping into the circle and fluidly dropping his black satchel.

Helen spoke: "Her hem caught on something. Then, boom, right off the edge."

"Hit her head?" He crouched beside Marian, whose eyes were again tightly shut.

"I don't think so," Helen said, her voice quivering.

Tula took up the young woman's hand, whispering, "It's all right."

"It's my right foot," Marian said in a loud voice, opening her eyes. "It hurts like hell."

"All right," Dr. Jack replied mildly. "Let's start there." Folding the gown back, he gently pressed his fingers down the length of her tibia. "Does this hurt?"

Deuce modestly looked away during the examination. Dr. Jack reached Marian's ankle and when he pressed down she howled in pain.

"Hmm," he said, nodding slightly.

Marian, who had raised her head to follow the course of the examination, asked, "What exactly does that mean?"

"Did that hurt?" he asked.

"Of course it hurt—I wouldn't be bellowing if it didn't," she said.

"How about this?" Dr. Jack cupped her heel and slowly rotated the foot.

Marian clenched her teeth, her eyes moistening. "Yes."

"Hmm." Dr. Jack pushed back a sickle-shaped hank of hair.

Marian's tone was panicked. "Is it broken? Do you think it's broken? It can't be. It can't."

"Well, I'm not certain it is broken, it might—"

"I'm booked for Galesburg tomorrow. I have to be

there. You'll just have to wrap it up or splint it or something. I'll manage."

Dr. Jack smoothed her gown and stood.

"I think it's broken but it could be just a bad sprain. You'll have to give it a day or two to see if the swelling goes down. Where are you staying?"

Darius Calhoun, the platform manager, wormed into the circle. "She can't stay a day or two. Didn't you hear the woman? She's due in Galesburg," he said, his small body quivering so that, with white pants and tufted eyebrows, he gave the impression of a fox terrier. "Then the day after that it's Blanchester and then . . ." he pulled a creased schedule from his pocket. "And then Vernon."

"At the very least this woman has a bad sprain and possibly a break," Dr. Jack said. "Can't one of the other lecturers with your group step in for her?"

"No. That's not how it works. Mrs. Elliot Adams is a First Day. She's always a First Day. The supervisor who is setting up the tent in Galesburg will be mighty upset if his opening act is stuck here."

Dr. Jack shook his head. "I'm sorry but I'm prescribing rest tonight. I'll check it in the morning. If the swelling has—"

From the ground, Marian shouted up, "I'm booked! This isn't possible. I'm booked!"

"She's staying at the Lamoine," Tula said. "All the performers stay there."

"Yes, yes, but . . ." the platform manager was saying.

Dr. Jack shook his head. "She's got to have someone looking after her, keeping her off that foot."

"I don't need anyone—" Marian started, but Tula interrupted.

"She can stay with me. We have a sleeping porch off the kitchen with a day bed."

"Fine," Dr. Jack said, dusting off his knees. "Thank you."

Mrs. Flynn grabbed Tula's arm. "But what about the welcome reception at the refreshment tent? The ladies are all set up."

"You'll have to tell them there's been an accident."

And so Marian, still protesting, was lifted onto a stretcher by four of the strongest stage hands, shoveled into the back of Mueller Florist's delivery truck which, fortuitously, was parked nearby, and transported down several bumpy streets, with the little platform manager trotting nervously behind.

After receiving the bad news from Mrs. Flynn, the members of the Ladies Welcome Committee despondently dumped the galvanized tub of ice and reclaimed their cakes that, in the heat, had slumped to one side like elderly choir members during a long sermon. As the ladies left the grounds, the first coin-sized drops began to fall. The thunderstorm, so long threatening, had arrived.

CHAPTER TWO
SIGNS AND SYMBOLS

THE NEXT MORNING, DEUCE WOKE to the buzzy rattle of the alarm clock. He reached across to turn it off. For the past two years, during sleep, the memory of his wife Winnie's passing would somehow be erased from his mind, and the empty space beside him was always a shock in the dawn's light. But this morning, even before he opened his eyes, he knew that she was not there.

For a few minutes he sat dull-eyed on the edge of the bed, his mind wooled in sleep. Absently, he thumped his feet against the rag rug and rubbed his knees. Below the open window, the floorboards were wet where it had rained in.

He switched off the rotating fan and shuffled to the bathroom. Even at this hour, the air was stuffy. A wrinkled sash hung from the newel post. In the bathroom, the mat was soggy. A hairpin stuck to the damp skin of his heel. Helen must have been running late for work.

As he dabbed shaving soap to his cheeks, Deuce thought of Helen's graduation day. It had been stifling on that day too. Helen had led her class across the lawn, up the aisle between rows of applauding families, and onto the bunting-draped outdoor dais. As valedictorian, she had taken her seat in the first row at the front of the stage, Deuce watching with amusement as her foot jiggled impatiently through Reverend Sieve's invocation, Miss Thayer's salutation, and the class history. Then it was her turn at the podium.

She had begun in the accepted manner, with references to "life's path," "beginnings, not endings," and "realizing our possibilities." She carried on for a good ten minutes in this fashion before veering abruptly into virgin territory. Deuce had straightened, suddenly alert.

"But these really are just platitudes, at least for the female members of our graduating class who are still denied full participation as citizens, as workers, even as we step forward to aid our nation in a time of war. Yes, we are fortunate to live in Illinois, a state where women have at least been granted limited voting rights, but none of us can earn a wage equal to a man's, or enter into marriage on equal footing."

A gust tossed the blue and yellow bunting. Miss Thayer and several of the young ladies clamped their hats to their heads. Hatless and unheeding, Helen continued.

"That is why tomorrow, when the 7:20 for Chicago pulls out, I'll be boarding it. The suffrage movement needs soldiers too, and I intend to join up. And I challenge each of the members of our class to join with me and journey out into the wider world."

Abruptly, she took her seat. Father Knapp gripped Deuce's arm.

"What the hell is she talking about?" he asked, in a barely controlled whisper. "Did you know about this?"

Deuce's mouth went dry. All spring Helen had chattered on about the Chicago Women's Political Equality League, the city's abundance of jobs for women, its profusion of respectable rooming houses. He knew she was going to go sometime, but he didn't think she'd be leaving so soon.

"Well?" the old man tightened his grip. Reverend Sieve, head bowed, was muttering the benediction.

"She's talked about it some," Deuce said. "I didn't take it seriously."

"There is no way in hell she's going," Father Knapp growled.

"No, of course not."

Helen rushed up to the two men, cheeks and eyes radiant. "How did I do?"

Deuce quickly turned away from his father-in-law. "You were wonderful, sweetie." He wrapped his arms around her. "Great day."

Helen laughed, pulled back, and gave Father Knapp a solemn peck on the cheek. His expression was as stiff as his old-fashioned collar. She glanced at Deuce with raised brows.

"Your grandfather—"

Father Knapp interrupted. "There is no way in hell you're going to Chicago."

"But—"

"And you did nothing but embarrass yourself up there." He flung his hand toward the stage. "Disgraced me too, *and* the memory of your mother."

When her grandfather mentioned Winnie, Helen's cheeks paled. The old man had struck a nerve. Although outspoken, Helen's vulnerability lay in wanting to live up to Winnie's aspirations for her. The old man knew this and, in the two years since Winnie's death, used his late daughter's memory to manipulate his granddaughter.

Deuce hated him for this. From the day he'd exchanged vows with Winnie, with a somber two-year-old Helen looking on, the old man had done nothing but stage manage every part of their lives.

"Look, it's too soon. Come work at the *Clarion* for a year, just like we discussed. Then the three of us can sit down and, you know, reconsider, and then . . ."

Helen glared directly into Deuce's eyes. "That's the kind of thing you always say. You're always compromising. You go along with everybody. Well, sometimes that doesn't work. You have to take a side."

She turned and stomped off across the wide lawn, her graduation gown billowing behind her.

Deuce started to follow but Father Knapp pulled him back. "Let her go. She'll cool down. She's got to learn that she's not going to always get her own way."

Remembering this exchange, Deuce wriggled uncomfortably as the razor scraped his left cheek. Even now, three months later, with Helen somewhat resignedly installed as bookkeeper at the *Clarion*, he knew things weren't settled. She could take off at any minute. Probably the only thing keeping her was Father Knapp's crack about Winnie turning over in her grave.

Yet, deep down, he was a tiny bit glad if it meant she'd stay. The house was too big for one person. Already, with Winnie gone, at least half of the rooms had gone fallow. On his rare visits to the parlor, the draperies smelled stale, his footsteps echoed on the parquet floor. What would living here be like when it was just himself?

He knew in his heart he should let her go. *Help* her go. But banging up against his father-in-law's opposition was dicey. The man had bought and furnished Deuce and Winnie's house, paid for Helen's painting, piano, and horseback riding lessons—none of which were within the reach of a newspaperman—and, most importantly, Father Knapp was a silent partner—the majority partner—in the *Clarion*. But Deuce loved Helen more than anything and refused to squash her dreams. The evening of the graduation ceremony, he and Helen had talked it through. She apologized for what she'd said and he admitted that he allowed himself to be swayed too often. Although unhappy these last three months, she'd agreed to stay in Emporia for one more year.

The metal clatter of the trolley's steel wheels on the tracks out front pulled Deuce's thoughts back to the steamy bathroom and the lather drying on his face.

In the bedroom, he dropped a hand towel onto the wet floorboards by the window. Over at the Lakes', the porch shades were drawn. Tula's houseguest must be sleeping in. He fingered the tangle of ties on the closet doorknob. Two striped affairs, some muted solids, and the lavender number that Helen had given him for his birthday five years back. He'd worn it once but the fellows at the barbershop had razzed him and that had been the end of it. "Don't want to stick out like a sore thumb," he'd mumbled to Winnie when Helen was out of earshot. Today he felt differently and yanked it off the rack with a snap.

On the dresser, a tortoise box held enamel lapel tacks and gilt watch fobs representing most of Emporia's fraternal orders and business clubs. Becoming a member of the Elks, Knights of Pythias, the Commerce Club, and all the others represented Deuce's slow but steady crawl up the social ladder.

Since the 1820s, when his ancestors first settled in what was to become Macomb County, there had been rumors about colored blood in the family. No Garland ever publicly confirmed it, but when he was nine, Deuce had been ushered into his grandfather's sick room. There, the old man, with skin the color of fallen oak leaves, solemnly explained that way back, Deuce's great-great-great-grandfather had married a Negress and it was a disgrace that haunted the Garland clan to this day. "But don't never admit it, boy. They can say what they like, but they can't prove it." Even without confirmation, whispers clung like cobwebs to each generation and Deuce never completely shook off the humiliation he'd felt as a small boy, teased in the schoolyard with shouts of "Nigger Deuce."

The taunts boiled up like welts whenever trifling disputes arose. As a child, it had happened over games of mumblety-peg and duck, duck, goose and he'd run home to the comfort of his older sisters. Later, the insult was occasionally flung during poker games and, more often, in disputes over the attentions of young ladies. Wounded, he had retreated to the type cases of Brown's Print Shop, where he'd worked as an apprentice. As he grew older, Deuce adopted a different strategy: rather than retreating, he'd moved heaven and earth to fit in. He took up the cornet when silver bands were the rage; ordered roast beef and mashed, same as all the regulars at The Rainbow Grill. When asked what he thought about a matter, he blew words as slippery and vague as soap bubbles until the questioner revealed his opinions first. "You got that right," was his pat response. None of this was all that difficult because he had a naturally pliant nature. It was his heart's desire to belong. He wanted nothing more than to be included. His nickname, Deuce, came from his earliest years when he ran after his older siblings shouting, "Me too, me too!" His first nickname was Two-Two, and eventually it became Deuce.

And what were the Elks and the Knights of Pythias and the others about, if not belonging? The handshakes, the toasts, the rituals, all separated insiders from outsiders. Then there were the levels, ranks, and orders to rise through, each with its own signifier worn on the lapel for all to see; recognition made tangible in bits of brass and gilt. He'd worked like a dog to win acceptance. But more and more, since Winnie's death, he yearned to rise above being nothing more than the mouthpiece for Emporia's prominent and powerful. Now, with the typhoid deaths, this urge became more acute.

He fastened on the usual array of pins and headed downstairs. Lifting the cake cover, he found a day-old biscuit. Breaking it open with his thumbs, he spooned on strawberry jam and reassembled the two halves. Bundling his breakfast in a napkin and dropping it into his pocket, something Winnie would never have allowed, Deuce retrieved his boater from the hall table and settled it on his head. He caught sight of himself in the hall mirror. Something prompted him to skew the hat to the left. He walked out of the house, letting the screen door bang behind him.

Deuce's two-story house, with its cedar shakes painted forest green and a wide-columned porch was considered substantial by Emporia standards. Three hoary chestnuts shaded the front lawn and a narrow strip of concrete led from the porch to the sidewalk. To one side was an open lot, waiting for Emporia's steady progress in the form of another solid middle-class manse.

On the other side, one step closer to town, was the Lakes' boxy four-square with its coat of whitewash where the never-married Tula kept house for her brother Clay. Devoid of trim work and shutters, its shallow porch and four rooms per floor held a certain charm for townspeople who were nostalgic for the rural life. It brought to mind Emporia's farming roots when this shady street, now grandly renamed Mount Vernon Boulevard, had been known simply as Route 7 and was used by farmers, like Deuce's grandfather, to bring crops to town. Even now, a cornstalk sometimes sprang up between the brick paving stones as long-dormant kernels, dropped from wagons, made up their minds to germinate.

Deuce's father had left the farm but not gone far, just six miles into town, to clerk for the railroad. But every summer he sent Deuce's older sisters out to Grandpa's. Deuce was the youngest of six, the only boy. He was still a toddler when the two oldest caught typhoid out at the homestead. The undertaker's wagon carried them back into town, along this very street.

He gazed abstractly down the embowered boulevard. Maybe I'll telegram the Springfield editor today and get permission to reprint that piece on adulterated milk. But his courage wavered when he thought of angering his advertisers and his father-in-law.

At the fork, where Mount Vernon slanted eastward, Deuce veered onto State, with its closely packed row of storefronts. A stranger in gray pinstripes, aggressively employing a toothpick to his molars, was lounging in the doorway leading to the second-floor photography studio

owned by Tula's brother Clay. There was something un-
savory about the man's stubbled cheeks. Deuce considered questioning the fellow about what his business was,
when a voice from behind broke through his thoughts
and the stranger was forgotten.

"Sure looks fine," Alvin Harp, the garage owner, was
saying, pointing to the canvas banner slung across the
street, shouting, *Chautauqua Week, August 12-19,* in a
fancy font.

Deuce grinned. "Surely does. Emporia has done herself proud."

"Those too." Alvin gestured with his chin toward the
red and yellow placards in the window of Fitzer's Market.

A wagon bumped down the street pulled by two
mules. A lanky farmer with shirtsleeves rolled up held
the reigns beside his straight-backed wife in her best Sunday dress. In the back, four youngsters gripped the sides,
ogling the store windows.

Deuce said, "I'd say Chautauqua is just about the best
thing to ever happen here. First of all, it brings the farm
and town folk together, and then there's the educational . . ."

His voice continued, but Alvin's gaze drifted past
Deuce's shoulder to a lanky Negro in overalls walking
toward them. Everyone called the man, who was a janitor at the depot, Smitty. As Smitty approached, Deuce's
editorializing ran out of steam. He pulled a watch out
of his vest saying, "Better get to the typewriter." Alvin
smirked, anticipating what was to come. Deuce was turning toward the *Clarion* when he caught sight of the colored man.

"Oh, uh, think I'll go over to the post office first,
though, and make sure Helen picked up the mail. See you

tonight in the tent," Deuce called over his shoulder. He hurried across the street, scarlet staining his cheeks. Alvin and everyone in town knew the rumors of Deuce's family history and those who were mean-spirited got a laugh over the excuses Deuce came up with to avoid crossing paths with the town's colored population. Alvin ambled off to the garage with a grin.

The newspaper building was owned by Father Knapp who believed in maximizing his investments whenever possible. Its exposed north wall faced a busy cross street. Over the years, Knapp had leased the wall to a succession of national concerns—Tiger Head Malt Syrup, Sweetheart Bread, and Coca-Cola—to use as a sign board. This went against the grain for Deuce, who believed that local products should command the town's allegiance. But asking Father Knapp to take a smaller profit was out of the question.

The painted Coca-Cola advertisement had been shucking off the building's raw bricks for a couple of months. Turning the corner, Deuce saw that was about to change. A sign painter and his helper were noisily hoisting a plank and themselves up the side of the building with rusted pulleys. Upon learning from the men that the new ad would be for U-Needa Biscuits, another big-time outfit, he threw the front door open with a bang.

"Morning, fellas," he called gruffly to the two young salesmen hunched at desks behind the counter. He took the iron stairs two at a time up to the newsroom. By the time he reached the top, he'd cooled down a little. The room was already thick with cigar smoke that clung like bacon grease to the rows of desks and stacks of old editions. Helen was at her place in the far corner. A potted geranium occupied her side-facing window that was now festooned with scaffolding ropes. The first time he'd laid eyes on Helen, Deuce was working at the print shop. Winnie Richards, as she was known then, came in to order calling cards. She'd recently moved to Emporia from Chicago with her father, George Knapp, the town's local-boy-made-good, and her young daughter, Helen. Her father let it be known that Winnie had been married to an up-and-coming banker who died of yellow fever when Helen was only three months old. The alternate version, passed around the town's watering holes and sewing clubs, was that the baby's father was the son of a prominent family, but had a drinking problem and was crushed to death by a train when he'd passed out on some railroad tracks. Deuce was behind the print shop counter when Winnie entered with Helen, a toddler wearing a frilly cap and a serious expression. Something about the little girl's grave brows contrasted with the silly bonnet had captivated him.

Smiling at this long-ago memory, Deuce approached her desk. "You're an early bird."

She lifted her head from the open accounts book. "Remember? I'm leaving at three to set up the women's booth at Chautauqua?"

"Oh, yes, yes."

Jupiter, the office dog, emerged stiffly from under Helen's desk. He made a show of rearing back to stretch his front legs before shoving his narrow snout into Deuce's palm.

"Any word on Mrs. Elliot Adams? Did she break anything?" Helen asked.

Deuce shrugged. "Things were still buttoned up tight when I passed Tula's just now."

Helen frowned at the ledger and erased an offending entry. "You should check on her. Include it in the article." She brushed crumbs of rubber onto the floor.

He pointed at her and snapped his fingers. "Good idea." He turned on his heel.

Helen nodded approvingly. One of the positives, the *only* positive, about remaining in town, was her role in nudging Deuce toward making the *Clarion* a real newspaper.

A volley of clattering sounded outside her window and she saw a pair of muscular hands pulling hard on a scaffolding rope. The rope was threaded through two pulleys that squealed in protest as they were set into jerky motion. A shock of black hair appeared above the sill—with another screech, the head and upper torso of a young man in white painter's coveralls. His thick hair needed trimming and his eyes were squinty—like one of N.C. Wyeth's sunburned pirates on the plates in *Treasure Island*. From the other end of the plank, a voice shouted, "That's it!" and the young man tied off the rope. Helen was staring when he suddenly turned and grinned, displaying brilliant white teeth against tan skin.

"Hello there," he said. "Admiring the view?"

"No. I don't know what you're talking about," Helen answered, her words clipped.

"Well, I'm enjoying the scenery, and I'm not talking about out there," the painter said, poking his thumb toward the buildings in back of him. He grinned again and his ears rose slightly. "Guess we're going to be neighbors for a day or two. I'm Louie Ivey."

Helen smiled tightly and busily began ruling off a ledger column.

"I think it's the polite thing to tell me your name, don't you—?"

He was interrupted by the gruff voice from the other end of the scaffold. "Hey, Louie, quit your gabbing and get started before the brushes dry out."

Louie cocked his head at his unseen partner. "Guess it's time to get to it."

"It's Helen," she said quickly. "My name's Helen Garland."

"Nice to meet you, Miss Garland. Guess I'll see you around—ha ha," he said loudly.

Smart aleck, Helen thought as she shuffled the *Clarion*'s July bills into chronological order. Still, she couldn't help looking up one more time as Louie, now with paintbrush in hand, began swabbing above her window, the bristles making a persistent scratching sound against the rough brick.

C HAPTER THREE
HOLIDAY IN A FLYSPECK

TOSSING A RAIN-SOAKED CUSHION ASIDE, Dr. Jack collapsed into a porch chair, his head tipped back, eyes closed. He tried to catnap, but quickly snapped upright. Where was Hazel Bellman with that coffee?

It had been a long night in the house at the edge of the Chautauqua grounds. A cannon of thunder had awakened Hazel Bellman in the early-morning hours. Poking her head into Jeannette's room, she'd been stunned to find the bed empty, stripped of blankets and pillows. She hurried downstairs. The front door was banging against the wall, sheets of rain drenching the carpet. Jeannette was curled in a fetal position on the porch settee, teeth chattering, soaked to the skin. The girl was burning hot. Hazel had screamed for Ted, who rushed down and gathered up their daughter. It had taken Dr. Jack hours of work but eventually he'd knocked down the fever and quieted the coughing so that now the girl slept peacefully.

Hazel toed open the screen door and stepped out with a loaded tray. She called to her husband, who was collecting branches torn from the wind-lashed maples, but he said he wanted to finish up.

"Are we past the worst?" she asked, handing Dr. Jack a steaming cup. She always had a mousy look, even at the best of times, but the strain of Jeannette's illness had pulled down the corners of her mouth until they formed permanent streambeds.

He sucked a mouthful of coffee between his teeth. "Can't answer that. What I'm afraid of is pneumonia. That on top of the tuberculosis." He shook his head.

Hazel's knees knocked under her wrapper. "I know. But not the hospital. Please, not that. Every time she goes in, I'm afraid she'll never come out."

Across the Chautauqua grounds, the Story Lady was leading a troop of youngsters in a song. The melody of that old chestnut, "Sunshine Bright," drifted onto the porch.

"We got her through the night. Now it's wait and see." He gulped down the rest of the coffee and stood. "Got to go, but I'll stop back later."

"You know what she was doing, don't you? Why she was camped out on the porch?" Hazel asked.

"I can guess. Jeannette heard last night's lecture and followed that woman's recommendation about sleeping out of doors."

Hazel nodded. "I could kick myself for letting her listen."

Dr. Jack shook his head. "If it's any comfort, I'll be doctoring Mrs. Elliot Adams later today and will give her a piece of my mind."

Two blocks away, Tula knocked twice on the door of the sleeping porch and entered, juggling a cup and saucer in one hand and a rubber ice bag in the other. Although it was midmorning, the room was dim, the shades drawn. Tula set the china and the dripping bag on a rattan table, pushing aside a pile of magazines.

"I've brought some coffee," she said to the elongated shape humped under a flannel spread. When there was no response, she tapped her patient lightly on the shoulder. "Mrs. Elliot Adams?"

Marian grunted and rolled onto her back. Her eyes opened and she grimaced. "Oh Lord," she moaned, reaching toward her lower calf that was entangled in the blanket.

"Here, let me help." Tula pulled aside the bedding. The ankle was red and swollen to the thickness of a small pot roast. "Let's prop it on these pillows, and here's an ice bag."

"Thank you," Marian mumbled. Squinting like a tabby in the sunlight, she examined her ankle. "I can't believe this has happened. I should be on the road this very minute. I've never missed a lecture."

"A Perfect Attender," Tula said as she sprung the shades.

"What?"

Tula waved her hand. "Nothing. Just reminded me of a prize our Sunday school gives out."

"I think what I will do," Marian said slowly, narrowing her eyes as she sipped the coffee, "I'll hire a driver. He can carry me to Galesburg. After that I'll manage on my own."

"Can I—" Tula was interrupted by the ringing telephone, a long and two shorts. "Excuse me, that's us." She hurried through the kitchen. "Coming, coming," she said.

The ringing stopped. Through the beadboard walls of the sleeping porch, Marian heard the murmur of Tula's voice. The lecturer surveyed her surroundings. An ironing board heaped with table linens stood in one corner.

Snowshoes, golf clubs, and a croquet set were piled in a dusty jumble before the altar of an overstuffed book-case. From a random pattern of nails driven beside the door to the kitchen hung a leather driving helmet with goggles, a rusted washboard, and a butterfly net. Tula's voice ceased; her footsteps approached.

"Somebody has a lot of interests," Marian said, waving a hand around the room.

Tula studied the walls. "That's mostly Clay."

"Your husband?"

"Oh, no," Tula said. "He's my brother. I'm a maiden lady."

Marian snorted. "Wise woman. I was married for seven months. Worst seven months of my life. I've got very little use for the male species."

Tula stifled a smile. "Really? You don't enjoy their company?"

"Their company's fine—for short periods. I just don't want to be restrained. They hold the reigns right now. But it won't always be like that. Especially when we get the vote. But enough," Marian said. "As I was saying, the solution is a driver. Is there someone in this town who does that sort of thing?"

"I think you're getting ahead of yourself." Tula pulled a wooden chair to the bedside. "That was Dr. Jack. He'll be here shortly. You're to keep that foot elevated and iced until then."

"Did you tell him that's not possible? I'm expected in Galesburg."

"He'll be here soon enough and you can tell him."

Marian puffed. "It's not for him to say, is it? I've coped with more than a twisted ankle over the years. This is nothing but a minor annoyance and I'll tell him so."

"You sound just like Winnie." Tula gazed absently out the window. "She wouldn't take orders from the doctor either, poor thing."

"Who?"

"My next door neighbor. She passed away . . . well, I guess almost two years ago."

Aggressively pushing the pillows at the head of the bed into a mound, Marian threw herself against them. "I'm not going to let any small-town doctor interfere with my work. And on top of that, it's ungodly hot in here." She kicked the covers off the bed, sending spasms of pain through her ankle. "Damnit!" she yelped.

Tula jumped up. "You need to lie still." She rearranged the pillows under the injured foot, repositioned the ice bag. Marian screwed her eyes shut, gathering herself. I'm nothing but a jumble of nerves, she thought.

While Tula was adjusting the sheets, Marian grabbed her hand. "I'm sorry, I'm just not used to lying around. On the circuit, we're constantly on the move."

She flopped back on the pillow, trying to remember the last time she'd spent two consecutive nights in the same bed, the same town. For the past seven years, she'd traveled the circuit in the summer and, come fall, shouldered a merciless schedule of Lyceum appearances up and down the eastern seaboard, until June rolled around again.

Her traveling life had begun three years after her recovery from tuberculosis. As soon as she'd been strong enough, she'd thrown herself into the cause of dress reform. She made the rounds of the largest settlement houses in New York, evangelizing to the shop girls and garment workers who gathered, after exhausting days of labor, in basement classrooms. A regular at the outdoor rallies held by the National Woman Suffrage Association, Marian soon began writing articles for the *National Suffrage Bulletin* and a couple of small progressive publications. She was unable, however, to break into the leading ladies magazines, despite the flood of write-ups she poured into their in-baskets.

Meeting Placidia Shaw changed all that. It was during a suffrage parade down New York's Fifth Avenue on a bright fall day. Marian managed to get herself assigned to the opposite end of a long banner carried by Shaw. An associate of the famous Chicago reformer, Jane Addams of Hull-House, Placidia Shaw was a well-known figure in her own right, most notably for her articles about slum conditions published in *Ladies' Home Journal* and *Collier's*. During the three-hour march, Marian discussed safe and hygienic dress so tirelessly that when they reached the end of the parade route, Shaw had agreed to help her get some of her articles published. Placidia had become her mentor. Marian's career on the road began when the older woman secured her a place as a lecturer with her own employer, the Prairieland Booking Agency. Now, considering these exhausting years on the road, Marian thought that, perhaps, staying with Tula a few days wouldn't be so bad.

Tula's mouth was moving.

"What?" Marian asked.

"Would you like a nice plate of eggs?"

Marian brightened. "Yes, please. Bring on the eggs!"

Tula was melting lard in the frying pan when a short

woman trudged up the drive pulling a wagon piled with bundles of soiled linens. Laylia did the wash for a half dozen of Emporia's lesser white households. The town's leading families used Mamie.

"I completely forgot this was wash day," Tula cried out. "We've had unexpected company. Come on in and sit while I get the things together."

Laylia sat heavily in the chair Tula offered. "Thank you, ma'am. Another hot one."

"There's cold water in the ice box. Help yourself," Tula called as she hurried upstairs to strip Clay's bed.

Laylia removed her black straw hat and fanned her face.

"So, any word on Emmett?" Tula asked when she returned several minutes later. She dumped her load on the kitchen floor.

Emmett, Laylia and Oliver's twenty-one-year-old son, was registered for the army and waiting to be notified when he'd be shipped out.

"Not yet. He still working at the garage. All fired up. Can't wait to get out. Just hope it's not Texas."

"Surely they won't send him that far."

"They got a colored regiment down there. But I read in the *Broad Ax* they had a riot. Colored soldiers and townspeople."

Tula frowned. "No, you don't want him in the middle of that."

Laylia shook her head, then pressed her palms to her knees and pushed herself up. Tula handed her the bundle of dirty linen. "Be back Thursday," Laylia called over her shoulder as Tula slid the frying pan back over the flame.

* * *

"Here we go," Tula said, resting a plate of eggs, bacon, and toast on the ironing board. She spread a large table napkin across Marian's chest. "I'm sorry Clay isn't here to say hello but he had an early sitting. He has a photography studio and it takes a good couple of hours for him to set up."

Marian put a generous forkful of eggs in her mouth, chewed and nodded. "These are excellent. I understand. Business comes first. That's what puts food on the table." She spread apple butter on a piece of toast. "Apropos of that, I hope someone thought to bring my things from the hotel."

Tula's hand flew to her mouth. "I'll ring up the Lamoine right away."

"And please, I need my lecture notes too," Marian called to Tula's retreating back.

Marian revised her talk daily, fiddling with the wording or adding a more current example. This late in the season, her typed pages were thick with penciled cross-outs and arrows pointing to scribbled sentences crammed into the margins.

Dress reform was no longer high on the list of issues pushed by suffragists. More and more, the cry focused on the vote. Younger women were already favoring a looser, more athletic clothing style. Some corset manufacturers had caught on and were replacing steel stays with elastic. Marian feared becoming irrelevant. Her reputation as a lecturer was built on an issue that was seemingly less and less germane. This fall, for the first time since she'd started, there was a five-week gap in the schedule before her first Lyceum booking.

A wave of anxiety washed over her. Can I afford to

stay here all week, even if I want to? She pushed the plate with the half-finished eggs onto the bedside stand. The fork and knife clattered to the floor.

On her way to telephone the Lamoine, Tula heard the noise and hoped Marian wouldn't try to retrieve whatever had fallen. That's all I need—for her to topple out of bed, Tula thought.

There was a knock at the front door. Deuce strode in with a broad grin, the screen door slamming behind him.

"Sounds like your patient is up and at 'em," he said.

"Just barely," Tula said, flustered. For a moment, her bustling efficiency dropped away, but she quickly composed herself. "Take your coat off. It's awfully warm."

She put down the receiver. He turned to drop his boater on the coat rack and she reached on tiptoe over his shoulders, hooking her fingers around his lapels. He shucked off his jacket and it slid smoothly into her hands. The fabric was warm with the heat of his body. She hung it up with a private smile.

Two months ago, Deuce had asked if he could escort her to the Elks strawberry festival. The entire evening he'd sat under the elms, attentively at her side. Since then, he'd often joined her on the porch for a short chat after the workday; and once, he brought over a cutting from his peony bushes that she'd admired, and twice, took her to the moving pictures. Tula, who'd had a crush on Deuce since girlhood, could hardly believe that he might be "turning to her," as they said, after all this time.

It had been thirty-four years since he kissed her, but the sensation of his lips, his cool nose brushing her cheek, was still fresh. Saturday evenings their crowd of bank tellers, shop clerks, and others not long out of high school, would blow into the Merry-Roll-Round, booted skates slung over their shoulders. Moving onto the wooden oval, Deuce and the other fellows would challenge each other to races while the young women linked arms in clusters of two and three. And all the while, Tula's eyes followed Deuce, at that time working as a printer's devil at Brown's: the concentration on his face as he zipped past, his head thrown back in loud laughter at one of Clay's off-color stories.

Then, one evening, as she'd skated arm-in-arm with Vera Driver, he'd darted up behind them, uncoupled their arms with a grin, and skated off with Tula. Round and round they circled. When her knees wobbled, he guided her to a bench beside the cubbyholes of street shoes and, without asking permission, kissed her. All that spring he'd skated by her side, walked her home, kissed her goodnight. Then Winnie Richards moved into town with little Helen, and Deuce had been swept away as neatly as he'd disengaged Tula's arm from Vera's.

Deuce pulled a notepad out of his back pocket. "Might I get an update on her condition from your illustrious guest?"

"Let me poke my head in first."

From the other room, a firm voice asked, "Are they bringing my things? Is that the doctor? Send him in."

"No, it's the publisher of the Clarion, Deuce Garland."

"Oh." There was a pause. "What does he want?"

Deuce called out, "We've met already. I helped you up when you fell. I only need a few minutes."

Another pause. "Could you come back after my bags arrive?"

He put his face to the crack. "I'm sorry, but I've got to

get back to the office. Deadline's coming up."

There was a clink of china accompanied by a heavy sigh. The scent of coffee and perfumed talc drifted past the doorjamb.

"All right, come on in."

Deuce entered and Tula slipped into the kitchen.

Marian took in the publisher, his wrinkled linen suit of a style fashionable five years ago, his too-eager expression, and, my God, a load of lodge buttons on his lapel! Her fantasies about relaxing in Emporia for a couple of days flew out the window. This is nothing but a hick town. Why on earth would I ever want to spend a holiday in this flyspeck? she thought miserably.

Deuce settled himself into a chair, glancing around the room. "More homey than the Lamoine. I'm sure Tula's taking good care of you."

"Yes, certainly. Now why are you here?" she asked, her voice impatient, her eyes narrowed. At every lecture, most men in the audience listened with frowns on their faces, shaking their heads. As if at her words, each woman in the audience would jump up and rip off her shirtwaist, corset cover, and corset. The remaining ten percent openly leered at her bosom, clearly assessing her as a loose woman. Which sort was Deuce?

"My readers will want to know the state of your recovery, Mrs. Elliot Adams, and whether you'll be staying in Emporia for an extra day or so."

"You can see my foot for yourself." She drew the sheet away from her lower limbs.

Deuce's face darkened in embarrassment. "That's pretty swollen. What does the doctor say?"

"He hasn't been here yet. So, there's nothing to report."

He tapped his chin thoughtfully. "My Helen will be disappointed. She sent me down here especially to check on your condition. She admires you greatly."

"That's kind. Please extend my gratitude." Marian picked up a book from the bedside table and flipped it open.

Deuce nodded. "I will. She's the one who was speaking with you just before your accident."

"Really? That girl?"

"Yep."

Marian closed the book, a finger marking her place. "Your daughter? Very progressive."

"Stepdaughter. And yes, she's full of ideas on the modern woman. I'm very proud."

"I'm surprised." Marian slid the book back on the nightstand.

"About?"

"In my experience, Midwestern newsmen are anything but progressive."

Deuce cocked his head, studying her upraised chin, the firm set of her mouth. "Have you seen my paper?"

He pulled yesterday's *Clarion* from under his notebook and handed it to her. She slowly leafed through the pages, pausing to read one or two items. From the kitchen came the sound of a broom whisking across the floor.

Marian returned to the front page, and flicked a column with her thumb and finger. It made a loud popping sound. "This is what I'm talking about."

Deuce leaned forward. "The locals?"

"This string of idle chit-chat." She read aloud: "*Bill Jones brought in a load of hay today. Thomas Hughes is recovering from a sprained hip. John Smith is putting a new porch on his Sylvan Street property.*" The newsprint crumpled into her lap. "This doesn't belong in a newspaper, and certainly not on the front page."

Deuce ran his hand through his hair. "Maybe not in a big city. I grant you that. But Emporia is a small town, and it hasn't been all that long since the pioneer days."

"All the more reason to raise the bar. Educate, not pander," Marian said righteously.

"Whoa, Nelly," Deuce replied, holding up his hand. "I wouldn't call that pandering. Those little items bring the community together. Not to get philosophical, but I sort of think of them as a mirror that shows us who we are."

Marian snorted lightly. "I already know who I am. I don't need a newspaper to do that. I need a paper to bring me the hard facts." She ruffled the pages again. "I don't see much in the way of that here."

Deuce winced. "I'm hoping to change that, but it doesn't come easy."

"You can't let that stop you."

"True. But, again, this isn't New York. Not so far back, Macomb County was just a handful of homesteads and Emporia nothing but a crossroads. The only way to grow was to help one another. Neighbors pitching in to put up hay, women spelling one another at sickbeds, those sorts of things. When it grew to the point where the town and county became incorporated, reciprocity was still the name of the game. Our banker befriends the railroad men, and Emporia gets a station. The *Clarion* boosts the town, and the great state of Illinois plants a college here."

Marian made a face. "One hand washing the other."

Deuce shrugged. "There are a lot of throwbacks here that stir up a fuss whenever something changes and—"

He was cut off by Tula, who stuck her head in the door. "Dr. Jack is here."

The doctor strode in and greeted them both. He set down his bag and began rolling up his sleeves.

"Here you go, doc." Deuce jumped up. "I'll wait outside, if that's all right, and then get the update, Marian?"

She motioned him to stay. "Can't keep anything from the press anyway."

"Let's get down to business," Dr. Jack said dryly, pulling back the sheet covering Marian's legs.

The doctor cradled the foot in his hands and prodded gently with his thumbs. She grimaced.

He ran his finger up the calf. "I'd hoped the swelling would have gone down by now, but since it hasn't I think there's a good chance the ankle is broken. Keep it elevated and on ice the rest of the day."

"That's—" Marian began, but Dr. Jack ignored her.

"I'll come back after supper for another look. If it's broken, it'll need a cast."

"After supper? Then you'll have to travel to Galesburg. I'm due there for a lecture tonight and I'm leaving by car today." She lifted her chin defiantly. "You can't prevent me."

"No, I can't," Dr. Jack said, gently repositioning her ankle on the pile of pillows. "But if you don't stay off of it and let it heal, it will only get worse."

"I can tolerate pain. We Chautauqua performers can endure anything."

Dr. Jack sat down. "Look. If the ankle is broken and you continue to travel, bumping on rutted roads, tramping in and out of hotels and up and down lecture platforms, you could erode the bone. It may heal crookedly.

Then you will be using a cane for the rest of your life. Or you might even get gangrene. And then they'll have to lop it right off. But I'm not going to argue with you. It's your decision."

Marian fell back onto the pillow, her lips hardened in a tight line.

"There is something else you need to know," the doctor continued, packing up his bag as he spoke. "One of my patients is gravely ill. Jeannette Bellman."

"Aw, jeez. I heard her coughing last night during the lecture, from all the way across the field." Deuce shook his head.

"Who?" Marian asked.

"A girl, just a couple years younger than my Helen," Deuce said. "Consumption—isn't it?"

Dr. Jack nodded.

"Oh, the poor thing. Don't I know what she's going through."

The violet shadows under Dr. Jack's eyes deepened. "She heard your talk and took your advice. Spent hours on an open porch in the pouring rain. Her mother found the girl in the middle of the night, half out of her mind with fever."

There was silence. Finally Marian, her voice soft, said, "But this will pass. I'm sure she will be stronger for it."

Dr. Jack raised his brows. "It's possible, but she's very weak and I'm praying that she doesn't develop pneumonia on top of the tuberculosis. She's a very sick girl right now."

"But I am living proof . . . this method works," Marian said haltingly.

The doctor picked up his bag. "It has been my experience, Mrs. Elliot Adams, that there are cures that may work for some and not for others. We're not all the same, you know."

Marian looked as if she was going to respond, then hesitated, her fingers hovering over her mouth.

Before Deuce followed the doctor out, he paused. "Don't think the worst as yet. She's got youth on her side."

Marian nodded.

The publisher lingered in the kitchen. "How's Clay taking this?" he asked Tula, inclining his head toward the sleeping porch.

Tula made a rocking motion with her hand. "He wanted to know if the circuit was going to pay us for her room and board. Said he was going to call the Lamoine to find out what their rates were. But I stopped him."

"At least he's thinking practically for once," Deuce said. "Not that he should be charging for her stay, but—"

"You don't have to say it. I told him just the other night that if he doesn't manage his finances better with this business than he did with the sheet music sales and the carpet sweepers before that, we'll be out on the street."

"Now, Tula, you know I wouldn't let that happen." Deuce patted her hand. She flushed, hoping for a gentle squeeze as well, but he pulled away, readjusted his tie.

She cleared her throat. "You've done enough for us. I just hope he's keeping a careful eye on his accounts."

CHAPTER FOUR
TOY LAMB

EARLIER THAT MORNING, shortly after Deuce strolled into the newspaper office, Clay had taken the same route into Emporia's business district. But unlike Deuce, when Clay turned the corner on State Street, he immediately knew who the fellow in the gray pin-striped suit lounging in the studio's entrance was.

Clay slowed his gait, making a pretense of fumbling for his pocket watch, while sizing up the stranger. A too-tight suit was stretched tautly across muscled arms, inflating the ruddy flesh of the hands and neck. Fresh off a farm, Clay thought. Maybe this won't be all that hard. He walked briskly the last few yards to the entrance, pushed past the stranger, had his key in the lock and the door halfway open before awareness registered in the man's sun-bleached eyes. But Clay wasn't fast enough. The bill collector's thick fingers fastened around Clay's wrist.

"You Clay Lake?"

"Why?"

"Because Mr. Lake has some debts he needs to take care of." A toothpick, lodged in the corner of the man's mouth, jerked up and down with his words. "Do you want to take care of this here on the street?"

The Reverend and Mrs. Sieve stepped out of a shop two doors down. "No. No. Let's go upstairs."

The two rooms that comprised Lake's photography gallery were stifling. The bill collector removed his suit jacket and tossed it on a chair while Clay opened a window. Despite the heat, his hands shook and the skinned look of his bony face became even more pronounced.

"Got some pretty fancy equipment here," the collector said, circling several cameras mounted on tripods. He lifted a black cloth hanging from the back of one and peered into the lens.

"Watch it. Those are expensive." Clay's jaw jutted out.

The man drew back and laughed. "Don't I know it."

Clay dropped heavily onto a chair. "So, you're here about the cameras?"

"Yep." The man flicked the toothpick onto the floor and inserted a fresh one in his mouth. "Those three you ordered from the Chicago Camera Company and never paid for."

Clay ran a hand through his hair. "Look, I don't have it. But I will. I just need a little time."

"You've had time. Didn't you get those notices?"

"Yes, but business has been slow. But now, I've got more sittings booked. Just today," he glanced nervously at the clock, "in a couple of hours. I've got a customer coming this afternoon."

"So you don't have the money now?"

"No. But if you'd just give me—"

"Not my problem. I'm taking the cameras." He surveyed the room. "Got any crates?"

"You can't take them."

The man paused. "Oh yeah?"

"But how am I going to make a living?"

The man shrugged. "And you're going to give me that expensive watch tucked in your pocket for my trouble."

After the downstairs door slammed behind the bill collector, Clay collapsed on a tufted chaise lounge that he'd paid a lot of money for, thinking it would be a nice prop, but none of his sitters wanted to use it. Too fancy, they said. He stared numbly at the ceiling, tracing the random paths of cracked plaster.

He was in the same position two hours later when Tula stopped by on her way to the druggist. Dr. Jack had advised Epson salt baths for Marian's ankle.

"Are you sick?" she asked.

"No. Yes."

"Your head?" She started to lay a palm against his forehead but he brushed her away and sat up.

"No. He took the cameras."

Tula looked around, puzzled. "Who did?"

"The bill collector!" Clay shouted.

Tula blanched, her fingers against her lips. "You owe money for the cameras, besides what you owe Deuce?"

Clay rose from the chaise, flapped his hand irritably. "Yes, yes. I owe money. I'm in debt. We're in debt."

Tula's chin trembled.

Clay kicked one of the wooden brackets holding up a painted backdrop of a marble pillar and the whole edifice collapsed.

"Oh, don't," Tula said. She pulled on one edge of the crumpled canvas to free it, then let it drop. "He took *all* the cameras?"

"No, I've still got that second-hand gear."

"Well then," Tula said.

Clay looked at the clock. "Christ. Mrs. Johnson will be here in half an hour. Help me set up, will you?"

Clay pulled a rickety tripod and an old camera from a small closet in the corner, fingering the camera's cracked accordion pleats and wondering if they would hold.

Tula set to work on the tripod. "So, what are you going to do about Deuce?" she asked, tightening the screws on the legs.

"Talk to him. Convince him to give me another extension on the loan. You could help soften him up for me, you know."

Tula flushed and straightened. "I don't know what you're talking about." She turned away, made a show of perusing the gallery of photographs Clay had mounted on one wall. She stopped in front of a portrait of an old couple. The woman was seated, the man standing behind her with his hand on her shoulder. Her arm was crossed in front of her bosom. Their hands were clasped as they smiled into the lens.

"You took this for their twenty-fifth, right?"

Clay was kicking a pile of canvas and strutting off to one side. "The Webbers? Yeah. She looks pretty good there. Who'd've thought she'd be dead in six months? And that old Henry would get hitched six months later?" Clay paused. "You know, it's been what, three years since Winnie died?"

"Two. So?"

"So, I know you're sweet on Deuce. You have been since grade school. And he seems to be taking an interest now. If you two got married . . ."

Tula pivoted. "It would solve all your problems? Is that what you're saying?"

Clay held up his hands. "No. Not at all. But, well, that too."

"I'm not listening to you."

"Hmm." Clay turned toward the window. With his back to his sister he continued, "You're going to have to be more forward. Reel him in."

"I'm leaving," Tula said, gathering up her pocketbook and hat and heading for the door. "I can't believe we're having this conversation."

"Why do I always have to be the practical one?" Clay asked himself aloud, after the street door slammed behind Tula.

Twenty-three minutes late for their appointment, Mrs. Johnson and her son could be heard mounting the gallery's narrow stairway. Clay listened from behind the studio door as they entered the outer waiting room. He let his hand rest on the doorknob for a count of twenty before giving it a brisk turn and greeting his subjects.

"Good afternoon, Mrs. Johnson. Please come in, I'm almost all ready for you. It's been a busy morning."

"I'm sorry we're late." She sharply yanked the boy by his arm.

Mrs. Johnson, an attractive young matron whose only flaws were a short upper lip and high waist, swept inside. Her four-year-old son Samuel followed, tugging uncomfortably at the short pants of his blue and white–striped suit.

"I just have a few more adjustments to make with the camera. Please take in my photo gallery while you're waiting," Clay said.

Mrs. Johnson approached a photo on the far left of

a portly woman with an open book on her lap, gazing abstractly off to one side. "Isn't this Flossie Batt?"

"Yes, I was privileged to capture her likeness shortly after her husband was appointed county judge. And in the photo beside her is Judge Batt himself."

Mrs. Johnson squinted at the heavy jowls and drooping mustache.

The next photograph, twice the size of the others, was a full-length view of a well-fed, carefully dressed man in his early fifties. He stood comfortably with one foot thrust forward and two fingers wedged in the small pocket of his vest, the pouches under his eyes and his large nose suggesting fleshy satisfaction.

"Oooo. This is wonderful." She tapped the brass nameplate screwed into the frame just like those on a painting. *E. Mummert—Mummert Power Shovel*, it read.

"He has one just like it hanging over his desk," Clay said.

"Do these nameplates cost extra?" Mrs. Johnson asked.

"Yes. The cost depends on the size and the number of letters, of course. Many of my patrons believe it's worth it. Let me just check in my price book . . ." Clay started to move toward a small desk near the door but Mrs. Johnson stopped him.

"Never mind. I don't think Mr. Johnson would agree to the added expense." She was turning away from the photo wall when an image caught her attention. The subject's folded hands were resting on a papier-mâché balustrade while, in the artificial distance, the Leaning Tower of Pisa could be glimpsed.

"Is this Jeannette Bellman?" Mrs. Johnson asked.

"Yes. That was taken a couple of years back."

"Poor thing! Look at how lovely she was. It's just heartbreaking."

The image showed a girl of about fourteen wearing a middy and pleated skirt. She was not pretty, but an appealing, eager expression played across her wide mouth. Her dark eyes caught the light in a way that reminded Mrs. Johnson of a sequined trimming she had ripped off one of her hats because it seemed too bold.

Mrs. Johnson clucked her tongue. "I passed her just last evening as we were walking to Chautauqua. She and her parents were sitting on the porch. She's lost so much flesh. It's a pity."

As his mother exclaimed over the town notables pointed out by the man in the white smock, Samuel slipped silently backward. Among some props in a far corner, he spotted a toy lamb mounted on a little wheeled platform. It had a gilt collar from which a tiny bell dangled. As soon as he was clear of his mother's reach, he ran to the corner and hugged the lamb's woolly body to his own. It emitted a dusty smell. He set the toy down, preparing to pull it across the floor, but then noticed the animal's rigid glass eyes. They were disproportionately large, with enormous black pupils. The irises were tinted an unnatural shade of blue. Samuel wailed in fright. The lamb wobbled on its wheels and tipped over.

"Here, here. You're not to have that." Clay snatched the animal from the child's grasp, placing it on a high shelf. Samuel bellowed more loudly.

Mrs. Johnson rushed over, handkerchief in hand. "What did I tell you about mussing yourself?" she scolded, blotting his dampened collar. "Stop bawling this instant."

Samuel promptly shut his mouth but continued to sniffle as his mother tugged on his clothing.

"If this continues, I'll have to tell the Story Hour Lady you won't be participating in the Chautauqua pageant," Mrs. Johnson said. Samuel inhaled in preparation for renewed wails but then thought better of it. "Mr. Lake, did I tell you that Samuel has the part of Old King Cole's page in the Mother Goose Festival? He's to wear real velvet breeches. They passed out the costumes yesterday. There was a little white shirt too, but it smells something awful and he refuses to wear it."

Mrs. Johnson turned to smooth her son's hair that had sprung loose from its anchoring of hair cream.

"I'll get everything aligned so we're ready to go," Clay said, retreating under the black cloth draped over his camera, making unnecessary adjustments to the eyepiece. This kind of disruption was one reason he hated photographing children. The sessions took twice as long and almost always seemed to involve tears. What he would have liked to do was pinch little Samuel smartly on the fleshy part of his arm. But I need this sitting, he thought. And about fifty more like it.

After the photographs were taken, and as Clay was ushering the mother and son out, Mrs. Johnson paused at one of the portraits near the door. A young woman with a slight, knowing tilt to her lips and an assured expression in her eyes clutched Elizabeth Cady Stanton's *The Solitude of Self* closely to her breast.

Mrs. Johnson snorted. "That Helen Garland has always read way too much for her own good."

CHAPTER FIVE
WALL DOG

FROM THE COMMUNITY BOOTH just beyond the ticket stand, Helen surveyed the track of beaten grass running across the Chautauqua grounds. Although it was two hours before the evening's performance, a few determined old folks were already marching toward the tent. As they passed the stall, none so much as glanced at the Equal Suffrage Club pamphlets she had artfully fanned across the table. Use of the community booth rotated among various Emporia organizations. Yesterday, it had been the Women's Christian Temperance Union. Tonight, Emporia's modern women, the suffragists, had their chance to bend the public's ear.

A bee circled the bouquet of Queen Anne's lace intended to pretty up what some might consider dry piles of literature. Helen stood to swat it away. She sat down again, adjusting the white and yellow suffrage ribbon pinned at her shoulder, her shoe absently knocking against the table leg. The WCTU had left behind a box of temperance song books. She flipped through one. Tried humming "Ohio's Going Dry" to the suggested tune of "Bringing in the Sheaves."

"Looks like you've got some instructive reading there." Louie, the painter from the scaffolding outside her office window, was leaning against the tent pole on one side of the booth. He had changed from work overalls into flannel trousers and a suit coat. There was a change in his gaze too, which seemed less forward, more thoughtful.

"I'm just passing the time before the crowds arrive."

"Looks like you might have awhile to wait."

"I'll get some takers." Helen resecured a tassel of hair that had come loose from her topknot.

Louie picked up one of the brochures, glanced at it, and tucked it in his pocket. "I think you might have gotten the wrong impression of me. I take these sign painting jobs every summer. Puts food on the table the rest of the year."

"Oh, really?" Helen said coolly.

"Yes, really. I'm an artist."

Helen sat up a little straighter. "That so?"

"I took courses at the Art Institute up in Chicago. Even won first place in a student exhibition."

A farm family passed, mother in the lead, followed by a weary-looking fellow with a sack coat slung over his shoulder and five dark-haired children.

Helen pushed the pamphlets around. "What do you paint? Landscapes?"

Louie threw a leg over the corner of the table. "Used to, but now I'm a cubist."

Helen's brows raised. "I've no idea what that is."

"It's revolutionary is what it is. Take a walk with me around town, and I'll tell you all about it."

"I can't. I'm the only one here." She motioned to the single wooden chair.

"I don't think anybody's going to miss you," Louie

said. "But okay. How about when the program starts?"

Helen hesitated. "Revolutionary? How so?"

"Give me an hour and I'll bring you up-to-date on the most advanced, modern movement in the art world since—since I don't know what."

The initial trickle of patrons had grown into a crowd. Not far away, Helen thought she glimpsed her stepfather's boater bobbing her way. "All right. I'll meet you under those elms at the edge of the grounds in twenty minutes," she said hurriedly. Louie saluted and sauntered off.

As Deuce's hat drew closer, the throng parted. Marian, seated in an ancient wicker wheelchair, emerged feet first. Then came the tip of a cane, which she was sweeping back and forth. "Coming through!" she called out. Deuce's face was flushed and sweat bloomed under his arms as he propelled the wheelchair across the bumpy pasture. Marian's healthy foot tapped impatiently on the footrest, her mouth determined, her free hand scooting along the rubber wheels to speed up the motion.

When she spotted Helen her face brightened. She waved the cane at the banner over the booth. "Working for the cause!" she cried.

Helen rushed around the table of pamphlets.

"Goodness, Papa, you didn't shove her all the way from Tula's on this bumpy ground?"

Marian jumped in. "Oh, no. He pulled the motorcar as close as he could to the ticket booth."

Deuce fanned his face with his boater. "Really, it was no problem."

"You know, I think I could just use this cane." Marian started to push herself up out of the chair. "I just hate being carted around like a sack of—"

Deuce pushed her shoulder down firmly, rolling his eyes at Helen. "I have strict orders from Tula that you're to stay in the wheelchair, remember?"

"Where is Tula?" Helen asked.

"Up at the Bellmans'. Jeannette's better and Hazel was finally willing to let someone else take over the nursing and get some sleep," Deuce explained.

"Thank goodness," Helen said.

Marian nodded. "Yes, it's tremendous news. Didn't I tell Dr. Jack she'd come around?"

"Speaking of Dr. Jack . . ." Deuce began.

A surge of ticket holders was making its way toward the tent. A loosely strung youth with wrists well clear of his cuffs tripped over Marian's back wheel. "Sorry, ma'am," he mumbled, lifting his hat.

"Slow down, son," Deuce said as he steered the bulky wheelchair out the stream of traffic.

"I just hate feeling like someone's old granny." Marian thumped the wicker armrest. "But the good news is that the doctor says it's only a sprain."

A pair of elderly sisters passed behind Deuce, murmuring to one another. "Such a pity about the Bellman . . ." They glared at Marian.

Deuce, unaware of the exchange behind his back, was fidgeting with his boater, rotating it through his fingers as if crimping a piecrust. He spoke up: "I'd like to check in with Dr. Jack. See if he's treated any more typhoid cases. Seems to me like there's fewer coming down with it. Has he passed by here, by any chance?"

Helen shook her head.

Marian continued with her train of thought: "Anyway, Deuce has been very kind to push me around in this contraption. I thought I'd go stir-crazy if I stayed cooped up in that sleeping porch any longer. But really," she turned to Deuce, and handed him his suit jacket that had been draped across her lap, "I'm sure Helen and I can manage from here."

Looking relieved, Deuce said, "Yes, I really need an update from the doc. You can get Marian inside, Helen?"

Helen's first impulse was to shout out, *Of course!* Here was the chance to talk with a famous suffragette, but . . . she hesitated. Her mind leaped to Louie and something stirred inside, tugging her away from Marian and toward the darkening trees at the edge of the grounds.

"I don't know if I can, you know, leave the booth. But I'm sure—"

"Of course not," Marian broke in. "You're doing important work. Deuce can commandeer someone. How about the fellow over there? This is just too frustrating. I don't know why I can't use this cane."

"No, no. Let me get you inside right now and I'll track down Dr. Jack later," Deuce said in what Helen recognized as his polite, out-in-public voice.

A few stragglers trotted past and then Louie and Helen were alone under the elms, the shadows vibrating with the rhythmic creak of late-summer crickets. Louie took her hand. For a short while they walked in silence. Everyone, except the very ancient or very sick, was at Chautauqua and the streets were quiet under the old trees. Ahead, twin rows of streetlamps shone along State Street.

"So, what's a cubist?"

"You heard of the Spaniard Picasso?"

Helen twisted her lips to one side. "Maybe."

"Okay. How about the Armory Show a couple of years back?"

"The one that was so controversial?"

"It started out in New York, then came to Chicago. I saw it and it changed my life. Changed my whole way of thinking. Before that exhibit, I was doing landscapes, snow in the woods, that sort of thing." Louie paused to light a cigar. A house cat silently descended some porch steps across the street and melted into the bushes.

"But now, whole different ball game." He made an expansive motion with his hands, fingers wide. An odor of turpentine eddied from his jacket.

"This way?" he asked, taking Helen's arm and pointing up the street with the cigar.

"Sure. Fine. All the streets end up in the same place anyway. Go on."

"So, in cubism, you think about something you might paint such as, say, someone's face. *Your* face, let's say. But instead of trying to get it to look as much like you as possible, like a mirror image, I take the pieces apart."

Helen raised her brows.

"The face is made up of all different pieces, right? Eyes, nose, mouth, nostrils, all that. And also, when I look at your chin, say, from this direction . . ." They were under a streetlight. Louie grasped her chin and tipped it to the left. ". . . I see it one way. But when I do this," he continued, pulling her face to the right, "it looks different. And when I do this . . ." He bent toward her, pressing his lips against hers. After a moment he said, "And when I do that, I don't see your chin but I feel it."

Helen pulled back, her eyes narrowed. "That just seemed like an excuse to kiss me."

Louie threw up his hands. "Not at all! Just trying to bring some of the world of modern art to the culturally impoverished."

"Now you're making fun of me," she laughed, thumping her handbag across his shoulders.

He grinned. "Just saying maybe you should get out more. Visit Chicago."

"I have," she said smartly. "And I'm moving there."

"Terrific. This is my last job of the summer. I'm heading back to Chicago in a couple of days. I'll take you to the Art Institute, give you some education."

"You really don't give up, do you? But it won't be until next year."

"Next year? Can't you make it sooner?"

Helen flung a hand up. "Too complicated." Inside, her mind was busy: Why *not* now? She was not going to change her mind even if Grandfather Knapp made her wait ten years.

"Say, what's over here?" Louie was saying. He took her hand and pulled her toward a stone building flanked by wide granite steps.

"It's First Baptist. My friend Mildred goes here." Helen allowed herself to be led down a shadowy concrete walkway along the side of the church.

"Is that so?" he said absentmindedly, as if he wasn't really listening. "What's in here, do you think?"

Helen started to answer and then realized that Louie wasn't really asking her a question. He pulled her under the small portico of a side door and put an arm around her waist. Helen glanced fleetingly over his shoulder at Reverend Carlisle's manse next to the church. None of the lamps were lit. Louie's other hand hung at his side, pinching the burning cigar.

"Put that out," she said and he immediately dropped it. The cigar emitted a small shower of sparks before it was ground out by his shoe. She put both her arms around his neck and, when he kissed her, his lips were pleasantly moist and firm.

After a few more kisses, Helen pulled him out from the doorway. "Let's keep walking."

They turned left onto State Street, passing a stray dog with a wiry coat who trotted by purposefully. A display in the sporting goods shop caught Louie's eye and he spent some time talking about the athletic prowess required to work scaffolding, as he examined the fishing hampers, golf bags, and medicine balls.

At the corner of Main and State, he stopped to light another cigar.

"How old are you?" Helen asked.

"Twenty-seven. That okay?"

"Yes."

"So, your daddy's a big shot in town," he said, leaning against a streetlamp.

"Stepfather. Sort of. But it's more my grandfather. He's president of the savings and loan."

They took a different route back toward the Chautauqua grounds. When the brick belfry of the United Methodist Church came into view, it was Helen who pulled Louie around the rear and down into an open basement stairwell. This time, after kissing her lips a number of times, he pressed his mouth to her temples, the space between her brows, and the tender spot just below her jaw where her pulse fluttered. She looked up at the rectangle of sky visible from the stairwell as he unbuttoned her shirtwaist. There were no stars visible, only a skim of clouds hanging in the warm night air.

Louie had smoothly freed her four top buttons and Helen felt his fingertips skimming her bare right shoulder in brushlike strokes. The sensation was dizzying, as if a cord below her belly, from deep within, was vibrating until her entire body thrummed.

"Did you say something?" Louie breathed into her ear. His fingers scooped inside her shirt.

"I need to get back to the tent before the program's over," Helen said, stepping away and securing her buttons. He protested, but she was already halfway up the stairs.

At the top she glanced at her watch and judged it would be about an hour before the Mystic Entertainer reached his grand finale. There were, she knew, at least two more churches between United Methodist and the Chautauqua grounds, and she meant to stop at each.

C HAPTER SIX
THE MYSTERIES OF HEREDITY

"YOU'RE SURE?" Marian asked.

The Negro youth sitting beside her in the driver's seat of the Packard nodded. "Yes'um. I carry Mrs. Mummert in her touring car when her gout acts up."

"You're positive you know how to operate this?" Marian repeated uncertainly.

He skated a finger around the glossy rosewood steering wheel. "This a *fine* machine." His cushioned voice knocked against the words like felt-covered piano hammers.

It was the morning after the Mystic Entertainer had conjured a cloud of Hindu spirits. The day was clear and already too warm. Just minutes ago, at ten a.m. sharp, Emmett Shang, Laylia's son, had tapped on the Lakes' front door. His hair was parted to one side with mathematical precision, his white shirt spotless.

When Marian had reluctantly come around to the understanding that she would be remaining in Emporia until the ankle healed, Tula cranked up the telephone. One call was to Nettie Harmon, the piano teacher, requesting that some of her more promising pupils entertain Marian in the afternoons. The other was to Harp's Garage, pleading for someone to take Marian on morning out-

ings in the Packard, now parked alongside Tula's garden-
ing shed.

Marian fidgeted in the passenger seat, searching for
the least painful position for her swollen ankle. "All right,
let's see how you do. Crank her up. I don't want to sit in
the driveway all day."

"Certainly, ma'am. I was . . . uh . . . just waiting for
you to get ready."

"I am ready."

"Yes'um, I see that." Emmett quickly got out of the
car and moved to the front of the grille. "I just thought
maybe you'd forgotten something."

"No, I did not. I'm crippled, not addled."

"It's just that when I drive Mrs. Mummert, she wears
a hat and veil. For the dust. That's all."

"Umpf," Marian snorted. "Nothing wrong with fresh
air. A little dirt never hurt anyone."

"No ma'am." Hiding a grin behind the Packard's
glossy hood, Emmett jerked the crank efficiently, slid behind the wheel, and released the handbrake in smooth
choreography. The auto rolled down the driveway.

"Any place special you'd like to see?"

Marian stared at a passing parade of lawns, porches,
and an elderly man pushing a mower. "Hard to believe
there would be anything special here."

Emmett bit his upper lip, considering. "There's the
courthouse, and Spring Lake's just outside of town."

She threw up her hands as if they were a white flag
of surrender. "Fine, fine. Anywhere." She eyed her chauffeur's erect posture. "Tula says you're registered for the
army?"

"Yes'um. Just awaiting orders. The training camps

aren't ready for us. That's what I was told anyway . . . This here is the business district."

A handful of shops on either side of the street slid by, mirror images of those in all the other Chautauqua towns Marian had visited.

"The train station's up ahead."

Marian shifted in her seat, unsticking the green kimono that was clinging uncomfortably to her thighs. In the open car, the August sun beat down mercilessly.

"Would you mind if I stopped at the station?" Emmett asked. "Mr. Harp asked me to pick up a package—if it's all right with you, of course."

"Oh, certainly! That will be the highlight of the excursion so far," Marian said dryly.

After Emmett disappeared inside, Marian billowed her garment. No relief. Across the street, a small park baked in the heat, its half-dozen young trees bent like buggy whips. For a long time, no vehicles passed. Finally, a horse-drawn wagon hauling a large water tank rolled by, sprinkling water on the dusty paving stones, and then all was quiet. She dozed.

Suddenly a train whistle blasted, waking Marian who self-consciously wiped a thread of saliva off her chin. The engine pulled into the station with a hissing gush of steam. A small greeting party quickly assembled on the platform, including a baggage clerk pushing a wooden dolly and a young couple, arms linked, kissing in the shade of the depot's overhang. Marian imagined they might be parting. A newsboy hawked papers as the train cars coasted by, then screeched to a stop. *Clarion* was stenciled in block letters on his canvas bag.

An old man debarked gingerly onto a wooden step

provided by the porter, followed by two business types. Then a familiar figure, her mentor, Placidia Shaw, stood framed in the passenger car's doorway. What luck! Marian thought. At least something positive will come out of this delay. Although they had lectured in tandem during Marian's first Chautauqua season seven years ago, now that Marian had been promoted to the position of first-nighter, their paths rarely crossed. Chautauqua performers were deployed in relay fashion, and so the two never again appeared in the same place at the same time. Placidia remained a "preluder," Chautauqua lingo for the lead-in before the main speaker. Still, they continued their friendship through letters and postcards, although, Marian realized, these had become less frequent. This summer, Marian and Placidia traveled down the line two days apart.

The older woman, clutching the same satchel Marian remembered from seven years ago, stepped onto the platform. She disappeared inside the station, emerged through the main doors, and walked briskly in the opposite direction. Marian remained planted in her car like a hobbled goat. A minute later Emmett stepped out—what in heaven's name had taken him so long? Marian pressed the horn frantically and, when he finally looked her way, waved vigorously. He rushed over.

"You all right, ma'am?"

"Yes, but that woman. I know her. Crank this up."

Emmett hastily got the Packard running, driving it down the block.

"Yoo hoo!" Marian called. "Can we give you a ride?"

The older woman paused, squinted, hurried on.

"Move up, move up," Marian said to Emmett, making swishing motions.

The Packard inched forward.

"It's me, Marian."

Placidia stopped again. "Oh, yes. So you are."

"Let me give you a ride."

"What are you doing here?" Placidia's head tipped to one side.

"Long story. Come on, get in."

Lifting several layers of heavy black skirts and petticoats, the traveler climbed into the tonneau seat behind Marian while Emmett tied her valise on the running board.

"It's so wonderful to see you," Marian said, twisting around, ignoring the pain shooting up her leg. "I just can't believe it!"

A few swift cranks and Emmett was back behind the wheel.

"How was the gate in this town? Standing room only?" Placidia asked, clasping and unclasping her hands.

"There was an overflow. Can I carry you to the hotel to freshen up before—" Marian began, but Placidia interrupted.

"No, no. Straight to the grounds."

"But you must be exhausted," Marian said, while at the same time noting that Placidia's nails were bitten to the quick.

"I have to make sure everything is set up properly. You can't trust those crew boys to do anything right." Placidia abruptly snapped open her handbag, shuffling through a number of papers that were covered in tight script.

"You must be wondering why I'm still here," Marian said. "You see . . ." Her voice petered out. Placidia was muttering to herself, pulling out a newspaper clipping only to examine it with a grimace and shove it back in her bag.

She's acting awfully odd, Marian thought. "Can I help you look for something?" she asked.

"No, I've got this well in hand. Go on."

Marian described the fall, the ankle, the interruption of her schedule. "The doctor says I must stay off it an entire week, but I'm thinking, if I could get a driver who would take me to Vernon tomorrow . . ." She paused and glanced at Emmett who seemed to be making of point of keeping his eyes glued to the road. "If that happens, I'll be back on track. Oh, I'm just so happy to see you. And still fighting the good fight for Hull-House."

"Here it is!" Placidia cried triumphantly, waving a pamphlet she unearthed from the valise. "Hull-House? That's all in the past. I was misguided. I have a completely new message now."

"Oh?" Marian drew back.

Placidia inched forward, her face suddenly animated. "Race improvement."

"I'm not sure what that is," Marian said slowly.

Eagerly, Placidia explained, "I had always assumed—well, we all did—that the problems in the slums, with the immigrants, were due to environment. You know, slumlords, poor sanitation, the industrial machine."

Marian nodded.

"But that was all wrong, don't you see? That view didn't take advantage of the new thinking, the new science that proves—proves *scientifically*—that it is heredity, not environment, that is the key to national vitality so that—"

"Just a minute," Marian said, holding up her hand. "You're saying that the solution to social problems is . . . is what?"

"Who marries whom and, of course, the number of children they have. That's it in a nutshell." Placidia handed Marian the pamphlet. "It's all in here."

The Packard bumped over an uneven set of trolley tracks. The sun continued to beat down. In the shade of a store awning, a mother was unfurling the hood of a baby carriage.

Marian read the brochure's title, *The Low Immigrant Gives Us Three Babies while the Daughter of the American Revolution Gives Us One.* Her cheeks reddening, she faced forward, crumpling the paper in her hand. She glanced at Emmett, trying to gauge his reaction. He was looking forward, his back ramrod straight. What in heaven's name was Placidia talking about? Had she lost her mind?

The remaining minutes of travel were made in silence. Marian directed Emmett to pull up behind the performers' dressing tent, fortunately pitched under a maple, and told him to let the superintendent know Placidia had arrived.

As Emmett ducked through a tent flap, Marian turned back to her friend. "Are you feeling all right?"

Placidia was shuffling pamphlets. "Yes, never better."

Marian had meant the question as a general entrée to feel out exactly how this drastic change in her friend had come about. Now that she looked more closely, Placidia did appear unwell. Her eyes jittered hectically; her skin had a greasy yellow patina.

At that moment, Placidia opened the door and began tugging at the handles of the heavy valise.

"Why don't you wait until Emmett gets back? He can carry that."

"I can manage."

Marian, attempting to lessen the tension, laughed lightly. "You're still the modern woman, I see. Taking on a man's job."

Placidia yanked the bag so hard it hit the ground with a thud. "Not in the least."

A smile crossed Marian's lips. "It was a joke."

Placidia looked away for a minute. Her words burst like a thundercloud: "Ever since I recognized you down at the depot, I've been struggling to hold my tongue. But I can't any longer." The older woman shook her finger in Marian's surprised face. "You and your ilk. Talking up dress reform so that our young women can venture even further from home, go to college, take up men's work, ride bicycles, golf, dance, and who knows what all? Have you given any thought to the consequences of what you are promoting?"

Marian's mouth dropped open in surprise.

Placidia continued, "No, I see not. I'll spell it out for you. The consequence is that nowadays the purebred American woman has less interest in raising a family. Birthrates are falling among our nation's native stock. And who is stepping in to fill the void? Why, the immigrant horde, of course. While our Daughters of the American Revolution have one child each, maybe two, the Italian, the Irish have three, five, eight. While our young girls play at being modern women, the immigrants breed like rabbits."

Marian's heart sank. This was not the woman she had known. Something must have happened to her mind. Hardening of the arteries? Marian had witnessed the curtain of dementia falling behind her own father's eyes, at first slowly, then rapidly. Marian wanted to leap out, pull Placidia to her, shake her, bring her back to her senses, but the older woman was stepping away from the Packard and Marian was trapped with the damned ankle.

"But don't think I don't know what you're doing," Placidia said, "and I'm unraveling it as quickly as you've knit it. Two days after your lecture, I take the platform and I don't hesitate to give our young women the message they need to hear." She angrily snatched up her bag and marched toward the dressing tent, calling out over her shoulder, "Just leave me alone!"

When Emmett returned to the car, Marian was staring without focus, fingers pressed to her mouth.

"Should I take Miss Shaw's bag?" he asked.

Marian shook her head. "She's already taken it. Let's just leave. I don't want to be here right now. Take me anywhere. I don't care."

"The lake?" His voice was uncertain.

"Fine. Fine. Anywhere."

On their way through town, the gas gauge bumped around *E*. Emmett pulled up to Harp's twin gas pumps, disturbing a bony cat who had been sunning itself beside an incinerator. It slunk off into the weeds. In the garage, a mechanic in striped coveralls, poking around the guts of a Model T, glanced up. Emmett unscrewed the gas cap and inserted the nozzle. The fellow sauntered over, wiping his hands on an oily rag. A second mechanic, emerging from the garage's shadowy interior, joined him.

The first one spoke in a laughing sort of way: "Ma'am, you must be the Chautauqua speaker with the snazzy motorcar."

Marian nodded. "Mr. Harp, thank you for letting me hire Emmett for a few days, and actually I have another favor—"

She was interrupted by the second mechanic, taller than the first but with the same dark features. "Mr. Harp is out on a delivery. We're his mechanics. I'm Wade, this is Merle. We don't see many Packards. Mind if we peek under your hood?"

"Go right ahead."

Merle turned to Emmett, who was screwing the gas cap on. "Since you're here for the time being, boy, go get me a clean rag. I don't want to dirty up this fine, fine machine."

Emmett's erect back disappeared into the station. Wade folded the hood open. Both men moved closer, as if approaching a shrine. Marian tapped her good foot restlessly. What is it with men and machines? she thought. The feral cat returned, skulking around a wooden tray of empty soda pop bottles beside an ice chest.

"What's that favor?" Merle suddenly asked.

"I was going to ask if he would give Emmett a few days off to drive me to Vernon and some of the other towns, until my ankle heals. That's all."

Emmett returned with a rag and a dripping bottle of Orange Crush from the cooler. He handed the rag to Merle and the pop to Marian.

"Why, thank you," Marian said. "Don't you want some too? I'd be glad to pay. You must be parched driving me around all morning in this heat."

She fished in her coin purse. Emmett climbed behind the wheel.

"Hey, boy, this lady wants you to drive her to Vernon.

Spend a couple of days out that way. What do you say?"
Wade laughed too loudly, Marian thought, for something
that didn't seem funny.

"Yeah, yeah! Hah! What'ya say to that?" Merle
guffawed.

Emmett sat stonily, staring past the heads of the two
mechanics.

An auto driven by a florid middle-aged man pulled up
behind the Model T in the bay.

"Guess we gotta get to work now. You take care of
this automobile. Don't let nothin' happen to her." Merle
snapped the bumper with a rag, then the two men sauntered back toward the garage.

"What was that all about?"

Emmett shrugged.

"Well, you must know."

"Merle's mad he didn't get to drive you, that's all. Mr.
Harp said he was needed here."

"It seemed more than that. Ah, here's a nickel! Now,
get yourself a drink." She pressed the cold bottle to her
forehead.

"No ma'am. Thank you, though. I'm not thirsty."

"You must be parched. Here." Marian held out the
nickel. "I won't take no for an answer."

"Look, ma'am. I can't drink one of those pops from
the cooler. The one time I did, paid my nickel and all,
Merle raised a big stink about drinking out of a bottle
that a colored man had put his lips to. He grabbed it right
out of my hand and broke it at my feet. Smashed glass
all over the asphalt, right where drivers pull in for gas."

"For crying out loud," Marian said. "This is what I
think of that." She extended her arm and poured the rest

of the orange drink into the dust. She smiled, but Emmett's face was neutral. "Let's go into town and get a soda for each of us."

Five minutes later, Marian was sipping another Orange Crush and, through the Packard's windscreen, perusing the flasks of colored water and stacked displays of dyspepsia tablets in the window of Sanitary Drugs.

"This tastes much better," she said, turning to Emmett who had a bottle of grape pop lifted to his lips.

"Yes. Thank you, ma'am. This hits the spot."

A slight breeze ruffled the oak leaves above their heads. Marian felt sweat dampening her scalp. Emmett's collar, she noted, was as starched and dry as it had been when he'd arrived on Tula's porch.

"So, what do you think about driving me to Vernon?" she asked.

His voice remained even but something flickered far back in his eyes. "Thank you, but that's not a good idea."

"Why not? I'll talk to Mr. Harp. And I'll pay, of course. Come on."

She sipped her drink. Emmett's gaze was fixed, turned inward. Finally, he said, "I'd like to. You're a nice lady, and this is quite an automobile. Who knows if I'll ever be behind the wheel of one of these again? Any riding I'll be doing will be in the back of an army truck, sure 'nuff."

"All the more reason . . ." Marian's voice trailed off.

"No, you see, Vernon don't allow no colored people to stay there. To spend the night."

Marian bit her lower lip. "I didn't think of something like that. How about you stretch out in the car? I've done that many a time and it isn't so bad. And surely the next town on the circuit will have a colored hotel. I think it's a fairly big town." She frowned. "Can't think of the name."

"No, you don't understand. See, Vernon, it don't allow no coloreds overnight. At the end of the day, you have to be out of town."

"Even if I give you permission to sleep in my car?"

"That don't make no difference."

"What happens if you stay? Do they fine you? I'll pay."

"No ma'am. They throw rocks."

"What!"

Emmett raised his brows. "Happened to my uncle's cousin. He's got a farm out that way. Went into town to pick up some seed corn, lost track of the time. It was coming on dusk when he stepped outside the feed store. A gang of young boys still in short pants had clustered round the door. All of them had stones. He started walking away; slow, then fast. But they followed and when he turned around, more had joined. Then he began to run. Down past the houses. The older men sitting on the porches egged the boys on. Told them to 'chase that old nigger out.' Then they threw the rocks. He got hit in the back, on the legs, one cut his head up pretty bad. He didn't slow up. Not until he was way past the town limits."

Marian listened in stunned silence. Finally she whispered, "That's terrible. I never thought . . ."

Emmett shrugged. "That's the way it is. I'm hoping the war, us colored soldiers having a chance to prove ourselves, will change some things. Some of my friends make fun of me for thinking that, but the way I think, can't hurt."

They sat in silence.

"If it's all right with you, I'm going to stretch my legs. I'll be right over there if you need me," Emmett said after a bit, pointing to the small park across from the depot. "Just blow the horn."

A sour taste rose into Marian's throat at the thought of small boys scouring the ground for the biggest rocks they could find. Going down the line, she'd heard that sometimes the circuit's Tuskegee Jubilee Singers stayed with colored families in neighboring villages. But Marian had always assumed this was because the place was too small to support a colored hotel; not that Negroes were run out of town at sundown like stray dogs. How many towns like that have I visited this summer? she wondered.

Three boys scrambled into the park. Two were tossing a baseball mitt back and forth, while the third, a smaller child, tried to snatch it. An arthritic granny carefully lowered herself to one of the benches. She pulled a hankie from her handbag and patted her face.

Marian's thoughts jumped to another bitter pill—poor, confused Placidia. She sighed heavily, pushing it all from her mind. Sweat had glued her thigh to the leather seat. She shifted her back so that it rested against the passenger door. From here, the scene before her—the same grassy expanse, scruffy kids, Emmett resting on his heels in the shadow of an elm—looked different. A trick of light perhaps. Or the sensation that sometimes happens when you are driving along and unexpectedly come at a familiar landmark from another direction.

She sounded the horn and Emmett trotted back. As he cranked the engine, Marian noticed Deuce standing on the far corner. He waved at her, and was beginning to step from the curb to cross the street, when a trolley approached with three brisk clangs.

It moved into the intersection and stopped, blocking her view. The bell clanged again and the trolley passed, rocking slightly in its shallow rails. The crossing was empty.

"Where did he go?"

"Who?"

"Deuce. Mr. Garland. I thought I saw him standing right over there."

"He must've gotten on the trolley."

"But I thought he was coming over," Marian said. "Guess he thought better of it. I gave him a hard time about his paper the other day. Not everyone can take criticism."

"I don't think it's that. He saw something," Emmett said, his voice matter-of-fact.

"What do you mean?"

Emmett hesitated. "Probably saw me standing here alongside you."

"So what?"

"Colored people make him nervous, is all."

"That's ridiculous." Marian turned back to the street. "The things you're telling me, I just find hard to believe. I thought they only happened down south."

Emmett lifted his shoulders under the white shirt. "Don't know about down there, but that's how it is here."

CHAPTER SEVEN
BENEVOLENT AND PROTECTIVE ORDER

DEUCE SLID ONTO A SEAT on the opposite side of the streetcar, glancing out of the windows across the aisle. He had a clear view of Marian, parked in front of the Sanitary, with that young Negro from Alvin's garage. I should have walked over and said hello, he thought, swatting his knee with a rolled-up newspaper. That would have been the polite thing. But the presence of Emmett had stopped him cold. He slumped in the leather seat while the trolley slowly lurched away from the drugstore. Why do I let that get to me? he thought glumly. He tried to focus on the passing view. Seeing all the red and yellow Chautauqua posters and banners gradually lifted his spirits.

Disembarking, he trotted up the steps of the Elks Lodge. Inside, cigar-smoking Brothers were lounging in the reception room's overstuffed chairs, ears alert for the dinner gong. The soft click of billiard balls sifted through a portiere-hung archway. Off to the right, in a side parlor, three fellows, including Clay, whose back was to the door, were huddled over a game of dominoes. Deuce started in their direction, but hesitated. Relations with Clay had soured in the last couple of months, ever since the June 1 due date for Clay to pay back his loan came and went. Deuce knew this was a risk when he advanced Clay the money. At least I didn't tell Father Knapp about the arrangement, Deuce thought. That would be another lecture.

One of the domino players spotted Deuce and waved him in with a grin and a raised glass. Ah, hell, I'm not going to let that get in the way of a couple of rounds with the bones, Deuce told himself.

"Hey, old man," Deuce said, clapping Clay on the shoulders with both hands. "How goes it?"

Clay jerked. Seeing who it was, he quickly dropped the glare and jumped up with an overly eager expression.

"Couldn't be better! Here, take a load off." He gestured toward the leather club chair where he'd been sitting.

"Hello, fellows," Deuce said to the other players.

Mack Abelman asked, "Where you been?" while Trot Carter nodded amiably, the cigar stuck in the corner of his mouth dusting the table with ash.

"Go ahead. Take my seat," Clay said.

"No, finish your game," Deuce replied politely.

"You finish for me. You're a much better domino player than I ever was." Clay nervously stroked the peninsula of hair above his forehead. "Remember when we were kids? You beat me every time."

"Wednesday—hash, eh?" Deuce was saying, pulling a cigar from the inner pocket of his jacket.

After a couple of games Mack and Trot excused themselves. "Going for another round," Mack explained, lifting his empty glass.

Clay glanced across the room. "There seems to be more of a turnout today. Probably because of Chautauqua. That afternoon program pulls a lot of the women away from the kitchens."

"Tula headed over that way?"

"No. Today's her day for baking. That means I can look forward to a good meal this evening. Helen learn to cook yet?"

Deuce grimaced. "She makes an occasional attempt, but I don't encourage it."

Clay nodded. "What say you come over for a regular meal?"

"That would be swell."

"Let's make it after Chautauqua, when that woman moves out of our sleeping porch," Clay said hurriedly, as if clinching a deal. "She's been nothing but a pain in the neck. I swear her voice is sharp enough to peel the paper off walls. And her ideas about women—how they should dress. It'll be a load off when she moves on."

Deuce pulled his lips down, raised his shoulders. "She's not so bad. How I see it, she's very opinionated, but that's her trade. I sort of admire that she speaks her mind."

"She's not living with you. That's all I've got to say."

The dinner gong sounded and the two men joined the throng pressing toward the dining room. Settled at a table, Deuce screwed around to survey the other diners.

A rotund man with unnaturally red cheeks and nose pulled out the chair across from Clay and settled in. "Mind if I join you?"

Deuce grinned. "'Course not, Henry. How's things in the tool and die business?"

"Nothing to complain about." He spread a napkin across his wide thighs, then leaned toward Clay and Deuce.

"Of course, complaining won't get me nowhere, nohow."

Deuce chuckled.

The waiter returned, laid three plates of corned beef hash, each topped with a shiny fried egg, before the men. They dug in.

"So," Henry said, pointing his knife at Clay, "your studio must be on a roll."

While maneuvering his slippery egg off to one side, Clay looked up quickly. "What do you mean?"

Pointing the knife at his own mouth, Henry swallowed audibly. "I mean that my brother-in-law Tom Hayes, you know Tom, who runs the delivery business over in Peoria? Well, he was the one that delivered that expensive posing chair to your studio two weeks ago. Didn't you recognize him? He was in town this past June for the Masonic picnic. Tall man, big nose?"

The color drained from Clay's cheeks. "I guess I didn't remember him. So, how is old Tom?"

"Same as always. But he couldn't stop talking about that chair. He was very taken with it. You know, he's always jawing about inventing something, making a bundle, cleaning up. Well, when he saw how smartly that chair was put together, with the hole in the back to prop up a baby, and then when he laid eyes on its price tag, he was just kicking himself."

Deuce paused with the loaded fork halfway to his mouth.

Clay turned quickly to Deuce. "I was meaning to tell you about the chair. It's the latest thing. My bottom line could use a small boost and you know how many doting mothers we have in this town. It's an investment. A sound one."

Deuce slowly set his fork down. "Just how much was it?"

"Not all that much," Clay said, glancing at Henry who was bent over his plate, trying to scoop a bit of egg yolk on top of some hash. "You know how careful I've been with the money. Every penny accounted for."

"Tom said . . ." Henry swallowed his mouthful followed by a sip of beer, ". . . it was fifty dollars."

Clay flinched. "No it wasn't. Closer to forty-five. There were shipping costs, of course."

Henry laughed. "You can get a first-rate, upholstered chair for thirty dollars down at Duncan's Furnishings and cut your own hole in it. Why, that piece you bought cost more than my ice box!"

Deuce examined the space between his plate and lap.

Clay said, "You know, I've had three sittings with that chair since it came. More will come once word gets around. It'll pay for itself in . . ." He paused, counting off the fingers of his left hand. "I'd say in two months at the most." His smile eager, his pale eyebrows raised.

Deuce shook his head as if clearing his thoughts. "Clay, you know the whole town is behind you. If there's a baby to be photographed, I'll be the first one to send the little nipper over. I'm just sort of disappointed that you didn't . . ." He paused, aware that Henry was listening intently. The financial arrangement between Deuce and Clay was supposed to be secret. ". . . that you didn't put in a small ad promoting this chair. That's all."

Clay perked up immediately. "Why, sure, that's a terrific idea. 'Course, you're going to give me a neighborly discount, right?"

Deuce, however, was not listening to Clay's response

or the banter that followed between Henry and someone sitting at the next table over. He gazed abstractly out the window, feeling as if lead fishing sinkers were dropping silently, one by one, into his stomach. What was Clay thinking? Three months in arrears and he's ordering expensive gimmicks? How many photographs of infants can he sell? But Deuce couldn't whip himself into anger. It hurt that Clay was banking on their friendship to push off making his loan payments.

Deuce stood abruptly, dropping his napkin onto the seat of the chair. "Fellows, I seem to be fighting some dyspepsia so I'm shoving off."

Clay jumped up. "Don't leave yet. Why, we've hardly gotten going here. Why don't I see if Huck could make something special for you if the hash doesn't agree? I'm sure he would."

Deuce shook his head. "No. Heading out."

"Think I've got a couple of Stuart's Tablets," Henry said, patting his vest pockets.

Deuce laid a hand on Henry's shoulder. "Thanks, but I've got some back in my desk drawer. I guess I'll be seeing you both tonight over at the grounds."

Clay, still standing, grabbed Deuce's elbow. "I'll stop by your office later. I have a photography catalog at the house that explains the income that can be made with . . ."

Deuce wanted nothing more than to get outside. He edged past his fellow diners, patting shoulders as he went. At a table near the door, the town's most prosperous undertaker cornered him to complain about a misspelling in an obituary.

Deuce listened impatiently. "Tell the family we'll rerun it. And I'll send a note of apology."

"That's all well and good, but I think—"

"Sorry, Campbell, I'm a bit under the weather."

Deuce passed into the reception room, which was, like the dining room, thick with cigar smoke. Now his gut really *was* roiling. Maybe I'm coming down with something, he thought. He grabbed the door handles, pulling Father Knapp, who was entering, almost off his feet.

"What the . . . Oh, it's you," the older man said, straightening. "Just who I wanted to see anyway. Where are you headed in such a hurry? They haven't stopped serving, have they?"

Deuce finger-combed his hair. "No, the kitchen's still open. I just have an upset stomach, and a pile of locals to write."

He stood to one side, expecting Father Knapp to push past. Despite his trim waist, Deuce's father-in-law was known for the formidable amounts of food he put away.

"That'll have to wait. You won't believe who I spotted going into the Alhambra just now."

Deuce shrugged. "No idea."

"Helen! At a moving picture in the middle of the day," Father Knapp said, his voice rising. "And with that sign painter. The younger one. If I hadn't been half a block away, I'd have yelled out, given him a piece of my mind."

"I'm not sure this is all that—"

"Of course it is. You are way too lenient. No wonder she got that wild notion of running off to Chicago." Spittle webbed the corners of the old man's mouth. He jerked his arm toward the door. "Get down there right now. We don't know who this man is, what his intentions are. Probably not good. I cannot, I *will* not see Helen go down the same path as her mother. And if you are unwilling to step up and act like a father, I've told you what I intend to do. She'll be living under my roof, under my rules."

The old man was working himself up into a fit.

Fear rose in Deuce's throat, but he managed to tamp it down. "Look," he said as soothingly as possible, "I'll handle it. You go have lunch and I'll talk to her."

"Make sure you do," Father Knapp responded, before striding into the dining room.

Deuce stepped outside. The outer door closed behind him. He turned right, toward the theater, but then stopped.

Let the girl be. Why force her to carry her mother's pail of stones? Just another ancient trouble passed to the next generation. He glanced once more at the Alhambra's marquee, then headed toward the *Clarion*, in the opposite direction.

CHAPTER EIGHT
BOOST, DON'T KNOCK

"YOU'VE GOT TO MAKE A TRIP out to the Sayre farm today." Dr. Jack's voice crackled like crumpled cellophane into the receiver Deuce held to his ear. "What I saw out there just now will make your skin crawl."

The doctor's words didn't register at first. Deuce was leaning over his desk to make sure Helen was still at work out in the newsroom. She was. It was the day after Father Knapp had spotted her with the sign painter. Deuce frowned, tipping back in his chair. "What'd you see?" he asked the doctor.

"A whole list of things that would be in violation of a sanitary code, if this county had one. I'm sure their hired hand has typhoid. He's had a fever for more than a week but they only called me out there this morning."

"Typhoid." Deuce's gut tightened. "I can't believe Jim Sayre'd let that happen."

"Well, he did. I've been telling you for weeks now that I've got more typhoid cases this year than I've ever seen. I think the Sayre dairy could be one of the sources."

"Oh Lord." Deuce dropped his face in his hand. "You're sure?"

"No. I need another set of eyes on this—yours. But

my suspicions are that the Sayres are watering down their milk with contaminated water or—"

"Jim wouldn't do that," Deuce broke in.

"Or," Dr. Jack raised his voice, "or they're using tainted water to cool down or wash out their milk cans. Either way, we've got adulterated milk."

Deuce squeezed his eyes shut, thinking of the editorial he should have reprinted months ago. "So what now?"

"I want you to go out there. See for yourself. We need to press for a countywide sanitary commission. You've got to write the column calling for a commission. I'm going to see if the last ten typhoid cases got their milk from the Sayres'."

"And if they did?"

"You and I take this to the county board of commissioners and demand that commission."

Outside Deuce's window, the sidewalk was crowded with farm families in town for Chautauqua. How many would cancel their subscriptions if he followed Dr. Jack's advice?

When Deuce didn't answer, the doctor continued, "Are you listening? You need to go out there. It'll light a fire in your belly. Weren't you telling me the other day that you've been trying to steer the *Clarion* in a new direction?"

Deuce thought of how he'd boasted to Marian that he was changing things, moving the newspaper forward.

"No, you're right. I'll head out there."

As Deuce put the receiver down he glimpsed the sign he'd tacked to his office wall during his early years as publisher. *Boost, Don't Knock.* "There's good in everybody. Bring out the good and never needlessly hurt the feelings of anybody." How many times had he repeated that admonition to his reporters? The sign had hung there for so many years, he no longer took note of it. On his way out of the office, he snatched it off the wall and tossed it in the waste can.

He swung by the house to grab a bite of lunch and to change his clothes. Nothing like a barnyard to muck up nice togs.

Attired in old pants and paint-spattered work shoes, Deuce was shutting the front door when Tula waved hello from her side yard. She stood knee-deep in her vegetable garden, clutching a handful of freshly yanked weeds. Marian sat nearby in a canvas deck chair, a closed book in her lap.

"Don't usually see you home this time of day," Tula said as Deuce approached. She tossed the stalks into a pile at the edge of the plot. He tipped his hat toward Marian.

"Needed a change of clothes for a trip out to the Sayres'."

"What's going on out there?"

Marian put the book on the ground and struggled to push herself up from the low-slung chair.

"Here, let me." Deuce strode over and pulled her to her feet. She grabbed a cane hooked over the chair back.

Tula joined them in the shade. "So, the Sayres?" she asked.

"I got a call from Dr. Jack. Typhoid cases are still way up."

"I heard the Smith children have come down with it," Tula said, shaking her head.

Deuce slumped.

Marian leaned both hands on her cane. "Who are the Sayres?"

"Farm west of town. Their dairy operation supplies a lot of Emporia's milk," Deuce explained.

"And Dr. Jack thinks they might be spreading typhoid?" Tula asked, a shadow passing over her face.

Deuce held up his hand. "Unknown as yet, and this is not for public consumption. But yes, something's not right out there. I'm going out to see for myself."

"I'm going with you," Marian said abruptly.

Deuce pulled back. "What?"

"I'm bored to tears. Sorry, Tula, but if I hear one more piano recital, I'll go batty. And this trip sounds like something worthy of Ida Tarbell."

Tula frowned. "Your ankle."

Marian lifted up the walking stick. "See? I've got the cane. I'll be careful."

Deuce rubbed his chin. "The footing is dicey around a barnyard."

"I take full responsibility."

"Well, I guess you can come, if you insist."

"I insist."

Five minutes after pulling out of the driveway, Deuce and Marian bumped across the railroad tracks at the edge of town. Off to the left was a dirt road, lined on either side with narrow houses, one room wide. Three colored children were huddled over something in a ditch. Then the open fields set in.

After ten minutes of idle talk about the evening's speaker, Marian abruptly asked, "If everyone suspects it's carried in the milk, all the dairies should be shut down.

Simple enough. Bring in the inspectors. Meanwhile, get milk from outside."

"There are no inspectors. Macomb County doesn't have a sanitary commission. That's one problem." Deuce swerved sharply to avoid a pothole. The Model T's left wheels bounced along the weedy berm. "Also, it probably isn't *all* the dairies. Why punish everyone when it's only maybe one or two unsanitary operations? And right now, Dr. Jack isn't even 100 percent it's adulterated milk. But something's gone wrong at the Sayre farm."

The auto turned off the road. Jolting slowly up the dirt lane, it brought them to a sun-hardened yard encircled by a farmhouse, barn, withered corn crib, and a couple of outbuildings, without a speck of shrubbery or grass to soften the scraped earth. Deuce climbed out and eased Marian onto her feet.

"Wait here," he said.

No one answered his knock at the back door of the clapboard farmhouse. After a couple of tries, Deuce gave up and returned to Marian.

"Let's see if we can't find the hand. Watch your step." He held her by the elbow.

An old-time log cabin sat off to one side; behind it squatted a single-seat privy, listing toward a weed-choked creek.

Marian sniffed. "I smell that outhouse."

Deuce lifted his head. "Me too. This cabin's the original homestead."

Inside they discovered the hired hand on a narrow bunk, shivering despite the stifling heat. With each breath his gaunt cheeks labored like leaky bellows.

"Jesus," Deuce muttered. Marian covered her nose

and mouth with her sleeve. A flap of oilcloth hung over the window, preventing any fresh air from entering.

Deuce bent down toward the man. "How you doing, Frank? I heard you were sick."

"Something's got aholt of me." The effort to speak sent him hacking. He propped himself on an elbow and spat a wad of phlegm into a rag clutched in his hand, then fell back on the grimy pillow. "Could you get me a drink?" he asked in a hoarse voice.

A pail of water and dipper stood near the bed. Deuce lifted the man's head and brought the ladle to the cracked lips. Beneath his fingers, Deuce felt Frank's gaunt neck and narrow skull.

"Did Dr. Jack give you something for the cough?"

Frank nodded.

"Where is it?"

"Here," Marian said. She handed Deuce a bottle of syrup from the table. That and a chair were the only pieces of furniture besides the bed.

Frank took a couple of sips with Deuce's help, then lay back and closed his eyes. The pair stood looking down at the sick man. After a minute, he drifted off.

"Jim or Maybelle should be around somewhere," Deuce said in a low voice. "I can't believe they'd leave Frank alone, sick as he is."

As Deuce and Marian walked toward the barn, a heavyset woman wearing a faded Mother Hubbard and sunbonnet emerged from a shed with a pail of slops in her hand.

"Afternoon," she called, putting down the bucket. "What brings you out this way, Deuce?"

He hesitated. He hadn't thought this part through.

"Got a city visitor here who was asking about farming and such . . ." Marian shot Deuce a glance, and he surreptitiously squeezed her arm. ". . . and my first thought was you all. Oldest farm family in the county, right?"

Maybelle nodded, directed her gaze to Marian. "We're the oldest. But I'm afraid you've come a long way for nothing. Jim's out working creekside and won't be back till dark." She paused. "Aren't you the unmentionables lady?"

"Women's dress reform," Marian said stiffly.

"Mrs. Elliot Adams has a packed schedule," Deuce added. "Don't think she can come back tomorrow, can you?" He turned to her with raised brows.

She picked up the ball. "No, unfortunately I can't. I know you're busy but—"

"Busy isn't the half of it," Mrs. Sayre said, her tone snappish. "Some kind of rot's moved into the alfalfa fields. Jim's trying to stave it off. I'm behind on my butter orders and the hand is sick again. And that's not even touching the washing or the windows I was hoping—"

Deuce quickly jumped in, "'Course, we don't want to be a bother. What say I just give Marian a quick tour myself and let you get on with your work? All those visits out to my granddad's farm as a kid, I think I know the basics. Do you mind?"

"I don't want to be rude, but you'll have to come back another day," Mrs. Sayre said, picking up the pail again and moving toward the house.

As soon as the farmwife was out of earshot, Marian said, "That woman was trying to get rid of us! She's trying to cover something up."

"You think so?" Deuce frowned.

"Yes. And you do too. I can see it on your face."

"Maybe so, but we'll just have to wait and try again tomorrow."

Marian exhaled impatiently. "This has to be investigated today. Can't we just get into the auto, like we're leaving, park it down by the road, and walk back through that corn?" She pointed toward the field closest to the barn.

"Hike all that way on that foot of yours?" Deuce shook his head.

Marian studied her ankle. "All right. On the way out, drive up close to the barn and then stop, as if there's a problem with the motor. Fold back the hood. I'll sneak out and into the barn. Drive down the lane, then meet me back here."

It was dim inside the barn, the floor scored with narrow whips of light filtering through the plank walls. The odor of manure and urine was strong. Two horses and a couple of mules were tethered to stalls on the right. Ropey cobwebs hung from the hay mow.

"What are we looking for?" Marian asked when Deuce returned.

"Milking parlor. Let's try over here." Deuce indicated a doorway on the left.

A row of open, bent-rod partitions, parallel to a long feed trough, ran down the center of the low-ceilinged room. Well-trampled straw covered the earthen floor. Double doors at the far end opened to a muddy feed lot and, beyond that, a herd of red and white cattle in a pasture.

"Is this it?" Marian asked.

"Yep. Those are the milking stations. Now we want to find the cooling setup."

"Which is . . . ?"

"Sinks of water to keep the milk chilled. Also need to find where they scrub down the milk cans after deliveries."

After a few minutes, Deuce found a large tub behind a stack of delivery crates. Full milk cans were lined up in a water bath below a dripping tap. He stuck his finger in the water.

"Tepid." He shook the water off with a quick jerk. "Goddamn."

"What's wrong?"

"This should be cold. When I was a kid, visiting my grandpa in the summer, it was my job to change the cooling water a couple of times a day."

Alongside the tub was a sink. A milk can was tipped on its side in grayish wash water in which a couple of dead flies floated.

"That's filthy," Marian said. "You've got to do something about this!"

Deuce felt the blood rushing into his face. "Let's see if we can find the water line that's feeding this sink."

He tramped through the double doors, with Marian hobbling behind. The outside air was slightly cooler.

The moment he saw the shallow trench running parallel to the barn his heart sank. An underground water pipe, which extended upward through the wall of the barn, had been partially dug out. It was cracked in several places. A second, jerry-rigged pipe entered the milking parlor through a roughly cut hole. This pipe ran above ground, down a slight incline toward the farmyard and its cluster of outbuildings.

"That pipe feeds the sink," Marian said.

"Looks like someone started to fix the permanent pipe and didn't finish. So this second line was added," he said. "I'm going to see where it's drawing water from. Should be the pump house above the well. Wait here."

"Not on your life."

"It's too steep for that ankle. I'll be right back."

Marian's jawline hardened. "Give me your hand."

They proceeded gingerly down the slope, through clumps of Queen Anne's lace and blue chicory. At the bottom was the concrete block pump house.

"This is where the pipes should connect to draw up well water," Deuce said in a constricted tone. "But look."

The pipe that they'd followed down the incline ran straight into the creek, and across the water sat the log cabin and privy.

He stared at the setup, his nostrils widening beneath closely clamped lips.

"So the water that's used to cool the milk, wash the cans, it's coming from here?" Marian asked, her voice rising.

"Looks that way."

"But that water is undrinkable!"

"Without a doubt."

"Contaminated by that outhouse?"

"Likely."

"For God's sake!" she shouted. "No wonder children are dying. You've got to do something."

Deuce exhaled raggedly. "I know." After a pause, he added, "I will." A dragonfly flitted across the water. Deuce shook his head. "I can't believe Jim would let something like this happen. You think you know a man . . ." His voice drifted off. After a moment he continued, "Let's head back. I'd like to reprint that Springfield piece in to-morrow's paper."

Marian, who had planted her cane in preparation to pull herself back up the hill, abruptly yanked it out of the ground and turned sharply on her injured ankle. "Reprint? This is something you've got to write yourself, man. You've got to describe what we've just found." She swung the cane around, taking in the barn, the creek, the outhouse.

"But I can't publicly accuse Jim Sayre of purposeful negligence. That's slander."

Marian snorted. "You've got to do way more than mouth someone else's words. You've got to do way more than make tepid suggestions about forming a committee—"

"Commission."

"All right, a *commission*. That isn't enough. You're mad as hell about this. I can see it in your eyes. And you've every right to be. Children have died because of this outrageous neglect." She threw her free arm out wide.

"We don't know that for sure. We don't know this is the cause."

"Oh, come on," Marian said, her voice full of anger.

Deuce examined the horizon. "No question that Jim's got to shut this setup down immediately, fix the pipe, and scrub everything down. I'll call Dr. Jack. We'll convince Jim that it needs to be fixed."

Marian impatiently flicked up stones with the tip of her cane. "How in hell do you think you and that doctor talking Mr. Sayre into doing what he should have done in the first place is enough? Someone should be held accountable."

Deuce struggled to keep his voice under control. "Look, I want the same outcome as you. But you don't know what small towns are like. Sometimes the way to get something done is doing it behind the scenes, instead of making demands and dragging everything out in public."

Marian's eyes narrowed. "If there's one thing I hate, it's pussyfooting. There are times you have to speak up, no matter what the cost."

She turned abruptly and stomped back up the slope. Deuce followed a few paces behind. When he picked her up at the barn ten minutes later, he made no attempt at subterfuge. Maybelle never showed her face. Deuce and Marian made their way in itchy silence back to town in the Model T. The trip seemed interminable.

The late-afternoon sun cast a tallowy haze over the cluster of shingled roofs, the green diadems of oaks and maples, the church steeples, and the courthouse dome. Deuce could hardly bear to think about being cast out from this place. But then he remembered his sisters, laid out in a single casket, their arms entwined, their closed eyes sunken into violet pools, their heads surrounded by dark mantillas of rippling hair.

Yanking on the brake in front of Tula's, he turned to Marian. "You're right. There has to be an editorial in to-morrow morning's paper, and it's got to be mine."

Marian nodded grimly. "Go to it, man."

After helping her to the door, Deuce drove straight back to the office, sat down at his typewriter, and tapped out what needed to be said.

C HAPTER NINE
HOUSE CALLS

FIVE SEWING NEEDLES TUCKED in an envelope of red foil. Two packets of headache tablets. A pouch of loose tobacco. A bar of soap. While Marian and Deuce were out at the Sayres', Tula was circling the dining room table, dropping each into a drawstring ditty bag. Trailing behind was old Mrs. Sieve, filling one sack to Tula's three. Tula tucked each filled bag, destined for an American doughboy, into the Red Cross box and picked up another.

Mrs. Sieve was a stout woman dressed in a shiny black taffeta and an ancient toque trimmed with jet-black beads that glittered moistly like compound eyes. She looped round and round the table, a bloated fly, gossiping about her husband's parishioners, tossing out bits of advice. Her voice droned on.

Tula wondered what Deuce and Marian had found at the Sayre farm. It was late afternoon, sun poured into the stuffy dining room and they were still not back. A headache bloomed behind Tula's eyes. She cast a half-filled ditty bag into the center of the table, suggesting it was time to call it a day. Mrs. Sieve quickly agreed but, instead of leaving, settled herself into a porch chair. Tula had no choice but to offer lemonade. As the women sipped, the pastor's wife launched into a detailed account of a recipe for fruit punch that Mrs. Herbert Kline had brought back from a visit to Indianapolis. It had become so popular at the wedding receptions held in the parlor of United Methodist that Mrs. Kline was overwhelmed with requests for the list of ingredients.

Across the street, Mrs. Ellingford threw a pan of dirty dishwater into a bed of hollyhocks alongside the garage. An approaching automobile raised a cloud of dust down the block. But it wasn't Deuce's Model T, only Vera Mummert in her Olds, waving briskly as she passed.

Marian finally returned, dropped off by Deuce, who walked her carefully to the porch with concentrated attention. Too much attention, in Tula's opinion. Even after Tula asked, Marian offered few details of the trip, only comments about how exhausted she was and was there any nerve tonic in the house.

Tula's headache did not go away. She was up nursing it half the night and into the next morning.

Next door, Deuce did not sleep at all. After setting the type on the editorial himself and watching the first pages roll off the press, he'd driven home and flopped into bed fully clothed, where he lay staring at the ceiling, unable to close his eyes. At first light, he gave up and padded downstairs. He'd just flipped over two fried eggs when he noticed Helen standing in the doorway, dressed for work except for her stockings and shoes that were clutched to her chest in a tangled bundle.

"Want an egg?"

"No, thanks. I'm running late already." She bowed her head with a small smile. "I didn't know you were up. I was trying to, you know, sneak out quietly."

Deuce cocked his head to one side. "Oversleep?"

"No, well, sort of. I need to talk to you."

"Good, because I need to talk to you too. Let's go sit out back." He shoved the frying pan to a rear burner. "Come on."

They settled on the back steps.

"You first," Helen said.

Deuce inhaled. "Marian and I took a ride out to the Sayres' dairy farm yesterday." He went on to tell her about the hired hand, the outhouse, the filthy conditions, and how Marian had convinced him to write an editorial. "So, get ready for some fireworks in the office today. I expect Father Knapp will be first in line, but there will be others."

As he talked, Helen's eyes opened wide. When he finished, she squeezed his hand. "I'm so proud of you. You've done the right thing."

Deuce smiled sadly. "I hope he doesn't try to take you away from me."

"Grandfather? I'm too old to be taken away. My mother married you, you raised me, he doesn't have any say at all."

Hugging her, he felt the wings of her shoulder blades, delicate yet wiry. "All right, your turn."

Helen busily untangled the bundle in her lap and began pulling on her stockings. "It's about Chicago. I really want to move there. As soon as possible." She stilled her hands, looked him in the eye.

Deuce's stomach knotted. "What brought this on all of a sudden?"

"It's not all of a sudden."

"I mean, I know we'd talked about it at graduation

. . . Anything to do with that young man who's escorting you around town?"

"His name is Louie Ivey. And no, it doesn't. Well, sort of . . ." Her voice trailed off and she fiddled with the shoelaces for a moment before letting them drop. "Yes, he lives in Chicago. He's an artist. A modern artist. And I guess hearing about all that's going on in the city reminds me about what I'm missing. Talking with Mrs. Elliot Adams too. The whole world is moving ahead, and I'm not going anywhere."

Deuce studied his fingers, permanently blackened with printer's ink. "But you promised you'd wait a year."

"But Grandfather is wrong. You know he is. I'm not my mother. I'm not going to be 'defiled,' if that's what he's afraid of. Do I have to live the rest of my life here, stunted and cramped because of what she did?"

"No, of course not. But there are real concerns. Chicago can be dangerous, especially for women on their own."

"What about Mrs. Elliot Adams? She travels all over by herself."

Deuce glanced over at Tula's sleeping porch. "She's older. Worldly."

"How do you get worldly except by getting out into it?" Helen snapped.

This is like getting your fingers nibbled by guppies, he thought. She was staring at him the same way Marian had yesterday.

He threw up his hands. "Okay. Let me think it over."

Smiling, Helen leaned over and kissed him on the cheek. "Thanks, Papa."

She ran inside, the screen door slamming behind her. Deuce winced, feeling as if he was caught in the middle of a walking bridge with slats too far apart. And now it had begun to sway.

Across the way, Tula rose to find Marian already up, dressed, and at the kitchen sink, filling the coffee pot.

"You're up early," Tula said.

"Usually I'm on the road before dawn, so this is late. Hope you like your coffee strong."

"And you're awfully chipper."

Marian herself couldn't completely explain her change of mood. "My ankle's better. See? The swelling's down by half." She poured two cups of coffee and took the chair at the table where Tula usually sat. "And here. Take a look at the newspaper. Deuce has done the right thing. And in a big way."

Marian slid the paper across the table. It was folded over to page four, where an editorial ran down the left-hand side. *Dairy Farm Conditions Deplorable; Underscore Need for Sanitary Commission*, ran the headline.

"The Sayre farm?"

Marian nodded.

"He'll catch hell for this."

"Maybe so, but it had to be done! You would not believe what we found there."

The women sipped their coffee in silence.

After a time, Tula rose and pulled out the frying pan. "Scrambled?"

"No. Nothing, thanks." Marian gazed across her cup. "I've been thinking that I should visit that girl with tuberculosis."

"Jeannette?"

"I think I should offer some words of encouragement.

I'm going to call Emmett right now and see if he can't drive me over."

"I'm not sure that's a good idea. Maybe you should wait until she's stronger. I don't even know if visitors—"

Marian shook her head, raised her hands. "You people are not direct enough. I can help this young woman now, not when she's recovered. What's the number for that garage?"

It was midmorning when Emmett pulled the Packard under a tree in the Bellmans' side yard. He scooted around to the passenger side and helped Marian out. She made slowly for the house, leaning hard on her cane.

He started to put his hand under her arm for support but she shook him off. "Thank you, I can manage."

Emmett shrugged and stretched out under the tree, tenting a newspaper over his face to keep off the sun. Marian stumped up the steep porch steps, pausing at the top to survey the bustle across the pasture. A band of men in short coats and braid-trimmed trousers were marching toward the Chautauqua tent. The Imperial Ringers had arrived. She'd spent the night with one of them a couple of seasons back. Squinting, she couldn't tell from this distance which one it was. They all looked alike.

"Yes?"

Marian, turning with a pleasant expression, took in the downturned mouth of a middle-aged woman filtered through the screen door.

"It's you," the woman said, taking a step back.

"Mrs. Bellman? I'm hoping to have a little chat with your daughter."

"She's sleeping."

"I'd be glad to wait."

Hazel Bellman's face was a stiff mask. In Emporia strong emotions were usually muffled by polite small talk, a holdover from the frontier days when survival depended on getting along. "Come in, then."

Marian limped through the narrow hallway and, following Mrs. Bellman's rigid gesture, into a small front room lined with furniture upholstered in cracked leather.

"Have a seat."

"How lovely," Marian said, taking in the floral wallpaper, the lace-draped mantelpiece cluttered with china dogs. "Might I trouble you for a glass of water?"

Mrs. Bellman disappeared into the kitchen. The house had a sweetish smell. From directly overhead came a hacking cough. Marian examined a needlepoint pillow on the sofa beside her. Mrs. Bellman reappeared bearing a tray when a fresh fit of coughing erupted. She set the pitcher and glasses on a side table with a clatter.

"I'm needed upstairs."

"I'll come with you," Marian said, levering herself from the sofa.

Mrs. Bellman, already in the hall, offered no encouragement.

There really was no second floor to the house. It was simply a space opened up under the eaves and partitioned into two rooms between a narrow hall. Stooping, Marian trailed behind Mrs. Bellman into a bedroom blooming with dry heat. The sweetish smell was stronger here, the cough louder. Most of the small space was taken up by a bed. Mrs. Bellman was bending over the patient, so that Marian's first glimpse was of coltish legs entwined in rumpled sheets. Then the mother turned away to dip a compress into a pan of water, and the girl's full form was revealed.

The flesh was wasted, the joints bulbous. Two sets of unnaturally long fingers plucked fitfully at the sheets. But it was the girl's face that weakened Marian's knees. Jeannette's nose was a sharp ridge of cartilage covered with translucent skin. Her crusted lips had sores at the corners. Within deeply sunken sockets, her pooled eyes glistened under thickened lids. A hectic excitement skimmed their surface.

She turned away, shocked by the sight of the sick child, ashamed that she'd pushed her way into the house. For what? she thought. I don't belong here. I never should have come. She stepped into the hall, intending to leave quietly, but Jeannette saw the tall figure and cried out in a weak voice.

"Mrs. Elliot Adams?"

Marian flushed, as if caught in a lie, but forced herself to answer brightly, "In the flesh."

With a disapproving glance, Mrs. Bellman drew back as Marian approached. Taking Jeannette's hand, as fragile as a bird's wing, Marian unstuck her tongue from the roof of her mouth. "I heard you were ill and wanted to offer comfort. I see, though, that your mother is doing a wonderful job with that. I'm not needed at all."

Jeannette smiled weakly. "Oh, no. I'm glad you're here. I'm getting better because of you. I listened to your every . . ." A fit of coughing erupted.

Mrs. Bellman rushed over, murmuring, "You mustn't talk," and held a glass to the girl's lips.

Jeannette pushed it away. The hacking continued, relentless as a metronome, but more nuanced, each phlegmy exhalation followed by a rough gasping inhalation.

Marian turned away, her vision blurred. Jeannette didn't have to finish the sentence. She'd heard the lecture; she'd followed Marian's prescriptions for sleeping outdoors. Marian's gut turned to stone.

Blotting her eyes on a sleeve, Marian forced herself to turn back to Jeannette. The coughing spell wound down. Mrs. Bellman dabbed ointment on the cracked lips.

"Your mother is right. You shouldn't be talking. How about I sit here with you until you fall back asleep? If it's all right with your mother, that is."

Jeannette's eyes momentarily shed their feverish glitter and danced playfully. She drew her finger across her mouth in a zipping motion, looking hopefully at her mother. A sinewy strength, Marian saw, still burned within the wasted body.

Mrs. Bellman pushed a damp strand of hair from her daughter's brow. "All right. If you promise to rest."

A few minutes after her mother retreated downstairs, Jeannette's lids fluttered, then closed. Marian stood slowly, pausing at each creak of the chair, but the girl didn't waken. School pennants were tacked above a small desk near the door. Marian peered at the Brownie snapshot of a basketball team, the girls all dressed in bloomers. A fuller-faced Jeannette stood at the center, gripping the ball, determined eyes meeting the camera. As Marian made her way downstairs, the heat from the roof formed a solid mass pressing down on her shoulders.

She climbed into the Packard, staring numbly through the windscreen. The newspaper rose and fell over Emmett's face and chest as he dozed under the tree. Across the grounds, groups of two and three sauntered into the tent. Marian thought of all the towns she'd passed through, all the lectures she'd given. How many other Jeannettes had been out there?

Shoes crunched on the gravel drive behind her. Dr. Jack, bag in hand, stopped beside the car.

"What are you doing here?" he asked.

"Nothing," Marian said quickly. "I mean, I came to see Jeannette. I'd heard she was sick."

"You shouldn't have come. You've done enough damage as it is."

I deserve that, she thought.

He turned away. She grabbed his sleeve. "But she's going to pull out of this, right?"

"I can't say."

"But surely—"

"Mrs. Elliot Adams, I'm needed inside. Just do me a favor, go back to Tula's. And don't come back here."

He strode off, taking the porch steps two at a time, and entered without knocking. Marian wearily called for Emmett to crank up the Packard. The heaviness yoked to her shoulders spread to her chest and stomach, down her legs and into her feet, until she felt as if she was made of stone. Like that famous hoax, the Cardiff Giant. A ten-foot-tall prehistoric man, his huge limbs and torso petrified into gypsum—in reality nothing more than a concrete statue buried in a field by a farmer looking to bring in some extra income by exhibiting it at local carnivals.

As Emmett drove her away from the Bellmans', Marian thought she felt the sharp crack of a stone hitting her spine.

CHAPTER TEN
ADVANCING ALLIES

"JUST WHAT THE HELL ARE YOU trying to do, ruin this paper?" Father Knapp shook with rage, standing on the other side of Deuce's desk, crushing the rolled newspaper in his hand. As Deuce had predicted, that morning his father-in-law was the first to push his way into the office.

Deuce sighed. "Sit down and let's talk this out."

"I'm not sitting until I get an explanation. It's not just your reputation at stake here. I've got a lot of money sunk in this paper. And what about Helen? You've put her in a pretty uncomfortable position in this town!" Father Knapp's dark brows drew together as he shouted, his features constricting like a fist.

Deuce crossed his arms, tucking his hands in his armpits. Best to let the man blow himself out. He was aware that Helen and the three or four reporters were listening to every word out in the newsroom. Helen had been warned, but the others must be in fear for their livelihoods. Beneath Deuce's feet, Jupiter shifted uneasily.

After five minutes of accusations and lecturing, Father Knapp screwed the newspaper into a wad, threw it down on the desk in front of Deuce, and sat down. "Well?"

"Well, I did what needed to be done. I'm not apologizing and there will be no retraction, if that's what you want. The dairy operations in this county need oversight. You know that. We all know that. Most municipalities have had sanitation inspectors for years, for God's sake. This editorial isn't stating anything that hasn't been obvious for a long time."

Father Knapp flapped his hand as if swatting flies. "Just because Fuller, Schuyler, Hancock, and all the rest of the counties in Illinois are doing it, doesn't mean crap to me. The people in Macomb County are good people. They'll do the right thing, take care of their own."

Deuce rose, leaned over the desk, and said in a barely controlled voice, "They aren't, though. Children have died. And it's we. *We* aren't taking care of our own."

"It's that dress reform female, isn't it? She's got you all stirred up. Someone spotted you two driving out of town yesterday. Did you take her along on your little scouting mission?"

"Nobody has got me stirred up except myself. This is something I should have done two months ago." Deuce's eyes were hard.

The banker picked a bit of thread off his trouser leg. "Which farm was it? The write-up didn't say."

"Wait a couple of days and you can read all about it in here." Deuce poked his finger at the twisted edition. "I'm still collecting the facts and want to give the dairy a chance to tell their side. I'd be surprised if it was just one operation causing the typhoid anyway. I don't want to brand some farmer as the villain when others are just as lax in their hygiene."

"That's it? That's all you've got to say for yourself?"

Deuce nodded. The two men sat in heated silence for

a number of seconds. Finally the banker stood, his face flushed, his eyes burning.

"All right, if that's how it is," Father Knapp said. "I'm going straight from here to my lawyer. And I'd advise you to pull out that agreement you signed when we set up this arrangement."

The slamming of the door woke Jupiter, who emerged from under the desk, blinking in the morning sunlight.

"Don't count on getting much shut-eye today," Deuce said. "I'm a'guessing there's a whole stream of angry county commissioners and dairymen, not to mention the ag agent, lined up outside waiting their turn."

By evening, Deuce was wrung out. He'd gotten a fair number of irate telephone calls and visits, but there were also some supportive comments, with Dr. Jack at the forefront. There were four kind notes left at the front desk and a silent handshake from the pressman, who had lost a niece to typhoid.

Glad this day is over, Deuce thought as he flicked off his office light. Then he suddenly remembered that he'd invited Tula to the bell concert. The strain of the day was pulling the muscles around his eyes into a steel band. The last thing he wanted to do was face the crowd under the tent. Surely she'd understand. Tula of all people would understand.

When Deuce knocked on the Lakes' screen door an hour later, Marian answered. She was wearing a faded cotton wrapper and there were deep lines etched on either side of her mouth. "Tula will be out in a minute," she said in answer to Deuce's good evening.

"Are you all right?" he asked, concern wrinkling his brow.

"Got a whopper of a headache. Great work on the editorial, by the way." Marian started to turn away.

The skin around her eyes, he saw, was pebbled with fatigue, the eyes themselves matte.

"What's wrong?"

"A headache." She suddenly slumped against the doorway. "No, that's a lie. I went up to the Bellmans'. That girl is at death's door. And it's my fault. I just want to crawl away, get out of here. But I'm stuck." She raised her foot.

From the front lawn came a cricket's sawing chirp. Fall's coming, Deuce thought. "Don't beat on yourself. She's a fighter. I've heard Dr. Jack say that a hundred times. She'll pull through. You'll see."

Marian's voice tightened in dismay. "She's very sick." She turned away again.

Deuce put a restraining hand on her arm. Unexpectedly, he heard himself suggesting they go to the *Clarion*'s offices. "It's quiet there and I have a bottle of whiskey in my desk drawer. We can talk."

"I won't be very good company."

"That's all right. Neither will I."

Tula emerged. "Sorry to keep you waiting. I couldn't find my seed pearl broach anywhere. Do you know where it turned up? In my sewing basket! I can't think how it got—" She stopped abruptly, her eyes darting to Deuce's face. "What's wrong?"

"Marian's got a headache, for one thing."

Tula turned to her houseguest. "Do you want some tablets? I think there are some—"

"She's not up to facing another night of crowds. And to be honest, neither am I. Father Knapp and some oth-

ers really put me through the grinder today. I'll get more
What for? if I show my face at Chautauqua this evening.
We're going to commiserate down at my office. But I
know how much you love the bells, and I'll run you over
there in the auto. Would you give me a rain check on our
date, just this once?"

Tula ducked her head, seeming to concentrate on but-
toning a glove, murmuring, "If she's got a headache, bed
is the best place." But when she raised her head again, she
said politely, "I'd appreciate that. Thank you."

As they entered the newspaper offices, Deuce flicked on
the overhead light. A scarred wooden counter extended
the width of the entire first floor. Beyond that were several rows of desks. Three calendars as big as windows,
courtesy of three different funeral homes, hung above a
bank of filing cabinets.

"The tour starts here," Deuce said. "Sales department—
want ads up front, salesmen at the desks."

Hearing the pride in his voice, Marian mustered a
smile. "It all looks very efficient."

"We'll take the freight elevator up to the newsroom
so you won't have to climb the stairs." He ushered her
into the cage at the back, closed the grille, and pushed the
throttle forward. Marian gazed up into the open shaft
as they rose, the big gear pulling them upward. The oily
cable creaked as it wound above her head.

Deuce pulled back on the throttle and the suspended
box swayed slightly. He pulled open the grille. "And here
we are."

The newsroom was cozier than the first floor. The ceiling was low and several desk lamps cast pools of light. A

black-and-tan hound trotted up out of the shadows, toe-
nails clicking like typewriter keys. Deuce bent to scratch
under the dog's muzzle.

"Who's this?"

"Jupiter. Great old dog." Deuce straightened.

The windows were open and the night was still. No
thunderstorms tonight. Why, for God's sake, didn't I pay
more attention to that storm when I was on the stage? I
could easily have cautioned— Oh, hell! Marian thought.

Deuce was saying, "Let's crack open that bottle."

He guided her to an office with *Publisher* stenciled
on its frosted glass door. Stacks of yellowed editions cluttered the floor and on a legal table another mountain
range of newsprint rose against the wall. Deuce pulled
out the leather chair behind the desk for her.

"Thank you."

"So, some whiskey?"

He opened a drawer and brought out a bottle and two
shot glasses. As he poured, Marian surveyed the room.
On one wall, a lithograph of Lincoln hung among printing samples. A not-unpleasant combination of printer's
ink and cigar smoke perfumed the air. He handed her
a glass and they clinked. The whiskey slopped over her
fingers.

He smiled sheepishly and handed her his hankie.
"Guess I overpoured."

She wondered what this man could possibly want
from her. He wasn't one of those fellows enraged about
her effect on their womenfolk—in fact, he seemed to
genuinely welcome her influence on Helen. But he didn't
seem to be inclined toward lewd speculation about her
unmentionables, either.

"So, what happened at the Bellmans'? Did Hazel give you a piece of her mind? She can be—"

Marian tossed back the contents of the shot glass. "I've never seen anyone that young so close to death. Her fingers. If she'd been holding a book, I could have read the title right through them. Christ. I never dreamed. You stand up night after night in front of the crowds, you stop thinking of them as people. They're just a blurry mass. You pour out the same words. And you know that only the tiniest percentage of those words will hit their mark, make a change. The bit about the consumption and sleeping outdoors, that isn't even my main point. It's just an illustration, for Christ's sake. To explain how I developed my philosophy about dress. But this girl, she took it to heart and now she's sick as hell and it's my fault." Marian stopped abruptly. "Could I have another?"

Deuce poured one for both of them. "Like I said, she's been sick a long—"

"It was all I could do not to burst out in tears in front of her."

Marian emptied the second shot.

"You're being too hard on yourself," Deuce said gently. "Chances are good Jeannette will pull through. She's had a couple of setbacks before and was able to get past them."

"But not this bad."

"Oh, they were just as bad."

"You're sure?"

"Yes."

She relaxed a bit. "What about your day? You caught hell, didn't you?"

"Yeah. I don't feel like talking about it now. But thanks for asking."

They fell into silence. Beneath the desk, Jupiter sighed damply. A crimson mortar board tassel swayed from the desk lamp as a weak breeze passed through.

Four blocks away, a couple was drawing apart. Pulling back from the pressure of Louie's lips on her mouth, his fingers on her breasts, Helen buttoned up her shirtwaist, wiped saliva from her chin. They were seated on the steps of the Garlands' back porch.

"So, will you write?" she asked, pretending to be occupied with smoothing her skirt.

"Certainly." His voice sounded firm. "And let me know when you escape from here and make your way to Chicago. I'll take you round to some galleries. I know lots of artists I think you'd be interested in meeting."

"All right. How about suffragists? I want to be a part of that right off."

Louie tapped his lips, gazed toward the grape arbor, a gray shape against the darkening sky. "Not sure. Most of the women I pal around with are artists' models or mistresses, or both. A few are painters themselves. Suffrage isn't on the agenda at any of the parties I get to." He moved closer again. "Now, since it's my last night in town, I think we should part on friendly terms." He slipped an arm around her waist and busily unfastened the buttons she'd just closed.

Later, one hand on the wire gate leading into the grassy alley, Louie handed her a note. His handwriting was an artful scrawl with strokes dashing at odd angles.

"I don't tend to room in the same place more than a month or two. But you can always reach me there." He pointed to the address. "It's sort of an artist salon."

After a final kiss, Helen watched Louie's white trousers flicker, then disappear in the dimming light.

I guess I should be feeling sad, she thought.

C HAPTER ELEVEN
REFUGEE

"HAS ANYONE SEEN KING COLE'S PAGE? Don't tell me he's run off again!" A red-faced young woman, surrounded by several dozen youngsters, was clapping vigorously. "If you don't stay in your places, we will never get through this."

A little girl dashed over, her long velvet gown dragging in the dust. "I'm hot," she wailed.

"You've strayed too! And where is that page?" the Story Lady shouted.

A young boy snatched off a ruffled collar as thick as a seat cushion and threw it on the ground.

"Jack-Be-Nimble, put that back on this instant," cautioned the Story Lady, pushing sweat from her brow with the back of her hand.

Withering noontime heat swathed the Chautauqua grounds. Behind the tent, the crew boys listlessly tossed horseshoes, producing an occasional clang. Seated on a pile of lumber and observing this scene, Marian and Helen waited for the afternoon program to begin.

Earlier that morning, Tula received a telephone call from Hazel Bellman, reporting that Jeannette had a restful night and was improving, which had lifted Marian's spirits.

She turned to Helen with a wry grin. "The circuit runs through twenty Story Ladies a season."

"No wonder." Helen covered a yawn. "Excuse me. Up too late. Not a job I'd take, that's certain."

"At least the poor girl's got the lungs for it," Marian said as the Story Lady bawled out another set of instructions.

"It's great having you to talk to. I'm going to miss you when you leave."

Marian shook her head. "It's time for me to move on. I'm a restless soul. Another day or two and I'll be back behind the wheel. But I'll miss you too."

Helen sighed. Marian's eyes followed several small knots of women strolling toward the tent. "Guess we better think about getting inside before all the best seats are taken." She picked up her cane.

"I wanted to ask you," Helen said in what she hoped was a careless tone. "You're familiar with Chicago, right?"

"Been many times."

"Have you ever heard of an artist salon called the Dill Pickle Club?"

"Of course. It's famous—among a certain set. I had a long talk with Emma Goldman the anarchist there one time. Why?"

Helen looked away casually. "No reason. Just a place on my list to visit when I move there."

Despite the heat beating through the tent's canvas walls, the superintendent moved briskly up the steps to the platform. With the week almost concluded, his once-white trousers were a dusty beige, but the part at the center of his head remained razor straight.

"Before I bring out this afternoon's speaker, I want to remind you of our big finale tomorrow night with the internationally renowned Bohumir Kryl Band. You will not want to miss this. And, of course, your own Chautauqua Committee is already hard at work planning next year's event. They'd really appreciate it if you all made sure to purchase a subscription for next summer. Do it now, while the inspiring words, the enriching songs are still ringing in your mind. Do it for the betterment of yourselves and your community. Just stop by the ticket booth after the show.

"And now, let's get right to our program. Miss Ruth Valentine is fresh from the front lines in France, and I know you will want to hear about her good efforts. She is one of a small group of American ladies who has undertaken the heroic task of relief work in villages formerly occupied by the Krauts."

A short young woman with freckled features and a turned-up nose stepped behind the podium. Marian relaxed in her chair, ready to hear a good tale. Her ears filled with the light whipping sound created by hundreds of handheld fans.

There was no coughing. Thank God no coughing. Jeannette was better.

"I have only been back in the States three weeks and I am not a professional orator. So please overlook any inadequacies," Miss Valentine began, her brows meeting earnestly. "However, the American people must understand what is happening to the French civilians during this terrible ordeal. Many households there have been reduced to the very old and the very young. All the able-bodied husbands and sons are off fighting. In those villages occupied by the Germans, all the strong young women were shipped to labor camps well behind the lines."

Gripping the podium, Miss Valentine described the conditions the American volunteers found when they were at last allowed to enter the French hamlets that the Germans had abandoned as they pulled back to the Hindenburg Line. In their retreat from the villages, the German soldiers had poisoned wells, chopped down fruit trees, and destroyed Picardy's sturdy stone houses. There was a young mother and her children sleeping on beds of rough planks amidst collapsed walls and open roofs, like huddled livestock. Another family of five had set up housekeeping in a hen house. One of the most pitiful cases was an old farmer whose entire family had been wiped out—two sons shipped off to the trenches, one daughter impregnated by a German soldier during the occupation and run out of the village, the other two daughters transported to German factories, and his wife dead of a broken heart. The relief worker had come upon him one day, wandering numbly among the sap-weeping stumps of what had once been his apple orchard. An old man with stooped shoulders, crying over his trees.

The images of pitiful French villagers, orphaned children, weeping stumps swelled in Marian's mind. Beside her, Helen listened open-mouthed.

Ending with a plea for donations, Miss Valentine removed her short-brimmed black straw hat with the high crown, the sort favored by suffragists, and tossed it out into the crowd to be passed from hand to hand.

"I am also sending out a call to the single women among you between the ages of twenty-five and thirty-five who can drive and speak French. There are hundreds of villagers in northern France who will welcome you with open arms."

Helen grabbed Marian's hand. "I'm going. I'm going to join those women, if they'll have me," she said breathlessly.

"You speak French?" Marian replied.

"No."

"Can you drive?"

"No, but I can learn."

"You're not old enough."

"But I look older. Everyone says so."

Actually, Marian thought, *I* meet the qualifications.

But Helen was continuing: "I've just got to get out of here and do something with my life. Make a contribution now! You must understand that, you of all people."

The crowd was sifting out. Marian and Helen remained seated, turned toward each other with knees almost touching.

"Yes, I see. But it certainly doesn't have to be shipping off to France in the middle of a war. That is something your father and grandfather would never agree to." Marian paused, gazed off in thought. "If I were you, I'd focus on the suffrage, now more than ever. It's been shoved to the wayside, but when the war's over, all momentum will be lost unless some of us hold down the fort."

Helen harrumphed. "What, manning booths like I did out there," she jerked her thumb toward the entranceway, "when not a single person picked up a pamphlet?"

"No, I agree you need to get out of Emporia. Have you talked to your father about Chicago?"

"Yes. He said he'd think it over. But he'll just side with my grandfather in the end."

Marian tilted her head. "If it would help, I know several reputable boarding houses and suffrage organizers. That might reassure him."

"That would be the great!"

A shadow passed behind Marian's eyes. Was this going to be a repeat of the situation with Jeannette? What if something happened to Helen in Chicago? But no, Jeannette was on the mend. Don't overdramatize, she scolded herself.

"We could go down to the paper and talk to Papa right now," Helen urged. "You can manage the trolley, can't you?"

Marian laughed. "Yes. All right, let's go!"

They found Deuce up in the composing room, an open space with raw brick walls and sooty skylights. To one side, a workman in grease-smeared overalls was crouching beside a machine that looked like a motor carriage tipped on end, its gears exposed. "Breakdown?" Helen called out as they approached.

Deuce, seated on a stool, was laying lines of type in a wooden frame. His sleeves were rolled up over muscled arms and he wore an ink-stained worker's apron. He smelled of sweat and oil.

"Yep. Linotype threw a cog two hours ago. George thinks he can get it up and running in time to make deadline, but I got nervous."

"You're setting the pages by yourself?" Helen asked. "Jeez. Couldn't you call in some of the composers?" She laid her hat and pocketbook on a stool and rolled up her sleeves. "I'll help."

"That'd be swell. There's a fairly clean apron in the back."

Helen trotted off. Marian randomly picked a letter

from the type case, rolling it between her fingers.

"So, you are not only the publisher, but you set type as well?"

"Not usually, not anymore. But when the linotype goes down, we all pitch in."

Marian glanced at the machine; the workman's upper body was now buried in its guts.

Deuce grinned.

Helen returned in an apron, a green printer's visor snapped over her forehead. "Papa, we need to talk to you about something."

"Now? It can't wait?"

"Marian's leaving soon and—"

"Oh, right," Deuce said, studying the floor for a moment.

"But if this isn't a good time . . ." Marian put in.

"No, it's a fine time." Deuce began wiping the grease from his hands on a rag. "Grab a stool, ladies."

"I have to get out of this town now. I just can't wait a whole year to get my life started. Boys my age are being shipped overseas to fight, for God's sake."

There was the click of a thrown switch and the linotype shuddered to life, emitting a perfume of oily heat. The workman bent over the keys, jabbing randomly and producing a mighty metallic clatter.

"You're still wanting to leave for Chicago sooner rather than later?" Deuce asked.

Helen's voice came out in a rush. "Marian knows the best rooming houses in Chicago. You won't have to worry about me being safe. And she said she'd write me a letter of introduction. To Mrs. VanWert. She's a leading suffragette, not just in Chicago but across the country.

Most of those pamphlets that our group gives out, she wrote them! And Marian *knows* her."

Deuce tucked his hands under his armpits and studied the floor. After a time he said, "You've certainly got your mother's will. But your grandfather will never agree."

Helen bit her upper lip. "I know. So what I'm thinking is that I just go, without waiting for his blessing. Pack up and get the first train out tomorrow."

"Leaving me holding the bag?" Deuce chuckled grimly. "Guess things can't get much worse between your grandfather and me."

A raw grinding of metal against metal sounded. "Got her going!" the workman shouted. The noise was cold, even in the furnace-like heat of the third floor.

Deuce took Helen's hands. Her fingers were long, elegant, the nails translucent ovals of pearl. Not like Winnie's stubby digits. Funny how some traits got passed from generation to generation and just couldn't be shaken off, while others melted away after a sui generis flowering, the petals extraordinarily lush, exotic, and never to be seen again.

"You have my blessing," he said hoarsely. "I will worry, of course, but I have every confidence in you. You have a good head on your shoulders."

As Helen threw her arms around his neck, Deuce caught a glimpse of Marian's face. It had softened in some small way. And it was then he sensed how deeply sad he would be to see her go.

CHAPTER TWELVE
ESCAPE

EARLY THE NEXT MORNING, while Helen dug in her handbag for an extra hankie, Deuce was pacing impatiently back and forth across the station platform. Twenty steps north. Turn. Twenty steps south. Still no train. He irritably yanked out his pocket watch. The 5:40 to Chicago was four minutes late. The sky lightened so that the water tower, just moments ago a soft wash of grays, was now hardening into its true self. Come on, damn it, Deuce thought, his ears equally alert to an approaching train and to Father Knapp's electric runabout that passed this way every morning. Not usually until six thirty or so, but it would be Deuce's luck that he'd be early and the train would be late. Today of all days. Tula, who was helping Helen locate the hankie, giggled loudly and Deuce quickly shushed her.

Marian approached. "She'll be fine."

"I know, I know. It's not her, it's her grandfather. I just don't want him driving by and spotting us. I want her safely on that train."

"If he shows up, I'll just crack him across the knees with my cane," Marian said, her mouth turned down wryly. She held up her empty hands. "Oh, look at that. I left it in the auto! Didn't even notice."

Deuce's shoulders relaxed slightly. "Must be a relief."

"I gave Helen the names of three good rooming houses. Two right off Halsted and another farther north. She also has a letter of introduction to Mrs. VanWert. So, no worries." She patted his arm.

"No worries," he said unevenly.

The putter of a motorcar sounded from the street. Deuce blanched. It passed the depot but there was not enough light to see who was inside. It kept on going, and Deuce exhaled.

Finally, a full ten minutes late, a whistle sounded far down the tracks as a belch of smoke appeared on the horizon. Two commercial travelers, sample cases in hand, hurried out from the station. The stationmaster dollied Helen's trunk to the edge of the platform. The train pulled in, brakes screeching. Deuce scooped Helen to his chest. Her shirtwaist smelled of starch.

"Thank you, Papa," she said.

He bent, carefully kissing the pale line where her hair parted. She pulled back and, sniffling, brushed at the damp blotches she'd left on his lapel.

Then it was a blur of leave-taking; the conductor hopping off with a step stool, Tula pressing an extra hankie into Helen's hand, the taller of the commercial travelers passing the cases through the car's window, and Marian standing erect to one side, a confident smile on her face.

"Use my name!" she called out.

Deuce, at last, found his voice. "Be careful, dearie!"

Late that afternoon, well past Helen's arrival time in Chicago, Deuce walked over to the Western Illinois Savings & Loan. Crossing the ornate lobby, he briskly approached the wooden fence that enclosed the desk of his father-in-law's secretary. Isabel Bechtold, now in late middle age, retained the cool manner and the blue glass paperweight that she'd brought to the position, straight out of Emporia Business School.

"Good afternoon, Mr. Garland," she said, turning from her typewriter and folding her hands expectantly on the blotter.

"Hello, Isabel. I need five minutes of Father Knapp's time."

She frowned. "He is in. But he said that he had a lot of paperwork and didn't want to be disturbed."

"I have to insist."

Isabel sniffed, but stood and disappeared through the pair of wooden doors leading to George Knapp's office. In a moment she emerged and swung open the little gate that separated her kingdom of notary seals, paper punches, and fountain pens from the public arena, and ushered Deuce in. "He'll see you now."

Father Knapp glanced up from a stack of papers. "Have a seat. Just got a few more pages to initial."

Deuce remained standing. He eyed the green leather chairs where nervous businessmen and farmers came begging for loans. I should have sent Clay over here when he first asked me for money, Deuce thought. Father Knapp would have clipped his wings right away.

"All right then." Father Knapp tilted back, frowning when he saw Deuce still standing. "Have a seat."

"This will only take a minute."

Father Knapp shrugged. "Suit yourself." The springs of his swivel chair squeaked as he shifted position. "I guess you've come to apologize about the editorial. You did a lot of damage, but I think I can help unravel some of it. Of course, things between you and me—"

"Actually, I'm not here to discuss that," Deuce interrupted. "I came to let you know that Helen left for Chicago this morning."

"What?" Father Knapp jumped to his feet. The chair rolled back and hit the glass-doored bookshelves behind him.

Deuce continued in a mild tone: "She has done a fine job at the newspaper and I think she will do just as well up there, so I gave her permission."

"*You* gave her permission? How dare you. That was not your permission to give!" Father Knapp's face was bright red. "You do not have custody of that child. I do."

Anger swept through Deuce, his muscles drawing tightly as piano wires. "She's not a child. She's of age."

Father Knapp sat down with a thump. "Never mind. I'll take care of it. Just give me the name of the hotel where she's staying. I'll get the sheriff to send a man up there." He picked up the receiver.

Deuce's voice was rigid. "I'm not giving you the name. Helen is a responsible young woman. She has a right to make her own way."

The receiver slammed into the cradle. Father Knapp opened his mouth as if to speak, then seemed to think better of it. He sat back in the chair. After a moment he said, in a calm voice, "All right. When Helen is found—and I will find her—she'll be back here living with me. And as of tomorrow, I'll be taking over the *Clarion*. You've been overreaching. You can stay on as editor, overseeing the day-to-day . . . with my approval, of course. I'll want to see a list of the articles before anything is printed. And I'll be hiring someone else to write the editorials. You can't humiliate me like this and get away with it. "

Despite the rage churning inside, Deuce managed to keep his voice level. "There is no way I'll work under those conditions. You don't need to force me out—I quit. And Helen is an adult. You can't control her. Women are changing. This town is changing. Wake up, man—everything is changing! And nothing will be as it was."

CHAPTER THIRTEEN
THE GLIDE

"You look like you could use a drink," Clay said from the front door as Deuce stepped onto the Lakes' porch. "Who put you through the wringer?"

Deuce exhaled heavily. "A drink would be mighty appreciated."

After leaving Father Knapp's office, Deuce had slowly walked back to the *Clarion*. He sat behind his desk, with the idea of emptying out the drawers, but couldn't stir himself to do it. *I should write a final column. A farewell to the readers*, he thought, but decided he wasn't ready to reveal his change of status to anyone just yet. At least for a day or so.

Deuce stepped inside, holding two rather limp bouquets of sweet peas. "I'm grateful that Tula decided to throw this get-together. Takes my mind off that empty house. It will be a tough go without Helen there."

"Glad to do it, old man," Clay said, clapping him on the back. "Hang up your hat and make yourself at home. Hey, Tula, Deuce is here."

After the exchange between Deuce and Clay at the Elks, Clay had sold off the posing chair to a gullible amateur photographer in the next county, at half of what he paid for it. He'd sealed the proceeds in an envelope and stuffed it into Deuce's mailbox. Since then, Clay believed they were back on good footing.

Tula, who had been quite aware of Deuce's arrival, had already removed her apron and patted down her hair. She emerged smiling from the kitchen.

"Just finishing up the shortcakes. Did you hear from Helen?"

Deuce extended the flowers.

"Aren't these lovely!"

"She telegrammed. Didn't say much except she'd arrived, gotten a room at one of Marian's places, and would send me more news tomorrow."

Standing on tiptoe, Tula kissed him on the cheek. "She'll be fine." How quickly things change, she thought. Only yesterday morning, Helen was gloomily entering debits and credits in the newspaper's ledgers and now—well—spending her first night in the city. And I was there to see her off. Like launching a ship!

After Helen's train pulled out, Tula had returned home to the unwelcome chore of canning pears. As she stirred the bubbling sugar syrup in a kitchen already overheated well before midday, Deuce's long face at the station swam into her mind's eye. Poor man. Nothing easy about seeing a daughter leave home. He needed a diversion. There was Chautauqua, of course. But tonight's program was the Jubilee Gospel Singers. The Negro octet with its spirituals, camp meeting shouts, and popular plantation melodies always made him uncomfortable. Why not a party? Just Deuce, Clay, and Marian. She'd pull out the Parcheesi board and serve nuts in those little paper cups left over from the garden club's tea.

"So, what about those streamers Tula put up? And

the table decorated and all? She's a real homemaker,"
Clay was saying.

Her cheeks flushed as she watched Deuce taking in
the green crepe paper and the card table covered with
her mother's daisy-embroidered tablecloth. The Parcheesi
game was laid out; the green, yellow, blue, and red wooden
markers arranged in their starting positions.

"Mighty snazzy," Deuce said. He picked up one of the
game's turban-shaped markers. "Haven't played this in
years. Since Helen was a kid."

An exotic scent—sandalwood?—brushed his nose.
He turned toward the kitchen where Marian stood in the
doorway, a coppery turquoise gown rippling like a river
down her tall frame.

"Evening, all," she said lightly.

As Deuce handed her the second bouquet, a dozen
silver bangles jangled down her arm.

"Thank you, sir. What's the word from Helen?" He
described the telegram and she nodded approvingly.
"Mrs. Richards will take good care of her."

Tula offered to put Marian's bouquet in water. "Lemonade all right with everyone?"

"I'm getting Deuce some whiskey," Clay said, heading
toward the dining room.

"I'll have some of that," Marian said. She surveyed
the game board, rubbing her hands together. "I can't wait
to get started."

Deuce pulled out a chair for Marian.

He took the seat opposite but then jumped up again
when Tula brought out a tray with cut-glass tumblers and
a pitcher of lemonade. "Let me help," he said, passing the
glasses.

Clay poured out the whiskey for Marian, Deuce, and himself, adding a dollop to Tula's lemonade.

"You're going to have to refresh my memory," Marian said. "I haven't played Parcheesi since I was a girl."

The path of play was in the shape of a Greek cross. At the four corners were colored lithographs depicting Victorian ladies in satin gowns prettily arranged among seasonal elements. These were the starting points.

Clay, who had been rattling one of the four dice cups, said, "There's really nothing to it. You move any one of your four pieces counter-clockwise around the board. The first one to get all their pieces in the house at the center wins."

"There's more to it than that," Tula said. "You see, you have to roll a six to get a piece out of your start space and then—"

"It's not six, it's a five," Clay interrupted.

Tula frowned. "I think it's six."

"My, isn't this a charming board," Marian said.

"I got it for my tenth birthday," Tula said as Clay examined the rule sheet. "I always loved these ladies on the corners. I thought they were so beautiful."

"It's five—see here, Tula? If you get a six you take another turn," Clay said, flapping the pamphlet under her nose.

"All right, all right, it's five. I believe you."

"I think it will come back to me as we go. Why don't we just start and see what happens?" Marian suggested.

The game began slowly; all had discharged their dice cups twice before Tula finally rolled a five and slid her yellow marker into play. Soon each player had at least one or two pieces on the board. For a while, the colored markers remained separate but soon some were moving ahead faster than others, and the reds, blues, yellows, and greens became jumbled. It was around this time that Clay, counting aloud, landed on the same space as Marian's foremost piece and returned it to her start spot.

"Back to start for you," he said, leaning backward with his arms crossed and a smug expression on his face.

"What?" Marian cried.

"I've captured your piece. You have to start it again."

Tula looked worriedly from Clay to Marian. "I forgot to mention that when—"

"I remember." Marian smiled thinly. "And isn't there a move called a fortification or something like that?"

"A blockade," Clay explained in a condescending tone. "It's called a blockade. When a player has two pieces occupying the same space, no one else can pass."

"Ah, yes," Marian said coolly.

Tula excused herself to bring out more ice. Marian and Clay bent over the rule sheet.

Deuce's attention slid away from the game, his gaze locking on a pair of china dogs on the mantle, then on the open doors of the phonograph. The tune of a popular fox-trot mushroomed in his head. He sipped the whiskey. Then his eyes fell on that day's *Clarion*, flopped over a stack of library books. Anger suddenly pulsed through his gut. Screw the old man. I'll start my own paper.

Gradually he became aware of a hand on his. His vision swam back to the room. Marian, for it was her hand, was staring at him. He drew in a slow breath, sat up straighter.

"It's your turn," she said.

A smile spread across his face. "So it is."

The game continued for some time, seesawing back

and forth as players had two, three, and sometimes all four markers in play, only to have them captured and sent back to the start. Tula concentrated on her leading pawn, moving it diligently around the path and leaving her other markers languishing in or just outside her starting point. Marian tried to keep all her pieces in motion at once. All Deuce wanted was to stay focused enough not make any foolish moves. Clay could be counted on at every chance to come in for an attack and bump others' pieces off the board.

In the end, it was Tula who was the first to triumphantly shepherd the last of her markers into the center. Clay's fourth soldier never made it home but rather spent its final minutes plodding around the path after first enduring capture by Marian, then by Deuce, and then by Marian again.

"Hah! Guess I got outmaneuvered. Ganged up on me," Clay said, his voice stiff with forced joviality. He flicked a pawn across the board with thumb and index finger. It snapped sharply against his nail. Tula stood, began gathering the glasses.

"Let me help," Marian said, reaching for Clay's empty tumbler.

"Not on your life," he said hastily. "You're our guest. Deuce'll lend a hand with the washing up—right, old man?"

"'Course," Deuce said rising, gathering the dishes in a neat stack. "What'll it be, Tula? Shall I wash or dry?"

Tula planted a hand on her hip, elbow cocked. "Can you be trusted with my best glasses?"

"We'll find out," he said, matching her light tone.

Good, Clay thought, catching the small smile crossing

Tula's face as she bent over the table. He quickly turned to Marian. "Why don't you and I go out on the porch, try to catch a breeze?"

Marian stood and shook out her gown. "If there's a breeze, let me at it. It's hotter in here than in the tent."

As Clay held the screen door open for Marian, he heard Tula laughing in the kitchen. Good sign. Outside, the cicadas screeched steadily, but there was no other sound.

Marian tipped the cat off the wicker rocker closest to the door and settled in. Clay balanced his rear on the railing just opposite her on the narrow porch.

"A little cooler out here," she said.

"So, what do you think of our little town?"

"Nice enough, but I'm a city girl . . ."

"You must be anxious to get back on the road." Clay pulled out a cigarette case. "Mind?"

"Not at all. I'll have one, as a matter of fact."

He raised his brows slightly, held out the open case, and, after she put a cigarette to her lips, bent to light it. She inhaled, shutting her eyes in satisfaction.

"Yes, I'm itchy to get behind the wheel. But Emporia, I will say, has more going for it than a lot of towns I've lectured in. More businesses. Better quality clothing stores."

"Sorry you never made it up to my studio. I've got all the latest gear."

"I'm sure in photography you have to stay—" She waved her cigarette around. "Damn mosquito. They say smoke keeps them away. Anyway, I'd think you need to be current."

"Oh, yes. Have to. My clients demand it."

"And there's the competition too."

Clay leaned against the porch column and exhaled a stream of smoke. "Not much to speak of, glad to say. Just a fellow two counties over and he's—"

"But what about that new shop going in on, oh, I forget the name of the street. You know, the one running parallel to—"

"What new one?" Clay sprang up.

Marian shrugged. "I don't know. I just noticed one of those *Coming Soon* signs when Emmett was driving me around. It was for a photography studio."

Clay tossed the lit cigarette into the yard. Goddamnit! That's all I need. Christ almighty. Everyone's got it in for me, he thought.

A clink of china came from inside. From where he sat on the railing, Clay could see through the living room, into part of the kitchen. Deuce had his head back, laughing. Goddamn him. Handed everything by that late wife of his and deserves nothing. Came from nothing. Worse than nothing.

Clay turned back to Marian. "Yes, well, I'll have to ask Deuce about that. He's up on all the news around town. Or maybe you could ask him for me. You two seem to be pals. Heard you went out to the Sayre farm with him."

Marian narrowed her eyes, as if uncertain how to answer. She stubbed the cigarette out on the porch floor. The cat padded over to investigate. Its tail brushed the inside of her knee.

"We're friendly," she said slowly.

"Well, did your *friend* ever tell you about his family?" A smile crossed his lips, and Marian was struck by its venom.

"You mean Winnie? Yes, I know he's widowed."

"No, I mean the Garlands. His *people*." Clay leaned toward her. She smelled the whiskey on his breath as he said quietly, "Did he ever tell you that he has nigger blood?" He drew back quickly as if he'd lit a packet of firecrackers and expected it to explode any second. But Marian didn't flinch.

"What are you talking about?"

"I mean," he said through clenched teeth, "that years ago somebody in the Garland family—Deuce's great-great-grandfather, maybe—cojoined with a Negro woman. Since then it comes out in all of them in some way—kinked hair, big lips, dark skin. Haven't you noticed how wavy Deuce's hair is?"

"No," she shot back, the corners of her mouth trembling with anger. "Who cares what happened between two people more than a hundred years ago?"

She could tell from Clay's manner that he had expected her to be shocked, aghast. She could never understand why people wasted so much time worrying about racial mixing. A couple of years back when she'd attended the horse races at the Empire City Trotting Club up in Yonkers, she'd seen the pale and willowy Etta Duryea on the arm of her Negro husband, Jack Johnson, the world heavyweight champion who had infamously defeated "The Great White Hope." The couple attracted attention, to be sure. Public outrage among the white community took the form of smashed windows in hotels that housed the couple, inflammatory headlines, and congressional speeches demanding stricter miscegenation laws. Johnson was hated as much for his flamboyance and flaunting of society's conventions as he was for beating a white man in the ring. Still, when she saw the pair, Marian had been more concerned about Etta's unnaturally tiny waist and ashen face than mixed marriages.

Clay, his mouth hanging open, stared at her in an uncomprehending manner. Finally he said, "A lot of people care. People in this town. Everyone knows this about the Garlands, about Deuce. Didn't you notice how he runs the other way whenever a colored shows up?"

Although she had clearly not reacted in the way Clay had expected, his revelation gave her pause. She thought she knew Deuce; if not all the details of his life, then the important parts: his worries about Helen, his ambitions for the *Clarion*. But he had hidden this. Just as with Placidia, Marian had been caught unawares, and she experienced another, very slight, leaking away of confidence in her own judgment.

Clay continued: "And why do you think Tula had this little get-together? So Deuce wouldn't have to squirm through that gospel concert. Everyone would be laughing at him."

"Then they are mean-spirited," Marian countered.

"Some might say Deuce is the laughing stock of Emporia."

"I don't believe that," Marian said. "Deuce has standing in this town. He is the publisher. He has many friends. I have seen people greet him with genuine affection."

"Yes, but it is always there, in the back of their minds. And now with that editorial. Well, he's a pariah for sure."

"That is ridiculous. And this is what I hate about small towns. So much nonsense, so much gossip. You say you are Deuce's friend but you are just a nasty man."

"Shortcake's ready," Deuce's tenor called through the screen door.

She stood abruptly, as did Clay, the tips of their shoes scraping against one another. Marian did not step back but rather purposefully brought down all her weight on Clay's foot, leaning forward. Tears came to his eyes as he grimaced. She applied more pressure, but he didn't yelp.

As Marian and Clay smoked and sparred on the porch, Tula and Deuce were amicably assembling the strawberry shortcake.

"You're in charge of the whipped cream," she said, handing Deuce a bowl and whisk and gesturing toward the ice box.

He saluted. "Yes sir. I mean madam. That didn't come out right." He laughed, sending a fizzy sensation coursing through her veins.

She began arranging the shortcakes she'd baked earlier in the day in individual bowls. Her thumbs broke through the brown crusts and into the soft, spongy centers.

"You gave me that Parcheesi game, you know," she said after a time.

"I did?" The clatter of the whisk against china paused for a moment.

"Yes, for my tenth birthday."

Deuce twisted his mouth to one side. "Something's coming back to me."

"We played Tourists' Curiosities," Tula said as she spooned strawberries onto the shortcake. "The lights were lowered and Clay passed around what he said was a mummy's hand."

"An old leather glove stuffed with damp sand!"

"Yes, and what else? Oh, the curious sea urchin!

Wasn't that my mother's pin cushion with the sharp ends of the needles sticking out?"

"Yes, and Earl Mummert stuck his finger and ran home crying!" Deuce said gleefully. "I need to remind him of that next time I see him. How's this look, by the way?"

He held out the bowl and Tula scooped a finger in the froth. A weak curlicue trailed in its wake. "Little more," she said.

She loaded the four plates, minus the topping, onto a japanned tray along with dessert forks and fresh napkins.

"Those were the days. We had quite a gang," Deuce said. "Sometimes it seems like yesterday. Just goes by so fast."

Tula guessed he was thinking of Helen. "She'll be fine. Really. You did the right thing."

Deuce nodded. "Tough, though. Really tough."

"Besides the tourist game, what else was there?" Tula snapped her fingers. "Famous Lovers. Oh, you boys hated that one."

Deuce shrugged. "No memory." He handed her the bowl to inspect. This time, the curl stood firm. She added dollops on top of the strawberries as she talked.

"It was sort of like Twenty Questions but the answer was a pair of lovers, like Hera and Zeus."

She handed the empty bowl back to Deuce. His head was turned toward the porch. Marian was saying something in strong tones. There was a certain look in Deuce's eyes Tula recognized. Criminently, he's infatuated with that woman and doesn't even know it, she thought. Her eyes misted with disappointment and anger. How could he turn to someone he'd just met, who had not earned his affection in any way? Tula was the better woman. Easy to say you're improving the woman's lot by sweeping through town and shaking things up. The harder part is staying put and trying, in little ways, to make things better.

The screen door slammed as Clay and Marian stepped inside. Marian blinked in the bright light. Deuce stood in the living room; his burnished cheeks, his silver hair, filled her vision. She moved toward him, and she realized with a start that she was galvanized by more than the simple urge to further enrage Clay. Fire wicked into her cheeks. For the first time she noticed that Deuce was the rare man who was taller than she. Behind him, Tula clutched the tray of desserts with a stiff expression on her face. Marian took the seat that Deuce pulled out. He scrambled to do the same for Tula but she ignored him. Clay grabbed a plate and carried it to the window.

Deuce brought a forkful of shortcake to his lips. "This is delicious!"

"Thank you. I'm glad you find it suitable," Tula said, her tone clipped.

Marian wondered what was wrong. All Tula's light spirits had drained away. Maybe some music would help.

"May we?" she gestured toward the Electrola.

In a flat tone, Tula said, "Pick whatever you'd like."

"Grand idea," Deuce said.

Marian put down her fork and walked to the cabinet. Crouching to flip through the phonograph records, she ignored the flicker of pain in her ankle.

"Too slow. Another dirge. What is this? Never heard of him," she said, shoving recordings back into their slots. "Now, this is more like it."

She waved a record at Deuce.

"Which one is that?" Tula asked.

"'The Gaby Glide.'"

"That isn't one of mine," Clay said, interrupting his contemplation of a streetlamp.

Tula pushed away her uneaten shortcake. "It belongs to one of the junior Red Cross girls. She brought it over to play while we rolled bandages."

Marian switched on the machine, placed the record onto the turntable, and settled the needle in place. She swayed as the voice of Billy Murray, the Denver Nightingale, filled the room.

Ev'ry body's raving 'bout the real Frenchy two-step,
Ev'ry body wants to do this smart fancy new step,
It's a funny bear . . .

One arm extended, hips swaying, Marian slid sideways toward Deuce, who was still seated.

"Did you see *Vera Violetta*?" she asked. When he shook his head she said, "I forgot. Broadway is a thousand miles away. This was the big number. Here, let me show you."

She reached out her hand and Deuce allowed himself to be pulled from his seat.

"I wonder if you should be dancing on that ankle," Clay remarked.

Tula's face was a rigid mask. "I'm going to clear the table." She deposited the dirty dishes on the tray with a clatter. Clay took to the porch, banging the screen door behind him. Neither Deuce nor Marian appeared to notice.

"You stand here," she said, positioning Deuce behind her. The warmth of his fingers radiated through the sheer fabric of her gown and the single layer of its undervest. She caught her breath, then continued, "We both face forward and you take my hand. By the way, did you know that some of these new dances are furthering the campaign for dress reform? You need free-falling skirts and low-heeled slippers to do them justice."

"I can see why," he said.

"Scooch closer."

The song came to an end, the needle announcing the completion of its journey with small staccato hisses as it bumped against the final groove.

Deuce's breath skimmed her neck and she relaxed back into his arms. Her limbs tingled with a delicious dissolving sensation that seemed to extend through the entire room and then beyond, until she imagined that Tula's house, the entire treelined street and the whole of Emporia itself with its dusty storefronts and creaky trolley, were all suffused in a golden glow.

A shrill ring from the telephone blew her reverie to bits. Both Marian and Deuce, who had been unconsciously swaying side to side in unison, froze. Their hostess hurried into the hallway where the telephone continued to jangle until Tula picked up the receiver.

"Yes." Pause. "Oh my God. Oh God." Tula's voice wavered but did not break. "Certainly. Yes, I'll be right over."

Marian stepped away from Deuce as Tula reentered the room, a handkerchief balled in her hand. Clay, slipping in from the porch, stood behind the sofa.

Tula exhaled heavily. "That was Dr. Jack. Jeannette has passed away. I'm going over. Her mother is hysterical."

"No!" Marian wailed.

Deuce grabbed his boater from the rack. "I'll drive you, Tula. It'll only take a minute to get the motor cranked up."

Tula lifted her hand. "It'll be just as fast walking. Anyway, you're needed here." She rushed through the back door.

Marian had collapsed into an armchair, her face as pale as custard. She sat in stunned silence and then tears formed, swamping her eyes and running down to the end of her chin where they fell, mottling her lap with nickel-sized splotches.

Deuce knelt beside her.

She whispered, "It's my fault. This would never have happened if it wasn't for me."

Deuce frowned, saying gently, "No, no. Jeannette had been sick a long time. For many months." He fumbled in his pocket for a handkerchief.

"But the pneumonia was my fault." Marian dropped her head, sobbing heavily. Deuce, still squatting, put his arm around her shoulders.

Clay walked out from behind the sofa where he had been silently observing the scene. "You certainly did go on and on about how sleeping in the fresh air was a curative. I remember that quite clearly."

Deuce shot him a look. "You weren't even at the lecture."

"I heard about it from clients. Especially as Jeannette got sicker. Marian's speech was mentioned whenever the girl's name came up. It's the talk of the town. Some say it's her fault."

Deuce rose to his feet. "You take that back."

Marian said hoarsely, "No. He's right."

"Yeah, listen to her. She's been leading you around by the nose all week so why switch horses now, as they say? I think an argument could be made that Jeannette would still be among us if she," he stepped closer to Deuce, "if your *lady friend* here, hadn't ever shown her face in this town . . ."

Deuce was no longer listening to the words from Clay's mouth but was focusing on his lips. He wanted nothing more than to wipe the smirk off Clay's face, to shut him up. Deuce felt the pressure of all those jeering taunts that had battered against his own ears as a boy.

Clay continued, "I for one wouldn't regret it one bit if I never laid eyes on—"

Deuce's fist skidded across Clay's cheek, smashing his lips into his teeth. Clay stumbled back, wiping his chin and looking with surprise at the bright blood smeared across the back of his hand.

Deuce abruptly turned back to Marian. "Let's go."

She stared up at him with a confused expression.

"Come on," Deuce said, extending his hand and noticing that it was wet with Clay's blood. He wiped it off with one of the crumpled napkins from the table.

Marian had trouble getting to her feet, even with Deuce's help. Her face wore a numb expression.

"Get the hell out of my house," Clay hissed through bloody teeth. He cupped a hand under his chin to catch the flow.

Deuce encircled Marian with his arm as they made their way to the door.

"I said get the hell out!" Clay shouted from behind them. "You're nothing but a nigger. You've been protected all these years by the Knapps, but you can't deny your blood. I may be at the lower end of the ladder, not one of Emporia's ruling elite, but at least I'm no nigger."

Deuce winced. Outside, Marian paused to steady herself against the porch railing.

"He's just talking out of his hat," Deuce said quickly.

Without seeing, Marian stared across the shadowy lawn. He tucked her hand in his elbow and guided her up the drive to his house.

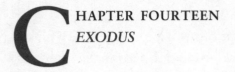

CHAPTER FOURTEEN
EXODUS

"Hope you don't mind a little dust."

Dabbing at her swollen eyes, Marian barely glanced at the room. "It's fine," she said, her voice thick.

Deuce guided her to the spare bedroom's overstuffed chair. "I'll see if Helen left behind some night clothes. Be right back."

Floorboards creaked as he passed down the hall. She stared dully at the Singer sewing machine shoved into one corner, a stack of yellowed *Collier's* magazines, the bed draped with a faded green coverlet, a set of Indian clubs. A jumble of castoffs.

Footsteps returned. "Found this," Deuce said, holding up a night dress, clearly too small for Marian.

"Thanks." She managed a tight smile.

"And clean towels in the bathroom."

She didn't answer. She felt his hand uncertainly hovering above her head, then tentatively stroking her hair. His touch was light. "Try to get some sleep. Things seem worse at night. My room is on the right if you need anything." He started to leave, then turned back. "About what Clay said . . ." Dust seemed to fill his mouth. For the first time since Dr. Jack's telephone call, Marian appeared to be listening. "It's true." Deuce squeezed his eyes shut.

"Some Garland, way back . . ."

Marian leaned toward him. "It doesn't matter to me." Her tone was soft.

Warmth spread beneath his ribs. "Thanks." He pecked her on the cheek, then stepped into the hall, quietly closing the door behind him.

After a few minutes, she heard the snap of a light chain. There was the sound of a faucet running, then the brisk tap of a toothbrush against porcelain. The chain snapped off and shortly after came the exhalation of bedsprings.

Marian rose from the chair, stretched out on the bed, fully clothed. The air hung thick around her. Above, the plaster ceiling formed an unbroken gray scrim. Feverish images unrolled across it: Tula's hand lifting the telephone receiver, her rictus of despair, the poor girl's bony, heaving chest. Marian sobbed heavily until the pillowcase was soaked through.

After a time she became aware of the silence beyond the open window. She got up and found her way in the dark, down the stairs and out onto the porch. The iron handrailing was cool to the touch. On the sidewalk, under the inky canopy of trees, Marian turned right. Most of the houses were dark. Half a block ahead, a light fell from open windows but, as she approached, it was switched off. Three blocks along she became aware of a heavy throbbing in her ankle. She had not done this much walking since the accident. Ten minutes later she limped to the grove at the edge of the Chautauqua grounds. The trees gave off the dusty scent of herbs. She leaned against a trunk, her ankle pounding with the beating of her heart. Close by, the tent lay dark and motionless. And beyond it, across an expanse of grass, the Bellmans' small house burned like a lantern, every window lit. After a time, she closed her eyes, but the image of the windows was imprinted on her eyelids. *I'm sorry. I'm so sorry.* Over and over the words ran though her head until her mind emptied and her lips moved automatically. She remained standing in this way until the rising dew seeped through her stockings and the sky began to lighten.

The walk back to Deuce's took a long time. She had to make a number of stops to rest her ankle that had stiffened during her vigil. The throbbing sensation had moved up into her calf. By the time she mounted the porch steps, a few people were out and about. A milkman made a delivery at the house across the street, the wire basket of bottles tinkling as he walked up the driveway.

Inside, the house was hushed. Deuce must still be asleep. She got herself up the stairs, pulling heavily on the banister. In the bathroom, she stripped down to her sweat-soaked undervest and slip. As she turned on the cold tap, she glimpsed the drained and haggard face in the mirror. Her hair stuck out in irregular tufts and the skin under her eyes was dark with strain. She wet down a washcloth and pressed it against her face, the nape of her neck. She started down the hall, pausing outside of Deuce's room. The door was ajar and the sound of steady breathing washed into her ears. Exhaustion swept over her. She had never felt so alone. Without thinking, she stepped inside. The pearly predawn light illuminated the outlines of a bed; the publisher's sturdy shape stretched out on the far side. The floorboards were cool. A current of air stirred the curtains, tugged at her slip. She crossed the room and slowly eased herself between the sheets, careful not to disturb him. But he must have been half awake.

"Come here," he whispered, maneuvering one arm beneath her ribs, the other around her waist. He pulled her to his chest.

"I don't—"

"I know. Just lay quiet." He gently kissed the top of her head. Through the thin weave of his undershirt he smelled of soap and sweat. After some minutes she exhaled heavily, releasing the taut coils in her arms and legs. Somewhere down the block a dog barked, then stopped. Silence radiated. Her thoughts swam languidly. She floated in a cool bath, her hair rippling, tugging at the nape of her neck. Tidal exhalations slipped in and out of her ears. Something roused her. She lifted her head from Deuce's chest, inundated with gratitude. In the dim light, her lips searched for his cheek. Instead, her mouth brushed the corner of his. He shifted slightly, their lips met. His tasted of whiskey and tooth powder. Suddenly he was kissing her throat, her forehead, running his tongue gently along the rim of her ear. She exhaled and slid her leg over his thigh. Felt the firmness through his combinations. A hot pulse of desire ran through her. She shuddered.

Deuce knelt, tugged off her drawers. Then moved to her undervest. She clutched the hem to pull it off. "No. Let me." He kissed her collar bone, brushed his tongue across her nipples. She reached down, feeling a springy erection pushing against her hand. His mouth nestled in the side of her neck while his fingers explored her breasts, rimmed her naval, sprung her legs, and slid two fingers deep inside. Marian wriggled. She pulled at his drawers. He quickly rose and slipped them off, then climbed back into bed, pressing the full weight of his body against hers. When he entered it was as if all her empty spaces were filled.

Afterward they lay without speaking. "I didn't mean for that to happen," Deuce said at last. "But I'm not sorry."

"Me neither."

He lifted her hand, kissed her palm.

After a time she said, "I have to leave today."

"I know. I don't like it, but I know. Now, get some sleep."

Deuce woke first. He eased an arm out from under Marian's head and slipped from the bed. Downstairs, he filled the coffee pot with cold water and took a jar of raspberry preserves and loaf of bread out of the pantry, in case she wanted toast. He was standing on the back porch sipping his second cup of coffee when she came downstairs.

"Morning. Find the towels?" he asked as she joined him.

She nodded. When he asked if she wanted coffee she burst into tears. "I just keep thinking about that poor girl." She covered her mouth and hurried back inside.

After a while she returned, dabbing her reddened eyes with a handkerchief. They sat side-by-side on the porch steps, gazing at the hedgerow concealing the alley.

"You know, Helen will be eternally grateful for your time here. She needed to get out, and you helped me see that. It's just that a father worries."

Marian blew her nose. "She'll be fine. By the way, how did her grandfather take it?"

Deuce sighed. "Not too well. As a matter of fact, he was livid. I've never seen him that angry. Even angrier than about the editorial."

"He'll get over it."

"Maybe. So anyway, he's taking over the *Clarion*."

"What! He can't do that."

"Unfortunately, he can. He's a silent partner and owns more than half." Deuce rubbed his jaw. "I didn't have the money to buy it on my own twenty-odd years ago. Then, when I did have the money, he wouldn't sell me his shares."

"You knew he might do this, didn't you? When you put her on the train yesterday."

"It crossed my mind."

"But you let her go anyway." Marian's tone softened. "What are you going to do?"

"Kiss you." He leaned over, pressing his lips against hers.

She drew away with a slight smile. "You know what I mean."

"Already did it. I quit."

"What?"

"I resigned. What else could I do?"

"But how will you earn a living?"

"I've been thinking of opening a small-job shop. You know, printing business cards and invitations. Things like that."

Marian took his hand, running her finger along the calluses at the base of each finger.

Deuce continued, "I'll be all right. You know, Helen's not the only one who's glad you came to town." She began to pull away. "Don't worry," he added, "I'm not going to try to persuade you to stay. I just want you to know I'm going to miss you."

She tucked her lips under her teeth. Why is this so

painful? she thought. Once she got on the road, she knew, she'd feel better. That's how I am. Choose a course, then don't look back.

"I'll miss you too."

He rose quickly. "Let me dress and I'll go over to Tula's and collect your things."

She smiled wanly. "Should I warn Clay?"

Deuce snorted. "No. I'm sure he's in hiding. Probably retreated to the studio. That's where he holes up when things don't go his way."

The remainder of the morning unraveled in the speedy fashion of all leave-takings. Deuce stood on his porch as Marian motored round the block, testing her ankle. Swiftly now, Emmett appeared, struggling to strap Marian's trunk to the rear bumper. When Tula materialized on the back porch, dark smudges under her eyes from sitting up all night with Hazel Bellman, Marian walked over, as if approaching the bench for sentencing. Tula, maybe out of pity, gave her a small hug before turning back to the house. Deuce took Marian in his arms, breathing in the scent of her hair, her skin, and committing it to memory. She pulled away and climbed into the auto. Her duster billowed out behind her. Then there was just the dust.

PART II

C

HAPTER FIFTEEN
BANGING AWAY ON LULU

So, I guess the big news from here is that the Gar-
land Weekly and Print Shop is up and running as
of last month. I got a good deal on a storefront
and the landlord threw in the apartment above
for the same rent. I sold the house. It was too big
for just an old widower anyway. The word from
Helen is that she's collecting fares on a trolley line.
From her letters home, she seems happy enough.
As for me, I think of you every morning when I
sit on the back steps drinking my coffee. I've had
to brush some fallen leaves off a couple of times,
and in not too long it'll be snow, but I'll be sitting
there just the same.

THINKING OF DEUCE'S LETTER, Marian scrutinized the
Picardy sky, cloudless and cold as steel. His note had arrived in the fall, four months earlier, while she was still in
New York. Now snow masked the frozen mud of eastern
France. Was Emporia, too, encased in white? A stiff wind
blew through the truck's open cab. She shoved her hands
under her armpits.

Nezzie, her partner on this day, trotted over and
hoisted herself into the passenger seat. She gave off the

odor, like all the women in the Fielding College Relief
Unit, of hastily sponged flesh combined with the lanoline
stink of wet wool. Give me another two weeks here and
I'll smell the same, Marian thought.

"We've got to go round back to the stable for the load
of blankets. I grabbed chocolate bars and a canteen of tea
for us," Nezzie said.

"How long do you think we'll be out?"

"Four villages to supply and these roads? Likely all
day and into the evening."

Under her coat, Marian's shoulders, already rounded
from fatigue, slumped further. Since arriving two weeks
ago, she had spent most of her days getting the vehicle,
a former delivery truck, up and running. It had broken
down in the fall, she'd been told, and towed into the
courtyard where it proceeded to collect fallen leaves, then
a heavy layer of snow. She'd spent long, solitary hours
cleaning the truck's carburetor, testing the plugs, and
pouring jugs of scalding water into the radiator.

At the stable Nezzie hopped out energetically. "Get in
the back. I'll hand the stuff up."

With difficulty, Marian maneuvered between the
driver's and passenger's seats. The skirt of the relief unit's
impractical military-style uniform constricted her hips.
She tugged the jacket, riding up her waist, back into place.

When the truck was packed, Nezzie leaped inside
and Marian released the brake with a yank. The truck
shuddered past the broken-down château that housed the
unit's mess hall. Nezzie waved gaily at the rest of the unit,
fifteen or so women, who were shoveling snow from the
main house's partially collapsed cellar. Several stuck out
their tongues in response.

She turned to Marian. "Aren't we the lucky ducks? If we hadn't drawn delivery duty, we'd be digging out too."

"I guess," Marian said with hesitation. "But isn't there a chance we'll get shelled or have a bomb dropped on us? You know, if we don't make it back in daylight?"

"Oh, we won't get hit! The chances are one in a million. Once you've been here for a while, you'll think nothing of it." Nezzie's mittened hand indicated the scarred landscape, the black smudge on the far horizon that Marian knew was the front.

They bumped along the snowy ruts in silence, Nezzie clumsily fumbling in her coat pocket before nipping off a mitten with her teeth. Fishing bare-fingered, she produced a cigarette with a grin.

"Did I hear you say you're from Boston?" Marian asked.

"Near Brookline. Know it?"

"No."

Nezzie puffed on the cigarette and idly surveyed the flat Picardy countryside with its open vistas of dormant beet fields. "Hard to believe we're only seventy miles from Paris."

After a couple of minutes Marian pressed on. "When did you graduate from Fielding?"

Nezzie exhaled a plume of smoke. "Class of '16. You know, you should give this truck a name."

Marian was calculating the difference in their ages. Ten years. "What? The truck?"

"Yes. Like Old Iron Sides or something. Let's come up with a good one—it'll be fun." Nezzie held out the cigarette, pinched between thumb and forefinger. "Want a drag?"

Marian shook her head.

"I know it's nasty. Pops would hit the roof if he knew. Turn here."

From overhead came the thrum of an engine—the steady drone of an airplane. A film of sweat spread across Marian's brow.

"Not close enough to worry," Nezzie said, leaning out with her face turned skyward.

They left the main road, jolting onto a country lane lined with bare trees.

Not far ahead, smoky threads rose from Canizy's broken buildings. At the end of an alley of trees, the road curved gently north, wending across another expanse of dun-colored plain. Suddenly Marian was in Deuce's car, driving back to town after that visit to the farm. The searing heat, sunlight beating down. Flat pastures rolled by. Beneath the floorboards, the motor putt-putt-putted, pushing up the temperature even more. A bevy of starlings rose in unison.

She started when Nezzie slapped the dashboard. "I've got it! Lulu. After that song the soldiers sing—'Banging Away on Lulu.'"

Marian smiled absently, still back in Emporia. "Yes. Lovely."

They jostled over a particularly deep rut and made the final turn into Canizy's single street. Marian steered around a jagged heap of bricks—all that was left of a dynamited church—and past blackened ruins that had once been trim cottages. Most were simply rubble, but here and there a single wall stood steadfast, the yellow or blue of its plaster keeping up a brave face. The destruction was still as much of a shock to Marian as it had been two weeks before when she had made her inaugural visit with a load of sewing machines.

A flock of little girls, all gripping black shawls tightly under their chins, ran out.

"*Bonjour, les filles!*" Nezzie called. "Hello, girls! Good to see you."

Most wore torn lisle stockings over sparrow legs, although some, Marian noted with a wince, had no stockings at all. The truck rolled to a stop and she yanked the hand brake as the children crowded around.

"What do you have today?" one called out.

Marian guessed that they were expecting the unit's traveling store, and not a load of scratchy woolen blankets. Once a week the truck was outfitted like a peddler's cart with bins of notions, lengths of cloth, soap, fascinators, sabots, and a brass band of tinware clanking from its sides.

Nezzie was rooting in the leather satchel at her feet, complaining loudly, "Where did I put the sewing kits?"

Another child jumped on the running board, her wind-chafed face serious. "Great Uncle says I may buy galoshes if you have them."

Nezzie leaned out the window. "I'm sorry, but we are not bringing the store today, *mes filles*, but I promise to make sure you get your galoshes."

When Marian had first arrived, she thought the villagers, who all seemed in search of galoshes to cope with the region's famously gummy mud, were asking for the filmy rubbers that American businessmen snapped over their shoes on rainy days. She soon learned that in Picardy, galoshes had patterned leather tops and cloglike wooden soles. More importantly, Picardy's galoshes differed from the all-wooden style worn in Brittany. This had become an issue when Marian pulled into the tiny crossroads of Ham with Brittany-style footwear, a mistake on the part of the regional Red Cross supply station, and hadn't been able to give away a single pair because the villagers refused to change styles. Remembering this, she thought of the fraternal pins on Deuce's lapels, authenticating him as a native Emporian in good standing. She smiled. Funny how important little things like that could be.

Nezzie returned to her excavations and at last pulled several paper packets of needles and cards of thread from her bag. "Ah hah! Sewing kits for all!" she shouted and was met with squeals of delight. "*Merci, madame,*" the children exclaimed before running off toward what now passed for their homes—barns, partially ruined cottages, cellar-ways with improvised roofs, chicken coops. It was really too cold to be out in the open. And who was there to greet them when they eagerly rushed in with their prizes? Very likely an ancient grandmother or crippled uncle, for Canizy, like all Picardy's villages formerly occupied by the Germans, was a town of the very young and the very old.

Nezzie pulled on her worsted mittens and tugged the scarf over her mouth. "I'll find Old Lalonde. Be right back." She hopped from the truck, trotting toward a barn from which issued a rag of smoke.

Old Lalonde was Canizy's acting mayor. A man of at least sixty, with the narrow eyes and leathery jowls of a pelican, he served in place of the official mayor who had been sent as forced labor to Germany. *Avec les boches,* as the villagers said. The Fielding Unit depended on the charcoal maker's immaculately penned lists of the hamlet's households, which included the names and ages of each inhabitant, to ensure an equitable distribution of Red Cross supplies. The Fielding Unit's director was constantly harping on the diplomacy needed to tiptoe around the village families, most of whom were members of interrelated clans mired in ancient blood feuds. Not so different from what I saw in Emporia, Marian thought.

A bony dog emerged from under an overturned and wheelless wheelbarrow, tentatively sniffing the air. Something about the color of its coat, or maybe the shape of its head, reminded Marian of Deuce's dog. What was its name? She could see it following them around the newsroom. This French dog was obviously starving; the span between its rib cage and hips shriveled against its spine. Marian dug into the pocket of her overcoat, hoping to unearth a crust of bread. Nothing. With effort, she leaned over, bumping her head against the gearshift, to check under the seat. There was a great deal of dried mud, a crumpled piece of paper that turned out to be a work order, and—what luck!—a withered apple. Grunting, Marian pulled herself upright. But the dog was gone.

Old Lalonde and Nezzie were striding toward the truck.

"I must check the quality of the blankets," he was saying. "If they are lightweight, each individual should receive two. That is only fair, no?"

Nezzie, trotting slightly behind, widened her eyes. An airplane passed overhead, and Marian tensed until she saw the red and blue of the Union Jack on its canvas wings.

The entire process took well over an hour. The acting

mayor fingered the blankets and contemplated his lists.
He argued with Nezzie when she contended that a family
of three who shared a bed should get three blankets, not
one as he insisted. Finally, he yanked the clapper of the
church bell mounted on a pole beside the tumbled sanc-
tuary walls. The response to the call was prompt. Two
ancients, weighed down under an assortment of skirts,
undervests, topcoats, capes, and open-work shawls, approached. From a partially collapsed garden shed, a
woman shepherded three young children toward the
mayor, who was forming a line with an excess of hand
waving and shouting, the pouch beneath his chin swaying. Two older men, one missing a leg and leaning heavily
on an improvised crutch, the other with a cap sitting atop
a bandaged head, took their places. Soon the tattered line
stretched halfway down the street. Old Lalonde made
various tick marks beside their names as each stepped forward to receive blankets. Many of the women insisted on
inspecting the closeness of the weave and the tightness of
the binding, as if considering a purchase from a fine shop.

After the last patron was served, Old Lalonde hurried off to make a permanent record of the disposition
of woolen blankets on this, the sixth of January 1918,
to thirty-seven residents—all that remained of the one
hundred households in Canizy, in the *région* of Picardy.
Tucked under his arm were two blankets, rolled together
so as to appear as one.

Marian settled her rump onto the running board,
wishing away the ache in her back and shoulders while
Nezzie racketed around the back of the truck, reordering
the tumbled stacks of their remaining stock.

"We've enough for our other stops."

Groaning, Marian pushed herself to her feet. With effort, she flipped up the engine cover to retard the spark, glancing up to scan the sky for telltale silver glints, but there were none. An old man, bundled thickly in brown serge, a crisscross of scarves, and a leather satchel slung across his back, wavered past on a bicycle. The downward stroke of his galoshes was so erratic that it seemed as if he might topple over. He rolled to a stop in front of a substantial home that was now broken open like a smashed bird's egg. The roof and one entire side had been torn away, leaving only a low addition intact. The lintel remained but the door was missing. After knocking twice on the empty casement, the man laboriously swung the bag to his hip and began thumbing through its contents. The mistress of the house emerged, wiping her hands on her apron and talking to the postman in an animated fashion. For a moment, Marian thought she was hallucinating. But no, the creak of the leather satchel, the faint tang of wood ash, was real enough. The pair was acting as if this were a regular, tranquil summer morning, rather than frigid winter in the middle of a cataclysmic war. As if the backyard gardens were embowered with spiky hollyhocks rather than muddy excavations left behind by soldiers searching for buried caches of coins. As if this were Emporia in August instead of smashed and gutted Canizy, fifteen miles from the front, with the constant threat of bombs dropping from above. She thought of the last time she'd seen Emporia. Deuce standing in the driveway as she drove away. I've done nothing but drive away, run away, all my life, she thought. She sighed heavily.

Nezzie abruptly slammed the truck's back door,

thrusting Marian back into the present. She hurriedly dabbed her eyes with the edge of a scarf.

"That went fairly smoothly, don't you think?" Nezzie said breathlessly.

Marian nodded. "Where to next?" she asked dully.

"Nesle. But really, I'd say we make a first-rate team."

The warmth of Nezzie's voice caught Marian by surprise. She brightened.

Nezzie tamped the end of a fresh cigarette against the dashboard. In an exaggerated British accent, she added, "Onward, my good woman!" Her nose and cheeks glowed as the match flared. "Want a puff?"

And yes, Marian did.

They had handed out the last of the blankets and were heading back to the château, as washes of lavender tinted the evening sky. It had been a long day but the near-empty truck rattled satisfactorily.

Nezzie spoke after several minutes of companionable silence. "I know who you are."

"What?"

"I know who you are. I've read your articles about dress reform and all that. I think you've done a lot of good. Most girls my age don't wear corsets anymore—and it isn't only because of the steel ration."

"Humpf," Marian puffed. "It doesn't seem all that important compared to this." She swept her hand across the view, taking in the empty truck, the scarred fields.

"I disagree." Nezzie yawned heavily. "Excuse me. I'm bushed. Mind if I grab a quick nap?"

"Not at all."

"You're not drowsy?"

Marian shook her head.

"You know the way?"

Nezzie curled against the far door, tucking up her boots, pulling the red tam low on her forehead. She shut her eyes. A few early stars broke out in the silent sky. Marian thought of the blankets tucked around sleeping children back in the darkening villages.

They were about six miles from the château when the far horizon erupted in a violent spurt of rhythmically pounding trench mortars. A scrim of reds and yellows dropped across the sky. The noise, even from this distance, was concussive. Marian's fingers clamped rigidly around the steering wheel. Nezzie, her head bobbing against the window frame, opened her eyes briefly and then shut them again. Steady, old girl, Marian thought, pushing well back in the seat and straightening her arms. They jolted on, past roadside stumps that looked like so many black coal scuttles.

After a time the road narrowed, then dipped below the fields so that the flares to the east were briefly veiled. Marian exhaled heavily. The sounds of the explosions were muffled. The truck rattled over a set of railroad tracks. A thin buzz, barely noticeable, quivered at the horizon. Over the course of a few minutes the drone slid into a steady hum. The sound grew louder, separating into the rumbling dip and surge of a powerful airplane motor. Suddenly a piercing whine descended through the night sky and exploded into light and ear-shattering noise only a dozen yards from the truck. A furious black fountain of earth surged through the open windows. Gravel and frozen clods of dirt rained down on the two women. Nezzie's lips worked frantically but her words were drowned out by the terrific noise of the blast that was slamming against Marian's ears. The truck tipped onto two wheels, smashing Marian against the door, before it righted itself and rocketed forward into the blackness. Stunned and half-blinded by debris, she wrenched the steering wheel toward what she prayed was the road.

Then came the dreadful whine of a second bomb cutting through the darkness. Closer this time. The force of the blast sent the truck spinning. Jerky patterns of dazzling radiance and blackness skittered past, as if someone were madly flicking a spotlight, on, off, on, off. A corner of the roof ripped open, pouring dirt and jagged shards of metal into the cab. Marian, fighting the urge to duck, locked her elbows and drove on, hoping to get away from the railroad tracks. Her right leg was shaking so violently it threatened to jolt off the gas pedal. She glanced at the passenger seat. Empty. Oh God. Where's Nezzie? She must have been thrown from the truck.

Marian raised her foot to jam on the brake when something rammed brutally into the truck's radiator. A direct hit, Marian thought frantically. Her bowels let loose. There was a wetness, a stink. A heavy thud of collapsing metal was accompanied by the smash of breaking glass. She jolted violently forward then backward, cracking her knee against the dashboard. Although her thoughts were scrambled, she was aware that the third bomb hadn't detonated—yet. But it will, she thought. It will. She twisted toward the door but the steering column had been knocked cockeyed, pinning her in place. Marian's heart thudded wildly. She squeezed her hands under the steering wheel, trying to push it forward. No go.

Suddenly, a fierce hissing erupted near the grille. I'm

going to die here, she thought. Blown into a thousand pieces in the middle of nowhere. Far away the trenches flared to life, momentarily illuminating a snow-covered field, white and uneven, stretching just beyond her reach. Jeannette Bellman's tangled white bedclothes flew into her mind—the girl's eyes glowing feverishly in the pinched, pale face. *I've got to get out.* Nezzie was lying somewhere close by, severely injured . . . or worse.

Marian shoved her hand inside her coat, touching Deuce's letter before pushing on the steering column with all her strength. This time it shifted incrementally. She tried to slide out but couldn't quite make it. The hissing roared louder. She pushed again and this time broke free, stumbling out of the cab. She bent over, hands on knees, catching her breath, but nothing could slow her racing heart. She straightened and ran down the road, eyes straining for a dark, crumpled heap. Suddenly the hissing gave out. Marian dived into a snow-filled drainage ditch, covering her head.

Nothing. After several unbearable seconds Marian rolled onto her back. The cold sky was sprinkled with stars. Maybe it had been a dud.

Marian rose stiffly to her feet, shuffling then trotting down the road. A low shape huddled not far ahead. Oh Lord! But it was only a boulder. A few large snowflakes fell, quickly followed by more. Clouds inflated like spongy balloons across the clear expanse of sky. Snow clotted her eyelashes. There was a dim glimmer up ahead that must be the railroad tracks and, before that, a smudge. Had it stirred?

"Nezzie!" she yelled. It was hard to tell in the half-light if the sooty form was moving, but yes, it seemed to be. Marian ran, seeing a body stagger to its feet, a flash of red across the forehead. "I'm coming!" She stumbled the last few yards, grabbing the young woman. They both collapsed on the road, Marian wheezing heavily.

"What happened?" Nezzie's face was as pale as the snow.

"We were hit," Marian panted, sat up. "Are you bleeding?" She pressed her fingers against Nezzie's forehead but felt only the tam's soft red wool.

Nezzie closed her eyes. "I don't know. I was having the most wonderful dream. Roast beef, potatoes, and the most delicious . . ." Her voice trailed off.

Marian yanked off the girl's hat, her fingers locating a lump the size of a plum at the back of the head. When she pressed it Nezzie yelped.

"You've got to move around. Here, stand up." Nezzie swayed against her. Snow fell thickly now. Cold crept up through Marian's boots, freezing the embarrassment that had run down her legs. "We've got to get under a tree at least. Something to shelter us. Here." She shook off the cape topping her greatcoat and put it around the girl's shoulders. "Do you remember if there were any blankets in the truck?"

"What?" Nezzie's voice was drowsy.

"Blankets?" Marian shouted.

Nezzie frowned. They floundered down the road. When the gray bulk of the truck loomed, Marian lowered Nezzie to the ground. The girl was quaking violently. Marian stooped to tuck the cape around Nezzie's knees and pulled the red tam more snugly over her ears.

The guns to the east were now quiet. A muffled silence pressed down all around. The truck had come to rest facing the tracks. Marian approached cautiously. Something was ticking faintly. Marian's heart hammered. There probably aren't any blankets anyway. I'll crawl in there, get blown to shreds for nothing.

The dim moonlight filtered through the snow, illuminating a massive shape smashed against the radiator. Marian halted, then slowly tiptoed forward. Only yards away she held her breath . . . but quickly expelled it with a great guffaw. She'd smashed into a colossal stump! Marian's raucous laugh filled the air. Tears of relief ran down her cheeks. An image of herself mincing up to the splintered stump rose in her mind's eye and she laughed harder.

"What's so funny?" Nezzie's voice came weakly through the thick snowfall.

"It's only a stump. Not a bomb. How stupid. I was sure it was a bomb." She was giddy with relief.

She pulled Nezzie up and walked her to the tailgate.

The cord lines that held the canvas flaps in place at the back of the truck were frozen. Thawing the knots with what seemed the last of her breath, Marian shoved Nezzie inside. She started to climb inside too, but smelled the contents of her bowels on her legs. She bundled snow into a handkerchief, shoved a hand beneath her skirt, and scoured off the mess.

The wooden flooring of the truck bed was splintered, the canvas walls snapped like storm-riven sails in the stiff wind, a faint odor of kerosene lingered from a previous distribution of lamps. She quickly pulled the rear flaps together and secured them as best she could.

"We're all right?" Nezzie asked groggily.

"Safe and sound."

Marian groped toward the toolbox stowed behind the driver's seat. Among the greasy wrenches, bits of wire, and oily rags was a flashlight.

"Now we can get our bearings." When Marian twisted the knob, a beam shone on two blankets left over from the day's efforts, and Nezzie's leather satchel that had been tossed backward. Marian unfurled one of the blankets beside Nezzie and lowered her onto it.

The girl was still shaking violently. Marian covered her with the second blanket and then stripped off one of her own scarves, rolling it up as a pillow and tucking it under Nezzie's head.

"Are you sure I'm not bleeding?"

Parting the dark hair, Marian examined the bump. It was a fierce purple. "No, but you've got a good goose egg. Let me see your eyes."

Nezzie's lids drifted closed again.

Marian jiggled her shoulder. "Try to stay awake. You could have a concussion."

Through the gap between the flaps, large snowflakes had given way to a finer, steady sifting that promised a thick covering by morning.

From the bit of Red Cross training she'd gotten before shipping over, Marian knew she needed to keep Nezzie alert until it was certain the lump wasn't growing and the girl's pupils returned to normal.

"Let's see if that canteen of tea in your satchel survived," Marian said loudly. "That will help things, don't you think?" When she got no answer, she squeezed her patient's arm.

"Yes," Nezzie said irritably.

Sorting through the bag's jumble of sewing packets, Marian unearthed the canteen, which she shook; it sloshed satisfactorily.

"Just a few dents. Like you," Marian announced with false cheer, unscrewing the cap. "Nothing to worry about. Let's get some of this in you."

She pulled Nezzie up so that the girl was leaning against her shoulder and Marian brought the spout to her lips.

"No," Nezzie protested, pushing it away.

"Dizzy?"

"Swimming."

"Just a little."

Nezzie drank and flopped back onto the pallet.

Marian took a small sip. "We're about five miles away from the château. We'd just crossed the tracks when the first bomb hit. It'll be a hike in the morning." She decided not to mention the heavy snow piling up outside.

The flashlight wavered. She snapped it off. "Dad blam it. I forgot about saving the battery."

"*Dad blam it?*" Nezzie giggled groggily.

Marian flushed, laughing nervously. "Guess I'm a little out of date."

Inside was blackness, but through the slits in the flaps, moonlight reflected off the snow in silvery tones of gray and slate. The black hulk of the truck, Marian suddenly realized, must stand out clearly among the snowy fields. We are exposed. Exposed and vulnerable. A gust of wind snapped against the truck. Tiny rooftops of snow were forming inside the back flaps. Marian tucked the blanket around Nezzie. Frigid air leeched up through the floorboards.

"Did we decide on a name?" Marian's voice was still falsely bright.

"Lulu?"

"Guess that's appropriate now, with the banging and all. More tea?" Marian held the canteen to the girl's lips. Nezzie managed two mouthfuls. "Better?"

Nezzie propped herself on an elbow and surveyed their surroundings. "Less dizzy but I must have hit hard. My right hip aches to beat the band."

Rolling up another one of her scarves, Marian tucked it under Nezzie's side. "This might help."

"Thanks. Are those your teeth knocking?"

"I'm fine. I'll be fine."

"Lay down with me. We can keep each other warm, huddle up. Like cattle."

Marian gratefully lowered herself to the pallet. Nezzie lifted up one side of her blanket. "Scooch closer." Her breath fell on Marian's cheek, her bundled form a great warm bolster.

After a time Marian snapped on the flashlight. "Let me check that bump again." Her fingers busily parted the brown hair. "I believe the swelling's gone down a little."

"Can I go to sleep?"

"Not yet. Why don't you tell me about how you ended up in this broken-down truck a dozen miles from the front?"

A bark of laughter issued from Nezzie's throat. "Is this some sort of test?"

"Just want to know if you can put two sentences together."

"My father is a minister. Believes everyone has a calling. One day he announced that mine was teaching. Not what I had in mind. But he was willing to send me to college. So I became a teacher. Then the war blew up and Fielding formed this unit. I joined immediately. Pops was furious but I told him they needed teachers and, since he'd pronounced that was my calling . . ." Nezzie expelled another harsh laugh, a puff of frosty breath jetting out toward the roof.

"And after this is over?" Marian asked.

Deep beneath the blankets and coats Nezzie shrugged her shoulders. "Don't know. I'm not going back to the schoolhouse. I know that." She yawned noisily. "So, now can I sleep?"

"Let me check your pupils." The small black vortexes shrank satisfactorily in the flashlight's glare. "Five more minutes."

She snapped off the torch and lay down, her head flat against the floorboards. Above, the roof struts creaked under their burden of snow. Jeannette's fingers were plucking reflexively on the white sheets pressing down, muffling, smothering. The words suddenly rushed out of Marian's mouth, the whole story about Jeannette's death. When she finished, tears were running down her face, encircling her neck.

"Maybe it was just her time," Nezzie murmured. "You'll never know for sure."

Marian scrubbed her face with the sleeve of her coat. The canvas shook above them, admitting a spray of snow. She pulled a hankie from a pocket and blew her nose. "I don't know why I fell apart like that."

"Bombs will do that." Nezzie laughed quietly before adding, "Sorry, gallows humor."

Marian didn't respond. She was thinking of the people in Emporia and the ancient postman and the housewife in Canizy. It takes courage to spend a lifetime with people who know your entire history, all your blunders, she thought. Marian shifted in the blankets. Deuce was brave. He took a stand and risked losing everything. Much braver than I, who was always spouting off and moving on.

The young woman yawned again. "It's been five minutes."

"All right. Get some sleep."

"Thank you," she said in a small voice. Her eyes closed.

Marian listened to Nezzie's warm, steady breathing. That, and the spatter of snow hitting the canvas, were the only sounds. At least, she thought, if another bomb falls in the night and crushes the life out of me, I'll not die alone.

The sweet smell of tea on Nezzie's breath mixed with odors of damp wool, iron, sweat, and something else, something warm and familiar. The waxy scent of the truck's canvas roof and walls sent Marian back to the Chautauqua tents. Her mind drifted to her first night in Emporia, the wash of faces in front of her like the smudge of fingerprints on the window of a train car—smudges that the eye looked past as it contemplated the distant hills. When had she stopped looking at the horizon and become aware of Deuce? Maybe she'd spotted the thick waves of silver hair, the head bent like a schoolboy over his writing pad. Suddenly an intense longing for him, the touch of his hand, the plucked strings of his Midwestern accent, opened inside her. His image slid beneath her lowering lids. Breath, warm and even, washed in and out of her ear; fingers swam across her skin. Abruptly she jerked awake. *I can't go back there.*

Nezzie was groaning in her sleep. Marian fumbled to

find the flashlight. Illuminated, the lump had grown no larger. The blanket had slipped to one side. She tucked it around the girl and lay back down. It would be a long night out in the open fields. But eventually dawn would come and the two would crawl stiffly from the truck and hike back to the château, the hems of their coats starched with snow, bracelets of ice encircling their mitten cuffs. A world away from the baking August heat.

C
HAPTER SIXTEEN
DEBITS AND CREDITS

As you asked how to reach me, I am sending the
address. As noted below, it is VERY IMPOR-
TANT to include "In care of the American Red
Cross, 2 Place de Rivoli, Paris, France" on the
envelope. Don't forget, because otherwise your
letter will never reach me. The crossing was ex-
tremely rough, but my fellow volunteers are pleas-
ant. None are much older than Helen. Our days
are long. Every village shelters nothing but heart-
breaking stories. As you suggested, I am keeping
a diary with the thought of publishing something
after the war. On the rare evenings when the guns
on the front are still, I smoke a cigarette in the
château's courtyard. One gets very sentimental
during wartime.

DEUCE READ MARIAN'S LETTER FOR the third time
that day. She had poured out a great deal of vitriol on the
uniform she was forced to wear, while on the next page
she'd described a tender scene of a young boy crawling
into her lap to have a story read to him. Under all that
outrage . . . He smiled, tucking the letter into his desk
drawer, and turned back to the jammed typewriter. Two

of the secondhand Underwood's sharp-edged struts had crossed yet again. He gingerly inserted his finger. Jesus, the damn thing bit me! He sucked blood from the cut, which wasn't as bad as he'd imagined.

Sighing, he toed off his shoes and slid his chilly feet under the desk, seeking out the warm fur of Jupiter's belly. The dog, deep in sleep, didn't stir.

Outside the storefront's tall panes, swollen snow-flakes eddied. Might as well be snowing in here, it's cold enough, he thought. But I'll be goddamned if I'm going to shovel any more coal into the furnace two hours before closing. Once in his rooms upstairs, with the oil stove cranked up for hash and eggs, his toes would thaw. It was really coming down out there. A tall figure, head ducked against the flakes, strode past. Deuce sat up hopefully, but saw it was Judge Batt. No chance of him stepping through the door.

Deuce's eyes followed the judge's rigid back as it moved off down the street. And what the hell? Was that a scratch in the gold leaf lettering he'd just spent a small fortune on? Deuce jumped up, startling Jupiter. The "S" in gothic font proclaiming *The Garland Weekly and Print Shop* was definitely nicked. Deuce's irritation was forgotten, however, when Mrs. Meyers, the butcher's wife, hurried into the office, brushing snow off her caped shoulders and woolen skirts.

"Good afternoon," she said in a warm tone, although Deuce saw that her face was strained and her clothes hung loosely from her once-sturdy frame. She had lost a three-year-old boy to typhoid. Hers had been the first letter of thanks that Deuce had received when the stories about adulterated milk were printed. Now that the *Gar-*

land Weekly was up and running, Mrs. Meyers, and most of the other families whose children had died that terrible summer, backed him by buying subscriptions and placing small advertisements.

Mrs. Meyers glanced at Deuce's stocking feet, but made no comment.

He hurried behind the counter. "How are you today? Any word from Willy?" The Meyers's oldest son had been called up a month before.

The woman raised her eyes to the ceiling. "Still at the Springfield cantonment, thank the Lord. I've been worried to death and he's not even over there yet."

Deuce nodded. "Nobody worries like a mother."

"But he is a good shot," she added, dabbing her nose with a hankie. "Even as a small boy with only a popgun, he had good aim."

"So you see?"

She smiled faintly.

"What can I do for you?"

She and her husband owned Meyers's Meats, a cramped butcher shop three doors down. Its cases displayed stew beef, ham hocks, and other cheap cuts that the Meyers's clientele could afford. Emporia's prominent families patronized the Quality Butchery two blocks over.

She inhaled damply and readjusted her cape. "The mister and I would like to run an advertisement. Just a small one, but regular. Every week." She glanced around the storefront's two desks, single chair, battered coat rack, and, at the back, the letter press. "How's business?" she asked, eyebrows lifted.

Deuce answered in a light tone, "Coming along, coming along. They say the first couple of months are the hardest for a new concern." He pulled a sheet of news-print from under the counter. "Why don't you take a minute and jot down what you were thinking of. I'll get a mock-up ready for you to look at first thing in the morning."

As Mrs. Meyers bent over her task, Deuce stared out the window where the snowflakes had slowed and were now swirling hypnotically. His thoughts flowed to Marian's letter. It had also been snowing where she was.

". . . along these lines, I think," Mrs. Meyers was saying. Deuce snapped back to the task at hand.

Running his finger along her script, he saw it had too much copy for a small ad, but it could easily be shortened.

"Thank you for your patronage. It means a lot."

Mrs. Meyers nodded briskly. "It's the least the mister and I can do. And we're not the only ones who feel that way. You stepped up and did the right thing, even though it was too late for our little Albert."

After she left, Deuce settled back on his chair, wedging his feet under Jupiter's belly. "Thank God for the Mrs. Meyerses. They're keeping us fed and housed, old boy."

Deuce flipped open the canvas-bound accounts book to that day's entries. Only three new subscriptions, two orders for business cards, and the Meyers's ad. Christ. He pushed back from the desk in disgust, disturbing Jupiter, who rose to his feet, circled twice, and lay back down. Outside, the snow had spent itself, draining away the remaining daylight and leaving only a steely twilight. Deuce began adding up the week's credit column but hurriedly slapped the book shut when Stroh walked in a few minutes later.

"No luck on that bridge repair lead. You sure about

it?" Stroh asked, tossing a notebook on the other desk. He and the pressman were the *Garland Weekly* and Print Shop's only two employees besides Deuce. Stroh's drooping lower lids lent his otherwise bland visage an air of ennui that suited a city reporter. Great poker face. When he'd blown into town a month before from Peoria, where he'd been fired by his editor for stepping on the mayor's toes, Deuce had felt like he was manna from heaven.

"Sorry. I thought I'd overheard something about that bridge over at the Rainbow. The lunchtime crowd is so darn noisy; I might have got it wrong."

"Not like dining with the Elks, eh?"

Deuce snorted.

After the blow-out over the editorial and resignation from the *Clarion*, Deuce had abruptly found himself eating alone at the lodge. No brother would share a table with him. And when his terms came up for renewal, he'd been quietly dropped from the church membership committee and the Macomb County Board of Elections. After that, he stopped participating in the organizations that had been such a large part of his life for so many years. He assumed he was no longer wanted. However, several months later, the commander of the Knights of Pythias telephoned Deuce and said he hoped he would see him at the next meeting. Grinning into the receiver, Deuce had replied, "You certainly will. And thanks."

Stroh poured a shot from the whiskey bottle in his bottom drawer, raised his glass to Deuce, and tossed it back. "So, how're we doing dough-wise?"

Sighing, Deuce rubbed his forehead. "Better pour yourself another and take a seat. I'm not sure I can make payroll tomorrow."

Stroh's brows twitched upward a fraction of an inch. "Again?"

Deuce raised his hands. "I know, I know. You've been more than patient. It's just taking longer to build up the subscriptions than I thought. How about you bunk with me upstairs for the next week? Save you from paying for lodging."

Stroh folded his arms and asked, "And how are things going to be different in a week?"

"I've got a long-standing loan that I've called in. That will be more than enough to pay you and Jake for the next two months. By that time, the *Weekly* will be rolling. I'm sure of it."

The lip of the bottle tinged against the edge of the glass. Stroh threw another back.

"All right. I'll bring my stuff over tomorrow. But if that payment you're counting on doesn't come in, I'm out of here. That daily in Findley has been after me. You know that." He shoved the bottle in the drawer and strode out.

"Damnit, Clay," Deuce muttered to himself. Since the night of Tula's party, since Clay had shouted what seemed to be the most vile of slurs at him, Deuce never again wanted to lay eyes on the man. Not easy in a small town. Actually, it was impossible. But getting back the money that Clay owed him would go a long way. Earlier that morning, Deuce had sent Clay a letter demanding that the photographer's loan be repaid in one week. Or I'll be forced to turn the matter over to the courts, Deuce had written. No more free rides, you good-for-nothing. He didn't know how Clay would come up with the money. Didn't know and didn't care. Let him sell every one of those cameras. Let him sell his automobile.

In the fall, when Deuce sold his house to start up the *Weekly*, he'd thought the proceeds would be enough to get the business on its feet. But the *Garland Weekly* was a slow starter and now Deuce needed that $1,200. The only reason he hadn't pushed Clay harder was for Tula's sake. There was no way around it now. But he'd make sure Tula was taken care of. She could work here if need be.

While Deuce was talking with Mrs. Meyers, Tula was struggling along State Street's snowy sidewalk, making her way to Jasper Watt's photography studio. It would have been nice to take the trolley, but there weren't enough coins in the change jar for the fare. It had taken her most of the day to work up the courage to make this trip. She was unaware of the ultimatum that Deuce had sent Clay but understood that her brother's business was in deep trouble—there was the unpaid loan but also, more telling, the lack of customers. Every time she tried to discuss the status of the studio's books with Clay he snapped, "I'm handling it," and abruptly left the room. Last night, when he'd finally gotten home, Tula had heard what sounded like a shoe slam against the wall between their rooms.

For some time she had thought about approaching Mr. Watts to ask if he might want to purchase some of Clay's equipment. She'd even suggested this scheme to Clay, but he'd brushed the idea aside. "How am I going to make a living without my cameras?" he'd asked irritably. In Tula's mind the most important thing was to pay off the loan to Deuce. When the business closed, as it surely would, she and Clay could likely get clerking positions somewhere in town, what with all the young men leaving for France. Those sorts of jobs wouldn't cover all their bills, but maybe if she also took in a boarder, they could get by. That back room where Marian had stayed was empty. But she knew he'd rather die than work in any position he deemed "inferior." These thoughts kept her awake night after night, along with the flushes of heat that raged over her body like a prairie fire. She was undergoing "The Change," as the ladies called it. While she picked her way through the snow toward Mr. Watts's, Tula's neck and chest were suddenly aflame. She unbuttoned her coat, unwound the blue scarf. Fortunately, there was no one to comment on her little performance since the sidewalk was almost deserted.

Hurrying past the entryway to Clay's second-floor studio, she imagined him upstairs, pacing nervously, jabbing at the coal in the stove with a poker. The trolley lumbered past with only a few riders. What with the war and the snow, Emporia was almost deserted. She turned down Main, past Deuce's old office. How many years had she gazed up as she passed, mooning like a schoolgirl? That was over. The day Marian left, she'd watched Deuce staring down the street long after the Packard had passed from view. And when he finally turned back to his own house, she'd caught a glimpse of his haggard face and understood how things were.

When she crossed Main and turned onto Court, the wind let up. The walk in front of Watts's studio was cleared and sprinkled with a carpet of ash. Displayed behind the plate glass was a single photograph of the youngest Walters child, squatting on chubby legs, its arm thrown around the neck of the family's spaniel, both positioned in front of Mrs. Walters's prized peony bush. It was a lovely image, so much more vivid with its open-air setting than the canvas backdrops Clay used. Mr. Watts clearly knew his business. Would he want to buy a bunch of secondhand equipment that probably wasn't of very good quality to begin with? Holding her breath, Tula entered the shop, setting a brass bell jingling overhead. Inside, two other portraits were displayed on easels. One was of the Reverend Sieve bent over a baptismal font, the round head of a placid infant cradled in his age-swollen fingers, the other of Floyd Van Meter shoveling corn into a burlap sack. Tula was examining these when a voice behind her said, "Can I help you?"

An adolescent girl, wearing a rubber apron, emerged from the back room.

Flustered, Tula said, "Oh, it's nothing. I wanted to speak with Mr. Watts but he's not here and that's all right. I'll come back—"

"He's here," the girl interrupted and called over her shoulder, "Daddy!"

Tula continued backing toward the door. "You needn't bother him if he's in the middle of something. As I said, I would be—"

"It's no problem, ma'am. We were just mixing chemicals."

"If you're sure?"

A man stepped through the doorway as the girl darted past him. "Dorrie, would you slow down!" He shook his head, rolling his eyes at Tula in false exasperation.

Jasper Watts, his bald head surrounded by a fringe of fading brown hair stippled with gray, appeared almost too old to have a daughter of Dorrie's age. But there was something youthful about the amused expression beneath the animated brows. His high collar and cuffs were brilliantly white, creating a dapper impression despite the rubber apron.

"I expect these children will put me in an early grave some day. How can I help you, ma'am?"

"I'm Tula Lake—"

"Oh, the photographer's sister?"

"I'm sorry to bother you. Maybe this isn't a good time?"

"This is a fine time. Why don't we sit down over here?" He gestured to the small seating area and hung his apron on a nail by the counter. "Let me take your coat."

Tula gratefully shrugged off her wraps, as another flush of heat was building up. She settled at the edge of one of the armchairs.

"So, what can I do for you?"

Now that she was here, Tula didn't know how to begin. She surveyed the studio with a birdlike tilt of her head until her eyes lit on a large photo. "That's a remarkable likeness of Floyd."

Jasper twisted to face the mounted portrait behind him. "I took that last November. You like it?"

"It's almost more a painting than a photo. He agreed to pose in the feed store?"

"Oh, that isn't a commission. I just happened to be there one day and noticed how the chaff floated out as he filled a sack. I asked if he'd mind if I ran and got my camera. I wanted to try to capture the husks suspended in the light. Fool around a bit. You like it?"

"Oh, yes. Yes! And is the one in your front window an experiment too?"

Jasper laughed. He leaned back, crossing his legs.

"That was a little bit of both. Mrs. Walters came in wanting a portrait of . . . Jimmy?" He snapped his fingers, gazing at the ceiling. "No, Timmy. It was Timmy. So, anyway, she had in mind the usual child on a hobbyhorse or holding a ball. I'm sure your brother has done hundreds of those. They're a photographer's bread-and-butter."

Tula, who didn't think Clay had done hundreds of any pose, smiled tensely.

"So I said yes, I could do that. But I had this idea of trying something outside. I'd seen a painting somewhere of a little boy in a rose garden. It took some convincing—including an offer to do the standard setup if this didn't work out—but I eventually talked Mrs. Walters into it."

"It's remarkable."

"And it has led to more commissions. Some customers are coming in and asking for a portrait at their place of work. You know, I tried to talk to your brother about this when I bumped into him at a meeting of the Commerce Club awhile back, but he didn't seem to want anything to do with me. I hope he doesn't feel I've taken away any of his business. With a county this size, there's plenty of work for two photographers."

Tula bit her lower lip. "As a matter of fact, the studio hasn't panned out as Clay thought it would . . ."

"I'm so sorry. I hope that was none of my doing! I would feel just terrible if—"

"No, no." Tula shook her head. "It was a struggle long before you came to town. I just don't think Clay's cut out for business. So," she inhaled deeply, "so I'm here, in fact, to see if you might want to buy any of his equipment. He might be closing the studio if things don't . . ." She dribbled off miserably.

"Closing!" Jasper's brows pulled together in concern. "Does he have other plans?"

"No. Yes. We'll work it out." She paused, then continued in a strained voice, "So, do you think there might be something . . . anything . . . you'd like to buy from his studio?"

From the rear room came Dorrie's announcement that she'd mixed all the chemicals and could she develop a print herself? Jasper excused himself and stood.

"Her late mother would say I indulge the children too much, but I'll be right back." He walked behind the counter. The smell of developing solution was strong. Jasper poked his head through the doorway. "Do you have the trays set up as I showed you?"

"Yes." Dorrie's tone was exasperated.

"And the timer is set?"

"Yes!"

"All right, then."

Tula gazed out the front windows. It was snowing again, and the reflected light illuminated her eyes and brow. When she heard him reenter the room, she started to turn.

"No, don't. Stay as you are," he said. "I think this would make a lovely photograph. Do you mind?"

A deep flush bloomed across her neck and cheeks. "You're joking!"

"Not at all." His voice was warm.

"But I'm not dressed for . . ." She began tugging at her shirtwaist, patting her hair.

"You were just admiring my other photographs. Trust me."

She shook her head. "I'm really not the sort of person for something like this."

"Oh, but I think you are. Why don't you arrange your hair as you'd like? Dorrie has combs and a mirror back there. While I'm setting up we can talk about that equipment. I'm sure there would be one or two things I could buy."

An hour later, from up in his studio, Clay observed Tula's winter hat traveling down the street toward their house. Something about that hat, which was a dated beaver affair and balding along the folds, further enraged him. As if it were the hat's fault, as if it were Tula's fault that he was in this mess. He'd spent the entire afternoon in this same spot; fuming at Deuce's ultimatum—a slap in the face, that's really what it was. Since the beginning of the new year, he'd been contemplating approaching Deuce, suggesting they let bygones be bygones and try to negotiate something since he still didn't have the money. But now that was out of the question.

He read the letter one more time, goading himself into righteous indignation. *Against all my desires*—what a pretentious load of hogwash. He snatched up his coat and headed out.

As Clay approached the *Garland Weekly* office, Deuce's bundled figure was stepping out into the street behind that goddamn mutt he took everywhere.

Anger boiled up in Clay's gut. "What the hell is this?" he shouted, shaking his fist, which held the crumpled letter.

Startled, Deuce turned.

"Is it a threat? Because if it is, you're fooling with the wrong man." Puffs of cold air trailed each word.

Deuce felt a dark flush rise into his face, but his voice was cool. "This is no place to talk. Let's go inside."

Clay nodded curtly. Deuce was unlocking the door when Jupiter pushed his snout into his palm, demanding attention.

"Okay, old fella." Deuce bent to stroke the dark head, thumbing the two tawny spots above the dog's eyes, the way Jupiter liked it. "Go on inside. Jupiter's due his dinner. It'll just take a minute for me to run across to the stables. Eli fixed up an empty stall for him. My landlord won't let me keep him upstairs."

Clay entered without comment. Deuce hurried the old dog across the street and into the dark warmth of the barn. Eli had already left for the day. A half dozen or so horses dozed in their stalls. Deuce pulled out a pack of beef trimmings from Meyers's Meats and dumped it in Jupiter's dish. He usually waited for the dog to eat and get settled in a mound of clean straw and covered with an old blanket, but he didn't want Clay snooping around unattended. He patted Jupiter's head and walked out.

Clay was pacing the floorboards in an agitated fashion. The minute Deuce walked in the door, he took up his diatribe. "I thought we had a gentleman's agreement on this. God knows, I've been trying to raise the money. I've told you that in good faith, but apparently a man's word means nothing to you."

"Now, Clay—"

"It's tough times out there, in case you haven't noticed."

"Of course I've noticed. Have you taken a look around here?"

Clay plowed on without pause as Deuce dropped wearily into his chair. "No, I don't think you have. In wartime, no one wants to spend the extra money on a photograph. That's a luxury! Sitters are few and far between. And that new studio? Do you think that's helping my business? Did you know Mr. Watts has a photo of your good friend Floyd set up in his front room? There's nothing loyal about that. I'll tell you another thing. This Watts—that's not his real name. According to some of the fellows at the Elks, it's Jacob Wasser—German background. No doubt about it. The same tribe we're fighting over in France is taking the business out from under my nose over here."

Deuce, who had been sitting back and letting Clay's vitriol wash over him, bolted upright. "Now wait a minute! Half the people in this county have German blood."

Clay snorted. "Watts, Wasser, whatever his name is, is a Hun. Once a Hun, always a Hun."

Gall washed into Deuce's mouth. "Get out of here. This conversation is finished." He jerked his thumb toward the door. "I'm sticking by that deadline for the money."

Clay, purple with rage, started to answer, but Deuce was already on his feet, yanking the door open, his features frozen. The photographer snatched up his hat and stomped out, his wild eyes glazed.

After slamming the door behind him, Clay turned blindly to the left, wading through the pile of snow clogging the curb and stomping down the street. His fury burned strong as he tramped Emporia's streets, muttering to himself all the while. At last he calmed down enough to make what he considered a rational plan. He'd get the last train to Chicago that night, without a word of explanation or farewell to anyone, Tula included. They'd wake up and he'd be gone and good riddance to the whole stinking town. There was plenty of work in the city not only for all those niggers streaming up from the South but for upstanding white men like himself. But before he left town, he'd take care of Deuce. He'd take care of him, all right.

On the way home to pack, he stopped at Meyers's Meats for half a pound of stew meat and at the feed store for a box of rat poison.

Before Deuce opened the office each morning, it was his habit to go directly over to the stables, feed Jupiter, and then escort the old dog across the street to the snug spot beneath his desk.

This morning, he waved at Eli, who was sipping his first cup of coffee, and headed down the aisle between the stalls. He first saw Jupiter's back paws, crooked at odd angles. Then the tongue stretching from between gummy lips, the eyes rolled backward. The old dog had vomited up his last meal. Deuce dropped to his knees, crying out, "No! Oh no!" over and over as tears ran down his face. Eli rushed over. When he took in the scene he folded his hands in silence, out of respect for the sorrow of any man who has lost a dog.

Deuce stroked Jupiter's knobby brows, the tawny punctuation marks above the glazed eyes. He had no doubt what had happened and who had done it. He bundled the dog's body in the blanket and carried it across the street. The apartment was silent. Deuce unwrapped the blanket and washed the vomit from Jupiter's chest, brushed his fur. He stroked the still head. From the linen cupboard, Deuce withdrew a clean sheet, gently swaddled the dog, and laid him out on the open porch at the back of the apartment. That evening he'd ask the Mummerts if he could bury Jupiter in the backyard where he'd played as a puppy.

Deuce wandered into the kitchenette, opened a few cupboards, then walked out, not yet ready to face a day in the office. In the bedroom he razored the dust off the old tortoise-shell box, his canoptic jar of fraternal pins. When he shook it, it emitted a mournful, tinny sound. These bits of gilt and colored glass that had meant so much to him were now drained of meaning. He considered tossing them into the trash but instead shoved the box into the bottom drawer of his dresser, next to a pair of trousers that needed mending and a couple of old suspenders whose elastic was shot.

CHAPTER SEVENTEEN
THE DILL PICKLE

As I write this, the girls are gathered around the fireplace at the far end of the mess hall. Nezzie is regaling them with a smutty story about a muscular youth modeling as an Indian for a female sketching class. Soon, I imagine, the loincloth will drop. You would instantly take to Nezzie. She is only a bit older than you with the quick mind, sharp tongue, and the bobbed hair of the modern woman.

As I stepped from the barracks early this morning, a fox darted out from some bushes and dashed past me. I was stunned by his beauty. For some reason, I have not been able to sleep as I used to. Me, who once bragged she could fall asleep on a pile of tent poles!

AS MUCH AS HELEN HATED the dense wool coat of her conductor's uniform in the warm days of early September, now, on this sub-zero February morning, she was grateful for every ounce of cloth in its unflattering flared skirt. She thanked the Lord for the military collar, snug under her chin. The wind gusting down Flint Street was fierce and damp with snow.

She hurried into a side door at the car barn, taking her place at the back of the cashier's line, just making the 3:45 a.m. punch time. A janitor was methodically sliding open the barn's massive doors, beyond which dozens of street cars waited in rows. In the rafters above, roosting pigeons beat their thick wings. One of the men farther up was cursing. Spotting her, he abruptly clamped his mouth shut with a resentful glare.

Helen marched in place to ward off the bitter cold. Every bit of her was chilled to the bone except her hands, which were snug in red wool mittens. They had been tucked in the parcel Deuce had sent for her twentieth birthday, along with a dictionary, a packet of hankies, and a box of chocolates. The mittens released a faint scent of cedar as she pressed them against her cheeks. She shut her eyes, imagining for a moment that she was back home.

Directly in front of her was a flabby fellow with a roll of fat showing beneath the back of his visored cap. A stale, unwashed smell seeped from his coat.

He turned, a smirk creasing his face. "What happened to the fancy footwork? Lost some of your starch?"

Ignoring him, she stared straight ahead. It had been a mistake, those first few months on the job, dancing in place as the line inched toward the cashier's window. That energy had drained away sometime during the winter. At first she'd been so happy to be in Chicago, to have her own room, and to have a job. A *man's* job. She'd just let loose a couple of times.

A bit of light eked through the sooty skylights. Same sky every morning. As the fat man shuffled forward she matched his step. Her neck spasmed. She ignored it. If she

paid no attention, it might go away. Then straight pins began prickling her gut. She squeezed her eyes shut. As the
line drew closer to the cashier's window, the constrictions
grew more urgent. *Calm down.* Then it was her turn at
the grille. The cashier, a ruddy-faced fellow who smelled
of whiskey, asked for her badge number and with a pencil
made a tick on a register secured to a clipboard. Then he
shoved a loaded change carrier toward her. She picked
it up and began strapping it to her belt but stopped. The
nickel-plated coin barrels seemed lighter, didn't they? She
hesitated.

Behind her someone grumbled, "Move along." The
toe of a boot bumped sharply against her heel. She shook
the carrier that should be full to the top with coins. It
rattled. The cashier had shorted her again. Should she
demand that he count out the coins? The line of men behind her would explode with curses. That's what happened last time. Helen felt certain that the cashier didn't
pull this stunt on the men. Maybe on the two other female
conductors working out of this barn, but they were on
the other shift and she never got a chance to ask them.

"Got a problem?" the cashier rasped, his eyes flicking
up and down her body.

She willed herself to keep her voice level. "Are you
shorting me?"

He spread his palms. "Look, sister, you accuse me of
that every other day. You want me to count it out?"

Helen sensed the roil of anger build in the line behind her. "No. Forget it," she muttered, moving aside.
Across the way she could see that Irvine, her motorman, was already seated impatiently at the wheel of
No. 5219. Christ, could she stand another day of this?

Irvine was a man of middle age, whose long face fell into drooping, phlegmatic folds. His eyes had a weary cast, which nothing, not even a midday intersection packed with harried pedestrians, automobiles, and peddler carts, could rouse. When they'd met on her first day of work, his initial words had been, "Won't hold it against you."

She'd been caught off guard. "What?"

"You being a female conductor. Just saying."

Helen had been opening her mouth to respond when a supervisor, who was showing her the ropes, swung into the car with a brisk, "Now this is what ya need to do in regards to collecting the fares."

Irvine rarely spoke more than a couple of words each day. This morning was no different. He mumbled a greeting, then cranked the controller, and 5219 bumped out of the barn and onto the Belmont Avenue line. Helen took up her post in the back, ready to collect the nickel fares as the passengers boarded. When the trolley reached the end of the line, which took about forty-five minutes, Irvine and Helen wordlessly switched places as the back of the car became the front and vice versa. Ships passing in the night. Despite the crowds pressing against her throughout the ten-hour shift, Helen felt alone.

In these predawn hours, most of the passengers were laborers; men in greasy or bloodstained overalls who worked in the stockyards, factories, or meat-packing plants. There were also a fair number of women who assembled paper boxes or ran mangles in commercial laundries. The first couple of months, she'd excitedly studied each passenger, as if she was a traveler in an exotic land.

Today, as the riders pushed past her, anxious to get out of the bitter wind, their faces were indistinguishable; watery eyes, red noses, pale jowls. As they pressed forward, shoving fares at her, Helen purposefully maintained a deliberate pace; slipping each nickel in the leather satchel around her neck, tugging the leather cord. The cord was connected to a fare register, a thick metal disk the size of a large clock with dials showing the number of fares collected, like a motorcar's odometer. Every time she pulled the cable, the dials turned to the next number and a bell rang.

By seven-thirty, every stop was jammed with passengers impatiently stomping their feet. The Packer Avenue throng was particularly rowdy. They shoved against the folding doors the second Irvine put on the brakes, those in the back crying out, "Hurry up, sister!" She ignored them. Coin, cord. Coin, cord. She'd done this hundreds of times since September, so it should have become second nature. But it seemed to require more deliberation each week and the anxiety about yanking the cord too many times had mounted. If, at the end of the day, her canvas bag of fares didn't exactly match the number on the register, she'd be accused of knocking down—stealing from the company—and would be fired immediately. This was all spelled out in the conductor's handbook, on page one in bold letters. She had come to hate the register, her guts twisting every time she yanked the cord. It seemed so easy to make a mistake in the crush of riders. To pull the cord too many times.

Why am I becoming such a nervous Nellie? I was never like this before, she thought. The car jerked away from the stop and the businessman in front of her lost his balance and stepped on her boot.

The nerves had crept up gradually. At first it happened only when a stop was especially crowded and the hands thrusting nickels at her came from all directions. Then her stomach began to pitch when she glanced at a stop coming up and thought it might be thronged. Now just standing in line for the cashier's window was liable to make her gut cramp up.

"Excuse me." A young woman wearing a thin coat over the office girl's uniform of shirtwaist and skirt squeezed past Helen's elbow. Even if the fare accidently comes up short and I'm fired, she thought, it's not as if I can't get another job. There's plenty of jobs out there. And look, she counseled herself, you're doing swell. Getting around the city from day one with no problem. I brushed right past those YWCA ladies hovering around the train station, handing pamphlets to the innocents from the farm. Didn't need them! And Papa so worried that last morning, seeing me off. All his little admonishments. His furrowed brows rose in her mind's eye. She teared up and had to quickly wipe her eyes on her sleeve as the trolley rolled to a stop and the doors flapped open.

At the end of her shift Helen endured another bout of nerves as she turned in the cash bag. But miraculously everything tallied, the lethargic cashier signed her receipt, and, for the first time that day, she breathed freely. It was dusk when she stepped outside the car barn and the sidewalk slush had frozen into icy ruts. She picked her way along Halsted. The wind let up slightly. She passed a brick wall plastered with yellow flyers, all reading, *Eight Million Women Wage Earners in the United States—They All Need the Vote!* A bubble of pride pushed into her throat. A wage earner and, what's more, in a man's job, she thought, smiling. But the smile faded.

Here six months and haven't gone to a single suffrage meeting. Not a single one. Let alone picket. Marian's letter of introduction to Chicago's suffrage league lay untouched in her bureau drawer. Each week she'd vowed to get to a meeting, but after a ten-hour day that began at four in the morning, it was all she could do to drag herself to the Shady Cottage Café for a quick dinner before collapsing into her bed at the rooming house. She hurried past the flyers and toward the steamy windows of the restaurant. The place was nothing special but she'd come across it on her third night in town and for some reason kept coming back. The roast beef was fatty, the mashed potatoes lumpy, but still she returned. And Marian's list of exotic-sounding restaurants lay with the letters of introduction, behind Helen's stack of rolled hose.

There was a small table near the window. Helen sat down, pulled off her mittens, and laid them to one side. A thick-waisted server, one she'd had before, passed by with a tray of dirty dishes and asked if she wanted the roast beef and mashed as usual. Helen nodded. When her little pot of tea was delivered, she warmed her hands over the steam rising from its spout before pouring a cup.

She would have liked to pull off her boots, her feet ached from standing all day and from the icy drafts swept into the car as passengers boarded and departed. That would have to wait until she got to the boarding house. She kept an enamel basin under her bed to bathe her feet each evening. What an old fuddy-duddy I've become! Doctoring aches and pains, eating at the same place every night. Still, when the waitress slid the oval platter of meat and potatoes in front of her, Helen took up her fork with relish.

As she was enjoying the last spoonful of ice cream,

a treat she allowed herself on Saturdays, the end of the workweek, the café door banged open and two fellows in overcoats hustled in. They were laughing and rubbing their hands against the cold.

Helen barely glanced up and so was surprised to hear, "Hey, it's the suffragette," and to see Louie the sign painter approaching with a grin. He called to his friend, "Get us a table, I'll be over in a few," before turning back to Helen. "So, you broke free? Good for you." His face had lost its summer tan, but his eyes still danced.

Her fingers strayed to her hair, mashed down all day by her uniform cap, aware of the mark it left on her forehead and the dried sweat on her scalp. Nothing to be done about that now.

"You didn't think I would, did you?" she said.

"Oh, I figured you'd get here by hook or by crook. Mind if I put my feet up for a sec?"

Helen shrugged, surprised to hear herself drawn into the playful sparring. "Suit yourself."

Louie pulled out the chair opposite and waved the waitress over. "Bring me a coffee, honey." He leaned toward her. "So, how do you like old Chi town?"

"It's swell. I've got a job at—"

"No, let me guess. Bookkeeper for the Women's Suffrage League? Union organizer?"

Had she really spilled out all her ambitions to him? "Trolley conductor."

He folded his arms and nodded appreciatively. "Not bad."

The waitress sat the coffee in front of him. "What'll ya have?" she asked.

"Nothing just yet." He sipped his coffee. "You're

earning your keep. Good for you. And I'd bet my bottom dollar you're knee-deep in the suffrage stuff."

Helen studied her hands. "Actually, I haven't . . ."

But Louie had already moved on: "You know, I've got an exhibit at the Dill. You should stop by."

Helen frowned. "What?"

"Dill Pickle Club. The place I told you about. You've been, haven't you? No? That's the place for the radical of the radical. Big Bill Hayward, Wobblies, socialists, anarchists, hobos, prostitutes, all the soap-boxers from Bug House Square. Sometimes Jane Addams shows with a couple of her Hull-House girls. The anarchist Emma Goldman was a regular, until she got arrested. And my paintings, well, they're the talk of the joint right now."

His lips were moving excitedly. What was it about them that were so attractive? Helen thought of the places he'd kissed her last summer and flushed.

"Come down tomorrow. Sunday's the big night there. Everyone shows up. It's the real deal and if you want to be in the know about activists of the fairer sex, you should be there."

Something inside told her to keep her guard up. "I can't." The words popped out. "I've got work."

"On Sunday?"

"Well, no, but very early on Monday so it's hard to, you know, I need to get to bed early . . ."

Why was she acting like this? Was it Louie she was backing away from, or the idea of not measuring up to the Pickle crowd? Just last summer this would have been the sort of thing she'd dreamed about doing, talked endlessly about to anyone in Emporia who would listen.

Now a chance to see Jane Addams in the flesh! And she was acting like a scared bunny.

"Here, I'll give you directions," Louie said, pulling a notepad out of his pocket and sketching a map. She noticed his paint-daubed fingers. Her gaze traveled back to his lips.

"Okay." Helen gave a small smile. "Show me where to go."

The next evening she found her way to Dearborn, a main drag in this part of town, with no problem. After several changes of clothing, she'd settled on what she considered her most highbrow attire: serge skirt and simple shirtwaist. With a thought to Louie, she added her close-fitting sealskin hat with the red rosette that matched the red mittens. Now, passing through the down-at-the-heels neighborhood lined with used book shops, barber training schools, and flop houses with dusty *Room for Rent* signs on display, she wondered why she'd bothered with her dress. After several trips up and down the block, she located a narrow tunnel between two ramshackle brick buildings that Louie had labeled "hole in the wall." She found herself in a dim alley smelling of urine and cluttered with dented dustbins. At the far end, an exposed bulb hung over an orange-painted entryway of what looked like a decrepit carriage house. That must be it. As she approached, she saw that the door was painted with a crudely lettered message: *Step High, Stoop Low. Leave Your Dignity Outside.* Just like Alice down the rabbit hole, Helen thought.

She hesitated, the butterflies in her gut getting the better of her. But then, all the visions rushed in of herself

marching in suffrage parades and rallying women laborers to the cause. She stepped inside.

The entryway was indeed low, with a wooden beam
just overhead. She heard loud voices coming from the top
of steep stairs. She climbed. The large, raftered room was
crowded. Clusters of two and three people faced off in
intense conversations. A number of them were shouting.
One man in particular, wearing a grimy sack suit reek-
ing of sweat, was yelling as loudly as if he were using a
megaphone. Despite the volume, the room was welcoming. Red, blue, and yellow chairs and benches were scattered about, some lined up in rows in front of a small
stage. A refreshment counter ran along one wall where
a middle-aged woman in an embroidered peasant shift
poured coffee. A sign resting beside a plate stacked with
sandwiches proclaimed, *Food for Thought*.

Abruptly, a redheaded man in a lumberman's jacket
approached Helen, arm outstretched. "Are you a nut
about anything?" he asked, shaking her hand vigorously.

"I, ah . . ."

"Then you have to talk to the Picklers."

She forced a smile. Behind her, footsteps mounted the
stairs and she quickly moved away. The man approached
the newcomer with his pat question, "Are you a . . ."

Plastered on a beam directly in front of her was a
crudely drawn cartoon of a man, his mouth wide open,
announcing, *We gotta change the system*.

A number of paintings hung on the whitewashed
wall to the right. These must be Louie's. She strolled over,
hands clasped behind her back as she imagined museum
regulars did. The first appeared to be a landscape. The oils
had been dabbed on so thickly that the hills and rooftops

were furrowed with brushstrokes, all rendered in vermil-
ion and cobalt and ochre. It was how she imagined Italy
might look. Had Louie been there? She looked around
for him. The space was filling up. Off to her right, several professorial types, with tidy four-in-hands and round
spectacles, conversed with an odoriferous man missing
most of his teeth. Two primly dressed women, hair pulled
back in buns that reminded Helen of photographs she'd
seen of Jane Addams, passed by holding hands and took
seats among the growing number in front of the stage. At
least half of the throng were women. Many clearly paid
no attention to their appearance. Frizzy, barely combed
hair, clean but unironed shirtwaists. But their eyes! They
had the eyes of zealots, of women in hot pursuit of a
cause. This is what I want, where I belong, she thought.
This is who I said I was back in Emporia.

Wouldn't the matrons and Grandfather Knapp be
shocked if they saw her here, in this hotbed of radicalism.
They'd be outraged. She imagined Mrs. Mummert saying
to her club women, "Did you hear about Helen Garland?
She's become a radical suffragist. Next thing you know,
she'll be picketing the White House and jailed like Alice
Paul."

She turned to the next canvas with a small smile. It
was a portrait of a man in a soft hat, a disconcerting jux-
taposition of sharply angled shapes forming the face. The
cheeks were shards of yellow and orange. A splinter of
blue formed half of the nose, the other half being a drab
brown. The mouth, although a jarring green, turned up
at one corner in a sly way. Louie certainly captured himself, she thought, despite the odd colors and shapes. Still,
the whole effect made her suddenly uncomfortable. From

across the room, someone was shouting, "Don't lecture me about the Old Testicle, you religious dogmatist!" Despite the fact that no one was paying her a bit of attention, Helen felt increasingly awkward. Where was Louie, for God's sake?

Just then he emerged from the stairwell. She waved, his eyes caught hers, and he squeezed through the crowd.

"What d'ya think?" he asked eagerly. "Sorry I'm late. Got into a debate with Flanagan and lost track of the time."

His breath came in short bursts, as if he'd run up the stairs. The scarf around his neck, in shades of walnut, matched his eyes.

"That's all right. And I like your paintings very much."

"Good. That's great." He slipped his hand into hers and gave it a squeeze. "Which one is your favorite?"

"Oh, I just got here. But of these two, this one," she said, gesturing to the landscape.

Louie pulled back, a surprised look on his face. "Really? That was sort of an early attempt."

Helen flushed, feeling as if she'd given the wrong answer. "The portrait is good too. I knew it was you right away. It *is* you?"

"Yeah, yeah. Sort of beside the point, but that's okay. I want to know what it is about the landscape that appeals."

Helen chewed her lip, trying to summon the words from the art lessons Grandfather Knapp had paid for when she was fifteen or so. She couldn't remember a one. "What I like is that they're not like the pictures in my grandmother's parlor."

Louie laughed. "Thank God." He kissed her on the neck. She flushed again. "Maybe we can skip the lecture. There's a church with plenty of stairwells just around the corner."

Helen pulled back abruptly. "No. I'm here to learn something, not monkey around."

"Ah, just for a while. We can get—"

He was interrupted by a voice from the podium: "Ladies, gents, and the rest of you, take a seat. It's time to get started and I know you'll find tonight's program well worthwhile."

Helen pulled away. "I'm staying."

A quiet groan sounded off to one side. In a darkened corner, Helen glimpsed the figure of a man leaning against the wall. A woman knelt at his feet, head bobbing rhythmically. Helen's hand flew to her mouth and she quickly joined the throng moving toward the stage. She dropped into a seat near the back. Her hands were shaking. Louie, seemingly oblivious to the display in the corner, followed her over, taking the chair beside her and sliding down on his tailbone.

The man at the podium was the redheaded greeter. After the audience settled, he continued. "If you don't know me, you should. I'm Jack Jones, former Wobbly, former anarchist, and current proponent of free speech of any sort."

Helen caught her breath. A Wobbly! Someone had shoved one of the Wobbly's radical pamphlets, advocating destruction of the wage system, into her hands as she walked to the car barn one morning. The Wobblies' ideas about overthrowing the system struck Helen as beyond the pale.

"The Pickle is dedicated to giving any and all ideas a respectful hearing. Tonight I'm pleased to host Red Martha, also known as Field Marshal Biegler. Fresh from an engagement on the soapbox in Bughouse Square, where she commands the respect of friend and foe. Red Martha will be arguing the point that the male is deadlier than the female."

There was a spurt of wild clapping and cheers. A few men booed. Someone shouted, "We've already heard from this coyote! Let's get the other side!"

Red Martha mounted the small stage. Like Marian, she was very tall but her face was plain as a sidewalk slab and her stringy dark hair was streaked with gray. She launched right into her talk, addressing the audience with her hands on her hips. As she talked, she bent at the waist to emphasize various points. "Let us agree that capitalism is the greatest evil ever invented. It pushes the lower classes further into the mud while the upper classes smell only the sweetness of the clouds. Can we agree on that?"

She dipped, and the crowd shouted its agreement, although the coyote speaker called out, "Prove it!"

She ignored him. "And who, I will ask, is responsible for the creation, promotion, and continuation of capitalism? The male of the species, of course." Another dip.

Helen slid restlessly in her seat, seeing where this was going. This sort of theoretical debate held no interest for her.

"It is no surprise that the captains of industry are all . . ." Red Martha talked on. Helen became aware of overpowering perfume saturating the air that seemed to be coming from one row away, where a woman was whispering to an unshaven fellow, her spit curl brushing against his ear, her unbound breasts pressed against his shoulder, her hand slipping into his pants. Helen abruptly looked away, trying to focus back on Red Martha. A number of people in the crowd had joined the coyote man and were heckling her. Someone in a Stetson was mounting the stage shouting that he wanted to open up the debate to the merits of birth control.

Helen inhaled shakily. Calm down, she thought. Louie took up her hand. She smiled stiffly at him. He abruptly shoved her fingers into his lap. She yanked her hand away and jumped up.

"Where're you going?" Louie asked.

"How dare you!" she whispered fiercely.

"Ah, come on. Don't you want to experience free love?"

"No, I don't. And this place isn't for me."

"Okay. Wait a minute. I'll walk you out."

"Stay away from me."

She rushed toward the stairway past a fringe of spectators at the outer edge of the benches. A handsome Negro man had his arm around a petite woman who was speaking to him in some Slavic language. The night air was frosty. Helen ran up the alley, toward the rabbit hole. A freezing wind, heavy with snow, pushed against her as she emerged. Across the street, the opaque windows of a vacant shop stared blankly. She hurried into the shelter of its doorway. Here since August, she thought as tears filled her eyes, and I'm back where I started. Alone with nothing.

She thought of the green-shingled house on Mt. Vernon Avenue, the familiar storefronts. But she clamped her mind shut against this assault. I'm not going back like a dog with its tail between its legs. That's what they expect. I'm staying.

The thick curtain of snow was parting. Flakes fell slowly past the sagging awnings, the lamp poles plastered with tattered flyers. The suffrage posters she'd seen on her way to dinner the night before suddenly flew into her mind. She swiftly searched her pockets for her mittens, and then realized she must have left them inside. She stuffed her bare hands into her sleeves and headed back to her room, to her desk with the stationery stacked neatly in the top center drawer. She'd write Marian's suffragist friend as soon as she got in, even if it meant only getting two hours of sleep before the alarm clock rattled, even if it meant no sleep at all.

C HAPTER EIGHTEEN
SPRING

The Clarion published a full-page rotogravure section last week with photographs of American women volunteering in France. I know how foolish this sounds, but I looked for you among all the faces. I hope you don't feel pressured by this confession. It gave me the idea to ask if you'd write a column for my weekly. I really loved the description of Canizy that you included in your last letter. From what you said, it sounds like those people are not so different from us out here. It could be a good thing to remind everyone of that.

THE WOMEN OF THE FIELDING COLLEGE Relief Unit labored in that part of the cellar open to the sky, a spring chapel of gentian, misty with pollen from a chestnut that once shaded the château's formal garden. Overstuffed burlap sacks were stacked against the old stone foundation and the women, Marian and Nezzie included, moved among the bags, chattering and laughing and bumping into one another. Last month, when snow still clotted the roads, the Fielding Unit had taken seed orders from its villagers. In Canizy, the grandmothers and old uncles had insisted on five varieties of spring lettuces, tapping Marian's clipboard for emphasis, dragging Nezzie to their tilled-up plots where the greens would flourish come April. Links said it had been the same in her village, except that early-, mid-, and late-spring peas were in urgent demand. The seeds had arrived in bulk and now the unit was dedicating every spare moment to dividing the thousands of tiny grains into fifteen- and thirty-gram packages and sorting by village. They'd set a deadline of the next day, March 21. This was the final push. Every flat surface in the cellar was crammed with dishpans, pails, pots, and kettles, all stuffed with paper bags.

Marian paused before a sack of turnip seeds, listening to the whack of a hammer echoing across the yard. The guns at the front were silent this morning. A carpenter, on loan from the Tommies, was helping Alice install the last of the shelves in the portable barrack that was to house the long-awaited library. It would serve the small schoolrooms that the unit had set up in four of the sixteen villages. Lulu, her radiator replaced, had made many trips across the greening countryside, delivering real desks and chalkboards to take the place of the rough tables and black-painted walls. The unit's four hand-me-down vehicles, recently passed along by Anne Morgan's well-endowed outfit, had also been pressed into service.

"Hey, no daydreaming." The Gish playfully thrust a sharp elbow into Marian's upper arm, grown muscular from loading the truck. The Gish, so named because of the dark smudges under her eyes that gave her the sorrowful look of the moving picture actress, dipped her hands into the sack of turnip seeds.

"Are your villagers planting turnips this season or not?" The Gish was wearing a hat that Marian had fashioned from a woven basket and two variegated pheasant feathers. It sat a little too far back on The Gish's narrow head. Maybe wadded newspaper could be stuffed in the lining.

"*Excusez-moi, mademoiselle.*" Marian consulted her list.

The unit had only two battered soup ladles and a tarnished serving spoon to use as scoops, so most of the measuring was done with cupped fingers. When Marian plunged her hands in alongside The Gish's, the dusty seeds gave off the unctuous aroma of spring violets. Marian closed her eyes, exhaling with a soft sigh. As the granules slid across her fingers, her hands brushed against The Gish's, combining with the muffled *thok* of the hammer in the distance and the pollinated spring sunshine. A thick ache, that so often preceded tears, rose in Marian's throat.

Nezzie approached, her mouth screwed to one side as she scrutinized her list. "Does this say *turnips* or *parsnips?*"

"You have the worst handwriting."

"I'm guessing turnips." Nezzie sank her hand among the seeds, joining hers to those of Marian and The Gish. The kernels made a rat-a-tat-tat as they dropped into the paper sack she held open. "Hear the latest rumor?" Her voice was casual.

Marian moved on to chicory. "Now what? The Red Cross has two dozen brass bedsteads for us to tote around? Our supply of toothpowder is running low and the director wants us to grind our own with mortar and pestle?"

Nezzie emitted her barking laugh. "No. Much less important. Two Canadian foresters stopped at the lodge just now. Apparently some Hun deserters are making noises about a German offensive set to begin at midnight. In this sector."

The Gish pursed her lips derisively. "Heard that before."

Marian let the handful of kernels dribble into her bag and examined Nezzie's strained expression. "Is this the real thing?"

Nezzie shrugged. "Who knows?"

"They *can't* be marching. Not now! Just when we're getting all the villages patched up!"

"It's just another rumor," The Gish said, her voice rising a little too high.

Marian cocked her head. "No guns."

The three women paused. The only sounds were the continued *thok thok* of the hammer and, in the distance, the strident voice of the director commanding someone to, "Come here right now!"

"You're right. Probably just whisper-down-alley," Nezzie said.

They returned to dusty bags, but the morning air had lost a bit of its glory.

In her camp bed that night, Marian turned restlessly onto one side, then the other, as if she were a heap of seeds pushed here and there by nervous hands. Her ears strained for the sound of guns. It was after midnight and so far nothing could be heard except the breathing of Nezzie on her left and Links on her right. Maybe it was just another rumor. The sorting marathon had continued well into the evening, and after a quick meal of rabbit stew, most of the women had flopped onto their beds, fully clothed. Across the room, The Gish slept, knees tucked up to her chest, frizzy hair splayed across the pillow.

After a time Marian, gave up on sleep and pulled a flashlight from under her cot, along with a bulging packet of letters from Deuce. It had grown so large over the last few months that she only took a few at a time with her on the road. She drew the blanket over her head to reread his most recent letter.

Seeing Jupiter lying there was one of the lowest points of my life. I couldn't get out of my mind how eager he must have been for the treat. How trusting. He was just a simple creature with no bone to pick with anyone. Never did as much as snap or growl. And yet, and I don't think I ever would have admitted this before, but maybe it's not a good thing to be so trusting. I always thought if I tried to see the good in people, they'd like me, and treat me well too. Or at least just let me be a part. I never wanted more than to belong, but now, not so much. Sorry this letter's turned gloomy . . .

Tears dripped from her chin. The strain of this war is turning me into nothing more than a blubbering sentimentalist, she thought.

She snapped off the flashlight and flopped onto her back, the blanket still covering her face, her eyelashes brushing against its coarse fibers. After a time she blew her nose wetly, setting off a small ripple of unconscious movement in the women around her. She tucked the letter back into the packet and forced her mind to designing imaginary hats until sleep finally overcame her.

It was still dark when Marian was jolted awake by a deafening cannonade of artillery. Her bunkmates were already up, pulling skirts on over flannel petticoats, grabbing up the wrong boots in the blackness. They stumbled to the lodge where they found the others, the air thick with fear. Small groups of women huddled together, wincing at every impact. The screeching of shells coalesced into an impenetrable fortress of noise. The usual concussions from the front that Marian had grown accustomed to these last three months now seemed, in comparison, nothing more than toy firecrackers.

Someone had started to make coffee but abandoned the task, leaving behind a heap of spilled grounds. With shaking hands, Marian brushed the mess back into the dented tin pot and set a pan to boil over the fire. She prodded the embers, feeling rather than hearing the poker clatter against the andirons. After a time the women settled uneasily onto chairs and benches, sipping the bitter coffee and shouting speculations on who was on the offensive. Even the most optimistic knew that it was the Germans, preparing to sweep out from the well-fortified Hindenberg Line as soon as the initial bombardment was over. The only question was whether the Brits, who guarded this sector, could hold the trenches. If they didn't, all the unit's work of the past six months would be destroyed. The villagers, who had managed to survive the initial German occupation in 1914, would be driven out of their homes. Marian patted the empty pocket over her left breast, wishing she had tucked her packet of letters in it.

At dawn, the women peered out into a hazy landscape. Even massive Lulu, parked only feet from the lodge, was invisible in the fog. Then, just as suddenly as it had started, the bombardment ceased; silence saturated the tissues of mist. Straining her eyes into the filtered whiteness, Marian imagined the British Tommies huddled in their chill trenches, her villagers trembling beneath the new iron bedsteads, waiting and listening as she was. Now the invisible orchestra of men and weapons turned from the cacophonous prelude to the main piece, the static of machine-gun fire.

This shift in noise galvanized the unit, as if a dam had burst. They shook off their terror. Someone gathered up the dirtied coffee cups for a wash. Links dropped another log on the fire. The women speculated on whether it would be possible to make it to their villages in the thick fog ("In this pea soup? Absolutely not!" the director said). Their pleas to set up a canteen were more successful. They'd serve the Tommies coffee and chocolate down at the intersection where the château's two-mile lane met up with the main road. In the meantime, Ruth, the most athletic of the group, was dispatched to gather information from passing troops. She was equipped with a flashlight, nearly useless in the landscape of clouds, and a walking stick to poke ahead of her like a blind person. Marian, Nezzie, and the others hurried to the pantry to take inventory for the canteen. Someone made a pot of porridge for the unit but Marian couldn't eat. Her intestines were cinched like a drawstring.

By early afternoon, the unit had loaded chocolate bars, apples, biscuits, and other canteen staples into three wheelbarrows. Someone remarked that the fog was thinning from chowder to consommé. Marian and Nezzie had filled empty champagne bottles, leftover from some long-ago revel, with milky coffee. Marian was tucking the last of these into the barrow when a figure stumbled out of the mist. It was Ruth, panting from exertion, yet trying to call out. Marian rushed over as the girl gasped, "They're falling back."

"The Tommies? Oh Lord. Did you seem them?"

Ruth nodded, her ribs still heaving. "Almost trampled. Gun teams heading west. Infantry. I ran."

"The director needs to hear this."

Marian put her arm around Ruth's waist. They stepped inside and were immediately surrounded. It had taken Ruth a good hour to get to the main road in the dense fog. No one appeared at first. Then several units of Tommies passed, marching quick-step toward the front. When she'd asked who was winning, they'd answered in confident tones. "No worries, miss. We'll push 'em back to kingdom come." That sort of thing. Her next encounter was with Canizy's antique postman, creaking steadily westward on his rusted bicycle. When he spotted Ruth he oversteered so that she had to jump into a drainage ditch.

Ruth said, "His breath was rattling so I thought he'd cracked a rib. I could barely believe it when he told me he'd been cycling the countryside all morning, collecting information. He'd ridden ten miles to the east where an ambulance driver told him that five of the villages in this sector, including Terezy, had already been overrun by the Germans and many others would probably be cut off in the next several days."

"No!" someone shouted. Several girls began weeping. Marian pressed a hand against her mouth, Nezzie squeezed Ruth's shoulder.

"The postman begged us to evacuate the other towns.

No one is doing anything about getting civilians out of harm's way."

"We've got to help," declared a voice from the back.

"Of course we will," the director said authoritatively. "Links, get my clipboard."

Marian, who discovered she was still clutching a champagne bottle, put it down on the trestle table gently, as if it were something precious. Villages shelled! The people panicked, wounded, some probably dead. She remembered one blind woman in Terezy who cared for seven children younger than five, only three of which were her own grandchildren. What had happened to them? All the beds and desks and blankets that the Fielding Unit had so painstakingly replaced, smashed.

"I waited around a little while longer, but when I saw the Tommies retreating I made a dash for it," Ruth said.

The director unfolded the unit's big colored map of Picardy on the table nearest the fire. Until this day, the director had prohibited anyone from marking it up, fussing that some remote intersection of two seldom used roads would be blotted out by a careless squib of ink. Now, in consultation with Ruth, she used her own pen to circle their precious villages. The rest of the unit crowded round in tense silence. The director drew an undulating line that cut roughly northeast to southwest. This marked the German advance, as reported by the postman. Marian saw immediately how cruelly Terezy had been separated from the unit's protectorate, like a pullet culled from the flock. Far to the west of the blue line lay Montdidier with its zipper of rail lines heading toward Paris, promising, like Jacob's ladder, salvation. Here the director drew a large star. All the women understood that between the advancing line of Germans and the evacuation point, chaos reigned. The main roads would be clogged with sweating, swearing British gunners pulling guns westward, their eyes seeking out high ground where they could block their wheels, point the muzzles eastward, and await orders. Crowded among them would be streams of mud-splattered Tommies, some supporting bloodied comrades, others stumbling alone. Officers would be shouting orders to unhearing ears. Within this noisy, stinking horde, the women could only hope, would be some of their villagers—those able-bodied enough to load up wheelbarrows and carts with their belongings, and flee.

But many of the townsfolk were too frail to walk or had nothing with which to haul even the smallest collection of goods. At least five of the hamlets were far off the main roads, remote dots on the horizon, and very likely knew nothing of what was happening. The director laid out what had to be done. Three women would be assigned to the roadside canteen. Everyone else would spend the rest of the evening, and on into the night, packing up the Ford truck for transport to Montdidier. All the materials vital to the unit's functioning—the precious records, basic medical supplies—would be crammed into the truck's cargo space along with barrels of crackers, apples, and flour. Once in Montdidier, they'd set up evacuation headquarters.

The Gish said in a hoarse voice what everyone was thinking. "But what about our villages?"

"I'm getting to that," the director said, her tone more patient than usual.

In the morning four drivers would maneuver the unit's remaining vehicles through the chaos to coordinate the evacuation and transport the frail, the sick, and the babies in arms. The director indicated the towns with a brisk tap of the pen—two were due north of the château, towns that had been reduced to populations at the extreme ends of the life span. Well west of the menacing blue line was Chaulnes, the most remote of their charges and least likely to have any hint of the Armageddon bearing down on it. The fourth destination was Ham, barely a quarter-inch from the German advance.

"The drivers will be racing the Germans—especially in Ham—besides dealing with panicked villagers and impassable roads. I don't have to say how dangerous this is. That's why I'm asking for volunteers."

The lodge fell silent, as if the fog had returned in full force, smothering even the smallest whimper. When a log thudded noisily into the coals, the entire unit jerked.

The director cleared her throat. "So. Volunteers?"

Twelve hands shot up.

Nodding, the director quickly pointed to her selections. "Isabel, Links, Nezzie, and Marian."

"Send me to Ham," Marian blurted.

The director tipped her head to one side. "You're sure?"

"I'm the best mechanic in case there's a breakdown. I insist."

"All right then. Let's have Isabel to Rouly le Grand, Links to Nesle, Nezzie to Chaulnes."

"You're sure?" Nezzie asked Marian as the director turned to other matters. "You could be killed!"

Marian's voice dropped. "If something happened to you, I couldn't stand it. It would be unbearable. I have to be the one."

* * *

For the second night in a row, Marian got barely two hours of sleep. The unit spent most of the night sorting out what to take and what to leave behind. The Ford was packed and unpacked half a dozen times. The women rotated duty at the canteen and every few hours, the relieved workers trudged back up the lane with discouraging reports of dazed and disorganized soldiers, horribly maimed ambulance cases. The women tried to buck up but at one point or another almost everyone decamped to the outhouse for a cry. At dawn, Marian and Nezzie had a chance for only the briefest goodbye before driving off in opposite directions.

In Ham, Marian found that only a few of the residents were capable of walking. The rest were loaded into Lulu with the barest of essentials and the entire town joined the massive jam of refugees, soldiers, and ambulances pouring westward. Many of the civilians were pulling carts with teetering loads of bedding, chairs, foodstuffs, and—hanging off the sides—pots and pans. Children riding on top, unaware of the danger, squealed excitedly each time the pile shifted beneath them. Marian's own charges were subdued. In the passenger seat sat the stoic Madame Broussard, one infant napping in a nest of blankets at her feet, her ancient hands stroking the delicate head of another asleep in her lap. Squatting in the rear, on bags of foodstuffs and blankets, were twenty-eight souls.

It took Lulu thirty-six hours to cover the twelve miles to Montdidier. Pulling past the city's steepled convent, Marian felt the tug of exhaustion, her legs ached unmercifully. She had barely taken her foot off the pedals since leaving Ham.

In Montdidier, Marian faced a confusing crush of

people, carts, and farm animals. Luckily she spotted a volunteer trotting briskly up the street, the woman's white headscarf with its embroidered Red Cross insignia flapping against her shoulders. The nurse directed Marian to the main square.

As she turned into the cobbled plaza, she saw a young boy untether a nervous cow from a hitching post, apparently to lead the animal toward the town's drinking trough. Marian quickly squeezed Lulu into the spot. Almost every inch of space in the square not occupied by animals or loaded carts was taken up by tables. Women in the traditional close-fitting white caps with strings tied snuggly under the chin, men in soft hats, and hordes of children sat patiently while volunteers moved among them with pitchers and baskets of bread.

Marian saw a number of her own villagers at the tables who, when they spotted her, wearily dipped their heads in recognition. The passengers in the back of the truck began moving restlessly about.

"Wait," Marian called out. "I'll get someone to help me with your things."

Beside her, Madame Broussard stooped to collect little Phillippe who was emitting fussy bleats. Marian turned to slide from the driver's seat, placed her right foot on the cobbles, and promptly turned her ankle, the same one that she'd injured in Emporia. The pain shot up her shin.

"Dang blam it!"

Madame Broussard touched Marian's sleeve worriedly. "Are you all right, madame?"

"Yes, yes," Marian muttered irritably. "I'll be right back." She hobbled into the square where two of her villagers rushed up, their faces haggard from the strain of

the past two days, filled with concern. Someone untied
a wooden chair strapped to the side of a cart and Marian dropped on it gratefully, feeling the pressure of fluid
already ballooning above her foot. She made eye contact
with The Gish who was threading her way through the
crowd.

"Are all our drivers in?" Marian cried when the girl
was within shouting distance.

The Gish wormed her way past a clutch of boys playing marbles and was at Marian's side. "Isabel is. Was. The
director sent her right out again. I don't know about the
others."

Marian bit her lip worriedly. "Nezzie?"

The Gish shook her head, and it was then Marian
noticed that she was clutching the unit's prize hen to her
bosom.

"Lulu's parked back there. I twisted my ankle before
I could unload the passengers. Most of them are too crippled to climb out on their own. Could you help?"

"Right-o," The Gish said, handing her the fowl, who
clucked indignantly, its sharp claws scrabbling to gain
hold on Marian's thighs. Suddenly the exhaustion, the
silly bird's frantic fluttering, the image she must have pre-
sented, sent Marian roaring.

That was how the director discovered her not ten
minutes later—hysterical, hobbled, clumsily clutching the
affronted hen.

"I was going to send you out to pick up stragglers
coming into town but . . ." she bent down and poked the
swollen skin of Marian's ankle, ". . . with that you can't
possibly operate the truck."

Marian sobered up immediately, levering the hen's

bottom down with a firm hand. "Nonsense. Of course I can drive, just give me an hour. What about Nezzie and Links?"

The director's hair, normally drawn upward into a severe chignon, was a ragged garden of wispy sprouts.

"We'll have a nurse look at that foot. We've managed to set up temporary sick rooms in the hotel over there." She pointed to a redbrick structure at the far side of the square. "Links is down at the rail station. The French government has left the work of feeding the refugees and getting them on trains entirely to us."

"What about Nezzie?"

"No word yet."

"But it's been two days. Has someone been sent to look for her?"

A large hog, directed from behind by an elderly woman whose lips were sunken against toothless gums, broke between them. "*Excusez-moi,*" the woman said daintily.

The director shook her head. The anxious voices of the people, the mooing and squawking, almost drowned out her words. "We're overwhelmed just coping with this right now." She gestured at the bundles of clothing, the overburdened carts and wheelbarrows.

"I'm going to find her," Marian declared, starting to push herself up from the chair.

The director pressed her down firmly. "No, you're not. After the nurse checks you, I'll decide where I need you most." She squeezed back through the crowd, clipboard pressed closely to her chest.

Fuming, Marian lifted her leg to examine the damage. It was the same throbbing roast beef that had been propped on Tula's day bed. How could so much have changed and yet she was back to this?

The Gish returned from her mission and Marian threw one of her arms over her friend's narrow shoulders so they could make their way to the hotel. The nurse, an Englishwoman with the moist coloring of a grub and the personality to match, pronounced that the ankle was badly sprained—and wrapped it securely with a strip of what might have once been a sleeve. After some argument with The Gish, Marian was persuaded to lie down on a cot for a short nap. She planned to make her way back to Lulu and drive out in search of Nezzie, but exhaustion overtook her.

She didn't wake until the next morning, sitting up abruptly and cursing herself. Through the hotel's tall windows, the creaking of carts and subdued calls told her the town square was still filling with evacuees. Maybe it was a caravan from Ham, maybe Nezzie had finally arrived! Marian swung her legs over the edge of the cot and tested her foot. It seemed able to hold her. She slowly rose, blood surging painfully into the tissues. She hobbled through the maze of cots. The hotel's umbrella stand stood unmolested by the front door and she plucked out a man's umbrella with a thick blackthorn handle. She emerged into the same frightened bustle of yesterday. None of the refugees, many still asleep on their bundles, looked like the villagers from Chaulnes, Nezzie's assignment, and there was no sign of the Dodge touring car. At the plaza's center, where a statue of the Virgin Mary presided from a pedestal, Ruth and Links were ladling out milk. As she made her way toward them, Marian was approached by the director who seemed to materialize out of nowhere.

"Any word from Nezzie?"

The director shook her head. Marian's gut twisted beneath her belt.

"I want you to relieve Links at the milk station. Lulu's needed to scour for stragglers."

Marian jumped. "I can go. See, no problem." She rotated her foot for the director, biting hard into her lower lip.

"Yes, there is a problem. You are not capable of operating that truck. You are, however, capable of ladling out milk."

Marian sullenly took her place beside the milk cans. A line of young mothers stretched in front of her, swaying sleepily on their feet and clutching swaddled infants. As Links handed Marian the ladle, she whispered, "Don't worry, I'll find her. I'll drive behind the German lines if I have to."

Marian felt the prick of tears behind her eyes and smiled weakly. She watched the girl's gangly body move into the crowd. The sky was now pearly gray. Marian dipped the ladle into the foamy milk. She thought of Deuce and their day at the Sayre farm when they'd discovered the milk bottles sitting in dirty water. Thanks to Deuce's reporting, Emporia's infants would be healthy. Let me do the same here, she thought.

Rose, one of the unit's regular customers at the château, was next in line. "Madame Marian, you are here!" Her round, peony face lit up, despite the hollows of fatigue beneath her eyes.

"And you and little Robert. I am so very, very glad." Her eyes brimming, Marian ducked her head and busied herself pouring milk into the bottle Rose had handed over.

Through the next hours Marian distributed milk to women who, just last week, she had delivered bolsters and shared coffee with. Each time, there was a burst of pleasure on both sides. By noon, the milk ran out. Links—and Nezzie—had not returned. At the hotel, the director, whose face was so desiccated that Marian felt a pang of sympathy, called the women together. She announced that the unit was to pull out of Montdidier. The French Mission was taking over the remainder of the evacuation. The Fielding women were to report to Amiens, where they were needed at a temporary hospital. More American forces were expected to arrive in early summer, and until the Allies pushed back, the unit would fill in at Red Cross canteens and clinics behind the lines. The resettlement work among their villages would not resume until the Germans were permanently cleared of Picardy.

"I am deploying you individually on the westbound trains so that you can accompany our villagers for at least part of their journey. Disembark in Amiens and someone from the Red Cross will meet you. Go and collect your things," she said, holding her clipboard aloft. "You're listed in order of departure here."

The women crowded around and Marian saw that her name was first. She opened her mouth to protest but the director looked so haggard, she remained silent. With a heavy heart she located her satchel and joined the throngs heading toward the station, leaning heavily on the umbrella and telling herself that since Montdidier was being evacuated, Nezzie would now be directed to Amiens as well.

The station was another scene of confusion, howling babies, and heaps of baggage. Near the tracks, The Gish, wearing the basket hat, was attempting to organize the passengers into orderly lines. She grinned and waved as Marian stumped over.

"Any sign of Links or Nezzie?"

The Gish shook her head.

"I'm to get on this train," Marian said desolately.

"I know. I have the list." The Gish's saucer eyes glistened. "We'll all be together again in Amiens. And if not there, after our boys beat the Germans, we'll go back to our villages and build them all over again."

Marian pressed her lips together, not wanting to break down in front of the refugees who were losing so much more than she was. The train gave a sooty blast, and Marian put her good foot on the iron step of the nearest car. She scanned the crowd for the face she wanted most to see. As the train jerked forward, Links appeared in the distance. Marian gestured frantically and Links pushed toward her. The train picked up steam. Links was still about a yard away. She shouted but the noise of the engine was too great. Marian gripped the handrail, swinging out as far as she could, feeling as if her arm would be wrenched from its socket.

"Nezzie—" was all Marian could make out.

Then, inexplicably, the train slowed enough for Links to grab the handrail and swing herself up beside Marian.

"There was an accident. Her car flipped!" Links shouted breathlessly.

"Is she all right?"

Links paused, then shook her head. "Didn't make it."

Marian let out an anguished howl. Suddenly Links was gone, jumping down to the platform as the train pulled away. Marian watched as the figure became smaller and smaller. When the train rounded a bend and the station was no longer in view, she collapsed with a moan on the floor of the vestibule. Beneath her, the couplings banged as if they were being forcefully torn apart. And not many miles to the east, Picardy's villages were occupied, once again, by German soldiers.

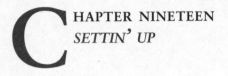

CHAPTER NINETEEN
SETTIN' UP

Excuse the scribble, but the Germans are making their big push to the west and our unit's headquarters will shortly be overtaken. We are evacuating our villages within the hour. Along the front, the guns pound ceaselessly; I can hardly think straight through the noise. There is no more time, so the act of sending you this letter must stand in for the words I intended to write.

"NOW, LET'S SEE IF THIS BABY RUNS," Deuce muttered to himself, slipping the last of the freshly greased bearings into place. Grunting, he rose from his knees. Here goes nothing. He flipped the switch of the job press. The thing started up just fine, as it had for the past three hours. But just as before, the screech of metal rubbing against metal quickly sounded and Deuce promptly snapped it off in disgust. Probably keeping the whole street awake, he thought. He consulted his watch. Almost a quarter to eleven. He'd been at it since about seven, when he'd tried to run a quick set of business cards for Dr. Jack and the press had started acting up. Since Marian's letter came, with its dire news about the Hun offensive, Deuce had found it hard to sleep and often worked late on nights such as this. He'd replaced the belts and greased the bearings twice already. No go. Disgusted, he dropped into his desk chair and poured out a jigger of whiskey. He stretched out his legs, unconsciously seeking Jupiter's soft belly, even though the dog had been dead more than three months.

Deuce caught the low whistle of a train. Two blocks away, Simon Maxwell, who was dozing in his Model T, Emporia's only public conveyance, heard it too. He climbed out to crank the engine and puttered down State Street. He parked in front of the station just as the engine was pulling in. Two women debarked from the passenger coach, blinking in the light thrown by the station lamps. Further down, intentionally overlooked by the Negro porter, a slender figure hopped from a baggage car and trotted into the shadows at the end of the platform.

Only when he was a block away did Emmett Shang pause to brush the dust from the khaki tunic and puttees of his uniform. The brass buttons on the army epaulets glinted in the dim light. It was hard to swallow, coming into town this way, on leave from the Official US of A Army and having to jump a baggage car, Emmett thought. *No colored coaches on this run, boy.* The courthouse clock sounded eleven. Goddamn, only five hours, then back on the train. But it was worth it. When Captain Frank had announced they'd be shipping out to Newport News in five days and, after that, on to France, he knew he had to get home one last time. It took some begging, but he'd gotten leave.

Trotting down Main Street, his mind was already home. Fried chicken, mashed potatoes, greens, dumplings, and biscuits with flaky sides, like golden gills. He chewed his lips in anticipation. Everything swimming in gravy.

Only in the army six months and nothing but skin and bones, his mother would tut-tut. Six months of drills, artillery practice and marching around the piney woods chopped down into a makeshift parade ground, eight-mile marches with a full pack, and all under the broiling Texas sun.

Only five hours, get going, fool. He picked up his pace. Not enough time to see the fellows. Tuck in particular. Tuck, who had needled him about wanting to join up. "You'll be nothing but a stevedore like all the other colored troops. Same old heavy lifting," he'd taunted. But Tuck was wrong. Emmett had landed in a combat unit, the 370th. Yeah, too bad he couldn't meet up with Tuck. He'd have been sure to tell him all about the colored females coming out to camp from Houston with pies and lemonade. "And sure enough, don't they admire a man in puttees," he'd have bragged.

Emmett turned away from the main drag and onto narrow Adams Street, a shortcut to the colored section, the single dirt street at the edge of town. Damn, the left puttee was unwinding. He knelt in front of an empty storefront to rewrap it. The street was shadowy. The only light came from a streetlamp on the far corner and, across the way and a couple of doors down, the glow from some business open after-hours.

The dank smell of concrete, maybe urine, rose from a basement stairwell at his back. Footfalls could be heard echoing a half-block away. He jerked to attention. Two men, one whistling off-key, stepped unsteadily into the streetlamp's cone of light. Emmett recognized Wade Johnson and his cousin Merle, the mechanics from Harp's Garage. Both had the unsteady gait of end-of-the-night drinkers.

Seeing the cousins coming up the street, he stepped back in the shadows.

". . . think about that?" Wade was saying loudly, punching Merle on the arm.

"I *said*," Merle began, then, "Whoa, what'da we have here?"

The two halted in front of Emmett. The air ballooned with the yeasty odor of beer.

"I think it's that boy from Harp's. Don't you think so, Wade?"

"Yes, but what's he doing here?"

Emmett stepped out. "Evening, Wade. Merle. Just heading home," he said, his voice stiff. He was turning away when Merle caught his arm. Underneath his khaki tunic, Emmett's heart quickened.

"Hey. Don't go rushing off. Let us get a look at you in that fine uniform." Merle's rubbery face broke into a too-wide grin.

Wade jumped in with a friendlier tone: "How's the army treating you?"

"It's not so bad. Sort of . . ." Emmett began.

Merle broke in: "Got you toting bales and all that? Bet you're not shooting guns . . . or driving Packards, are you?"

"I'm in a combat unit." Emmett stepped back, legs quivering. The iron railing that edged the stairwell pressed against his thighs. He couldn't help but think of the riot that had erupted in Houston a couple of months before his unit rolled into town. Regular colored soldiers fight-

ing the police. It had ended badly. Thirteen colored soldiers hanged, and lots more colored skulls cracked open
with batons.

"So where's your gun?" Merle asked, his eyes flicking
across Emmett's puttees, the brass clasp of the Browning
belt. "If you're combat you've got to be carrying a gun.
Or a knife?"

Emmett shook his head, frantically searching the
street, the lighted windows of the store across the way.
The volume of Merle's rough voice grew, bounced against
the walls of the shuttered stores.

Inside the *Garland Weekly*, Deuce put down the jigger,
startled by the shouting. He rose cautiously and approached
the window. There was movement in the shadows across
the street. Two figures—no, three. Wade Johnson's thick
mat of black hair. The other fellow was surely Merle. The
third? Deuce couldn't make out.

"You know, Wade, I think this boy has a knife on
him! Don't ya? Hah!" Merle lunged forward.

Suddenly, Emmett Shang's face heaved into view,
constricted in fright. His eyes roved frantically up the
street, his head twitching this way and that. Then his
gaze locked on Deuce, the dark eyes pleading. Deuce was
out the door in two strides. Up ahead, he caught a flurry
of movement. The soldier pulling away from Merle, the
larger man advancing until Emmett was bent back over
the railing. As he ran toward the group, Deuce heard
leather soles skittering frantically on the concrete. An
animal howl sprang from the soldier's throat as he disappeared into the darkness of the stairwell. The two cousins
paused, caught sight of Deuce, and turned and fled up the
street. He shouted at them to stop but they ran on. Heav-

ing, he clattered down the steps, to the dark heap at the bottom. In the dim light, Deuce could make out Emmett's twisted form. One leg was splayed out cruelly. Kneeling beside the head, Deuce shoved his hand under the skull; it came away sticky. His ear to the soldier's lips, he couldn't be sure whether he heard breathing or not, his own was coming so rapidly. Running back up the stairs, he tore into his office and called Dr. Jack, then the sheriff. Before heading back down the street, he took the stairs up to his apartment two at a time and snatched a blanket from the bed and a flashlight. Back in the stairwell, he covered Emmett with the blanket, then went to stand at the top. A pair of headlamps appeared.

"Down here," Deuce said to Dr. Jack, ushering him down the steps.

After a minute, another car pulled up.

"What happened?" the sheriff called down from the sidewalk. He'd apparently been sleeping when Deuce's call roused him. A tuft of his hair stuck up in the back like a fowl's tail feather and his vest was buttoned crookedly.

"Just hold off a minute, Johnson. I need Deuce's help," Dr. Jack said, kneeling beside Emmett.

The cellar way was dank and there was a sharp ammonia scent of cat piss. Deuce squatted down on the other side of the cramped space.

"Hand me the light," the doctor said to Deuce. He drew up Emmett's lids—first one, then the other. The soldier's face was illuminated, the young man's lips pulled back in a grimace of fear. Dr. Jack handed Deuce the light and placed his fingers on the neck.

"So?" the sheriff called down.

Deuce glanced at Dr. Jack, who murmured, "Pulse is very thready."

"Damnit." Deuce rose.

The sheriff was leaning over the railing.

Deuce said, "I was working late, heard some shouting. When I looked out, I saw Merle and Wade. They were arguing with a third person. I couldn't make out who at first. Their voices were getting ugly, though. Then one of them, not sure which, lunged at the fellow and I saw it was Emmett. I ran out the door and up the street. My head was down part of the time. When I looked up again, I heard Emmett cry out but didn't see him. Merle and Wade were leaning over the railing here. Then they caught sight of me and took off. That's it."

"You're sure it was Merle and Wade?" the sheriff asked, running his fingers through his hair.

Deuce nodded. "Positive."

The sheriff sighed wearily. "All right. I'll go over to their place right away. Last I knew they roomed at the American House."

Dr. Jack called out, "Before you go, Dan, get someone to drive out to the Shangs' place and bring the family back. He's slipping away on me and they should come quick."

A slight breeze kicked up, stirring the awning above a nearby store. The canvas flapped erratically. Deuce opened his mouth, then closed it. The name calling and taunts filled his ears for a moment. "I'll go," he said, his voice low.

"What say?"

"Said I'll go."

* * *

Five minutes later he was driving down Armstrong Street, into the shabby section of Emporia. Pillared porticos and trim brick gave way to narrow houses with rickety porches in need of paint. At the railroad tracks, even those shells of civilization fell away. The brick paving and streetlamps stopped abruptly. Asphalt shone dully in the headlights. On the right, Deuce caught the dump's cacophonous odor of decay, fermentation, and cloying sweetness. He saw without seeing the row of discarded doors, broken shutters, and splintered pallets that formed the fence.

Just beyond the dump was the Flats, a street of skinny wooden shanties. Every window was dark. Far away a bullfrog hummed, but otherwise elongated shadows of silence stretched between the houses, under the elms. As the Model T puttered past the thin-walled shacks, its vibrations did not go unnoticed. This Deuce knew. His hands shook on the steering wheel. He gripped it harder.

He had no idea which house was Laylia and Oliver's. He should have asked the sheriff. Six places or so on each side, that meant odds of one in twelve. Might as well try this one. He pulled up to a dim façade and stepped outside of the auto. A chill wind raised goose bumps on his arms. When he'd dashed out of his shop at the sounds of an argument, he hadn't stopped to put on a coat. Only now did he become aware of the grease on his hands from the press's bearings. His shirtsleeves were still rolled up. Nothing to do but wipe his hands on his pants and roll down his sleeves.

He mounted the porch steps and gingerly tapped on the door. He tried again, louder. Someone grunted inside. The slap of bare feet on wood sounded and the door

swung open. Deuce stiffened. It was Smitty, whom Deuce
had seen, and avoided, dozens of times at the train station
as the janitor leaned on his mop, waiting for the passengers to board so he could swab out the men's toilet. But
tonight, instead of frayed overhauls, Smitty wore snappy
blue-striped pajamas. Someone had ironed a crease down
the trouser legs. They eyed one another. Smitty's face was
an impassive mask.

"Sorry for the late hour, but I'm looking for the
Shangs," Deuce said.

"This ain't the Shangs."

Deuce realized he'd never heard Smitty speak before.
The edges of his words were rounded.

"Could you tell—"

"Who is it, Daddy?" A pretty woman with a heart-
shaped face and a row of spit curls across her forehead
appeared beside Smitty. When she saw Deuce, she covered
her mouth with her hand and drew back into the shadows.

Deuce continued: "Could you tell me where they live?
It's urgent. There's been an accident. In town. Emmett's
been hurt. And now . . ."

"Emmett in the army."

"I guess he's home on leave or something, because
he's right up in town. Please." Deuce hoped the quiver in
his voice wasn't noticeable.

"Serious?" Smitty asked.

Deuce nodded.

"All right. Let me get some clothes on and I'll take
you . . ."

"Hurry," Deuce said.

Smitty quickly emerged, calling back through the
door, "You get dressed too."

The two men hustled down the road. Three houses down Smitty nodded. "This they one."

Oliver answered the door. Even as Deuce was opening his mouth to speak, Oliver, taking in the strained faces of both men, stepped back with a moan. "Emmett?"

Deuce jumped in, his tone urgent: "There's been an accident. Dr. Jack is with him. I'll drive you and Laylia. We've got to hurry."

Five minutes later, the Model T was heading back toward town. Smitty sat up front with Deuce. In the back, Oliver stared dully at the dark houses at the edge of Emporia while Laylia wailed and prayed next to him. "Please, Lord, don't take my boy. Please, sweet Jesus . . ."

On her other side, Smitty's wife, who they'd picked up on the way out, tried to comfort her. When Deuce turned down Adams Street, he saw several autos and a wagon parked near his storefront. As he pulled up to the stair-well, Dr. Jack and another fellow were gently lowering a body, completely covered in a white sheet, onto a stretcher on the sidewalk. Laylia screamed and began clawing at the door handle even before the auto came to a stop. Oliver slammed open the door and reached in for Laylia.

Smitty also began to climb out but turned back. "Thank you." He stretched out his hand and, after a moment's hesitation, Deuce shook it, his eyes tearing.

The last thing Deuce saw before releasing the brake was Laylia, supported between Oliver and Smitty, stumbling toward her son's still form.

In his rooms above the shop, Deuce sat numbly for a long time, his head in his hands. After a while his mind turned to Helen. How precious our children are! he thought.

The next afternoon, the sheriff telephoned Deuce, asking him to come over to the courthouse to give an account of what he had witnessed the night before. As a clerk took notes, Deuce described hearing angry voices, seeing three figures, and immediately recognizing Wade and Merle. Had he seen a knife in Emmett's hand? No, not during the scuffle and not at the bottom of the stairwell. Merle and Wade, who had been picked up for questioning earlier that day, had insisted that Emmett pulled a knife. They'd admitted that voices had been raised, over what Wade called the "uppity attitude" Emmett had acquired in the army. But the cousins contended that Emmett, after words had been exchanged, had started to lunge at Wade with a pocketknife, lost his footing, and tumbled over the railing. Was that scenario possible?

Deuce bowed his head in thought, tapping clasped hands against his lips. No, he felt sure that it had been Wade who had moved toward Emmett, not the other way around. But, after questioning, Deuce had to admit that the lighting was poor and that during the several seconds it took him to run up the street, he didn't have his eyes on the group the entire time.

At the end of the session, Deuce stood up. There was a sour taste in his mouth.

"Gotta tell you, unless some evidence turns up, it seems like it's going to be your word against theirs."

"I'm not afraid to go up against them in court. I know what I saw and didn't see. And it's not just my word. What about the knife they claim he had but wasn't there?"

Hank shrugged. "The investigation isn't closed, just letting you know how I see it right now."

Deuce shook Hank's hand and passed out the door. He stood a moment on the courthouse steps in the watery spring sunshine. His eye caught a flyer plastered to a light pole announcing the dates of the coming summer's Chautauqua. Someone else was in charge of publicity this year. So many things had changed.

When there was a death, it was the custom in the Flats for the body to be laid out at the house for several days. Two days after their son's passing, the Shangs held a settin' up. The morning of the wake, Deuce telephoned Tula.

"I'm thinking of going over to the Shangs' place today."

"I think you should."

"Want to come with me?"

"Just a minute," she said. With her hand muffling the receiver, Deuce heard her say something to someone. "I'll be in town this afternoon, so why don't I come over to your office at two and we can go from there?"

Who was she talking to? Deuce thought. Had Clay come back from Chicago?

Tula arrived at his offices twenty minutes late, unusual for someone so punctual. Deuce noticed she wore a blue dress of a particularly flattering shade. Her skin shimmered, as if pollinated. The letterpress, now fully operational, at least for the moment, was noisily churning out a stack of flyers for St. Paul's parish picnic, the big do-up for the town's small and clannish Catholic enclave.

"Be with you in a minute," Deuce called out, feeding the last couple of sheets into the press.

Tula set a large leather satchel on the counter and wandered over to the typesetting area where that week's issue was about half finished. The letters were backward, but she could read enough to see that Deuce had put Emmett's obituary on the front page.

Her eyes welled up and she dug into her handbag for a hankie, pushing aside a jumble of wadded shopping lists, safety pins, and the small silver vanity case with its cake of powder and mirror she'd taken to carrying.

She was noisily blowing her nose when Deuce approached, wiping his hands on a greasy rag. She gestured toward the obituary. "Laylia will be so proud."

Deuce rolled down his shirtsleeves. "Needed to do it, even if it costs me a subscriber or two. Stroh, my city reporter, is moving on, and I'm going to try to cover the county news myself. That'll save me some."

"Money that tight?"

"Could be worse." Deuce buttoned his cuffs. "So, ready to go?"

On their way out, she picked up the satchel.

"What's that?"

"One of Clay's old cameras. Jasper taught me how to use it and I thought that Laylia would like a keepsake of Emmett."

"Jasper, eh?"

Tula blushed.

On the drive out to the Flats, Tula's mind turned to the widowed photographer. She couldn't help thinking about him, despite the fact that she was going to a visitation.

Tula and Jasper had been spending quite a lot of time together. He'd bought a few pieces of Clay's, although she suspected he didn't need them, and what he didn't buy he helped her sell to other photographers in the area. And he was teaching her how to take and develop prints.

She stroked her fingers, stained with fixative from the darkroom, and secretly smiled. In the red glow of the darkroom lantern she'd been courted, among the drippy prints hanging from a wash line and the shallow enamel basins of developing fluid. The darkroom was small, a closet really, so that when they worked side-by-side, their shoulders and elbows were constantly touching, as if magnetized. His hands steadied hers as she poured the sharp-smelling chemicals into basins arranged on the waist-high counter. After several lessons, as she gazed at a print slowly transforming beneath the still waters, he slowly ran his fingers along the curve from her lowest rib to her hip and back again. Just the act of stepping into the darkroom, slipping the rubber apron over her clothing, felt as if an electric current had been run through her.

Two weeks ago she was clipping a print to the wash line when Jasper's lips pressed against the base of her neck. She froze in shock and pleasure. His hands encircled her waist. The clothespin dropped with a ping. He fashioned a necklace of kisses, then traced her chin, her mouth. Fanned fingers moved up her body, cradled her breasts. Surely he could feel her heart dashing against her ribs. The rubber apron was untied, collapsed heavily at her feet, the blouse unbuttoned, the skirt unzipped. Someone was laughing. Is that me? Murmured breath conversed with her collarbone. It's like swimming in fizzy water. "No corset?" A trill of giggles. A gown of air, only her stockings, her shoes. There was not enough room to bend and unlace in the ruby-tinted space. She was airborne, enthroned gently on the counter, its corrugations rippling beneath her. Suddenly shy, she covered her breasts. "My rosy goddess," he whispered. He modestly turned, removed his shirt, his trousers, his drawers. Effervescent, she wrapped her legs around his waist and pulled him to her. "Got you," she said. His member was larger than she'd expected, never having seen one in the flesh. It sprung between them, as if their party of two was now three. Jasper cupped her bottom and pulled her forward beyond the lip of the counter, then began gradually, gently burrowing into her folds. When he was inside, the fullness expanded, it seemed, to every inch of her body until she was nothing but sensation.

Flushing at these thoughts—how had they arisen?—Tula shook her head. They passed into the Flats and the Model T pulled up to the Shangs' house, with its line of callers stretching from the road to the door.

"I didn't think there would be so many people," Deuce said. Despite all his good intentions, he was having a hard time shaking off the nerves.

Tula adjusted her hat, pulled down her sleeves, drew on a pair of gloves. "Laylia and Oliver are very well respected in the community."

They joined the line behind a middle-aged woman with stooped shoulders. It was Elsie Ross, housekeeper for the Broadheads. The woman nodded politely.

"Sad turn," Tula said.

"Yes ma'am, it is. It truly is. But the Lord giveth and the Lord taketh away." Elsie drew a hankie out of her bosom and blew her nose.

At the base of Laylia's porch, a pussy willow was budding. Rocks twice the size of cantaloupes and thickly painted in bright reds, greens, and yellows were arranged along the beaten dirt walk. When a man in a shiny black

derby at the front of the line stepped inside, the mourners shuffled forward two paces. No one spoke. Several
women hummed "Balm in Gilead" in low tones. Clouds,
which had blanketed the sun all morning, moved away.

The women's throaty humming vibrated inside
Deuce's head. When it was his turn to step inside, it took
his eyes a moment to adjust from the bright sunshine. The
closest he'd come to a colored person's house was two
nights before when he'd knocked on Smitty's and then
the Shangs' doors. Now he was inside. It smelled tart but
not unpleasant, like aging wood. There were a dozen or
so mourners seated around the room's perimeter, some
praying, some moaning. The black-suited minister was
whispering something in Laylia's ear. Straight ahead was
the open coffin. Deuce quickly looked away and began
examining a picture of Noah's Ark—the same version
that hung in the ladies' parlor of First Presbyterian.

The coffin was mounted on sheet-draped sawhorses.
Emmett's face was still, the expression neutral; anything—
acceptance, sorrow, recrimination—could be read there.
The young man was in uniform; the soft, wedge-shaped
cap arranged carefully on his head, the brass buttons per-
fectly aligned. Deuce's gut lurched. It wasn't right that
Emmett was dead, that all those other boys were going
off to war, and Wade and Merle, who had contributed
nothing, swaggered around, boasting about how they'd
defended themselves.

He focused on the seams running up the back of Tula's
kid pumps, followed her to the circle of mourners. Oliver sat beside his son's casket. He wore a dark sack suit,
the trousers pulling around thighs muscled from work
on track crews for the railroad. When he saw Deuce, the

grieving father rose. The men nodded at one another. Laylia was seated slightly apart from her husband and the other mourners, regal in a black dress with jet beading on a wide collar. She cradled a puppy.

"Thank you for coming, Miss Tula," Laylia said. She was rocking back and forth. "I surely didn't expect you to."

Tula shook her head. "I'm so very sorry. I know how proud you were of Emmett going off to fight. Who would have thought?"

"The Lord works in mysterious ways." Laylia tucked her lips under her teeth.

Her broad face was stoic, but when Deuce looked into her eyes he saw oceans of grief. Mothers bear a special burden, he thought. He had seen the same look in his wife's eyes in those final weeks, when she understood that she was dying and would be forever separated from Helen. In Laylia's case, she was the one left standing alone on the shore—but it seemed that a mother's sorrow was just as deep no matter who had died and who was grieving. It was the fact of separation that cut so cruelly.

Laylia's eyes fell on him. Tula was offering to take Emmett's photograph, explaining that she and Deuce would set up the lighting and camera, if the family would want a likeness as a keepsake. Laylia was slowly nodding. Tula passed to the old aunty seated next to Laylia.

When Deuce moved in front of her, she stared up silently. After standing on the bank for so many years, he waded out into the current and took her hand in his. The flesh was warm.

"Oliver and I thank you for what you done for Emmett. And then driving out to bring us to him."

Deuce shook his head. "We shouldn't have to thank one another for an act of human decency, but I'm glad I was able to do it."

"So am I," she said.

He moved along, completing the circle of mourners. His chest opened up as if the load of stones that had been pressing on it for a lifetime had at last lifted.

A week later, the inquest ruled Emmett Shang's death as accidental. While the coroner disregarded the contradictory testimonies of the cousins and Deuce, he had no doubt about what had happened. The whole thing turned Deuce's stomach. He published an account of the inquiry, including the testimony of all the witnesses, on the front page of the *Garland Weekly*. And he wrote an editorial, reminding his readers of the sacrifices soldiers of both colors were making in the Great War.

The *Clarion*, on the other hand, devoted not a single word to the soldier's death, as if it had not happened, as if Emmett had never existed at all.

C HAPTER TWENTY
KNOCKING DOWN

After Marian left, I took over the sleeping porch and made it into a proper sewing room. Thiedick's had a good price on matching braiding for the shoulders and frog closures. Do you think I am too old for the military look? What are the women wearing in Chicago? When I wash up the supper dishes, I can see how Ralph Mummert is renovating your old house. Just yesterday the wallpaper man showed up and stayed all day. Last Sunday, the church custodian put too much coal in the furnace. It was so warm that Mrs. Sieve napped through the whole service! I wish you had been here; we would have had a good laugh. This is a sketch of a dress I'm working on.

FROM HER POST AT THE REAR of the trolley, Helen dimly noted the store windows, filmed with grime, slide by in the first light of this mid-April day. Her eyes burned from lack of sleep. The suffrage meeting had run late last night as members tugged this way and that. Some believed supporting the war effort should be the priority. Others, including Helen, were adamant that this was the ideal time, with so many women taking men's places in the workforce, to press forward with the suffrage agenda. She'd arrived back in her rooms with a voice hoarse from shouting and the league's newspaper that she'd wrung into a baton during the heated discussion.

The car rocked gently side to side as it passed sidewalks still lined here and there with traces of snow. She was on the brink of dozing off, like old Mrs. Sieve, she thought, when Irvine abruptly hit the brakes, the metal wheels squealing against the rails. Helen was instantly wide awake. What was going on? The next stop wasn't for a couple of blocks. She stood on tiptoe to see above the seated rows of fedoras and toques. A large touring car, operated by a woman in a glossy fur coat and matching hat, was whipping past the front of the trolley. Irvine, no doubt cursing the lady driver under his breath, turned the crank and they were underway again.

The wealthy woman in the touring car looked very much like the women Helen had seen last night at the Chicago Political Equity League. Most of the members were large-bosomed and earnest matrons. No one under forty, Helen had guessed, and among the well-heeled assembly, none were working girls. She yawned loudly and stamped her feet to stay awake. Working girls don't have the luxury of evening meetings, Helen thought. At least this one doesn't.

The front of the trolley clattered over a junction, then came the echo from the back wheels. Helen hung on to the oily grab pole. Irvine drew back the brake lever, more smoothly this time, and Helen called out the next stop. No one stirred in the crowded car. On the corner, at least a half-dozen people were waiting. The first to board was a man in a homburg. As he deposited a nickel in her palm, she yanked the cord, registering his fare. Next was a young woman in a crocheted tam. Then five or six businessmen squeezed in. Toward the end was an office girl in a tailored suit, then Louie stepped on board, a slow grin passing across his face.

"Fancy meeting you here," he said, making it clear from his tone he was not surprised at all. I don't have the energy for this playing around, she thought. He pressed a nickel into her palm, then took the opportunity to squeeze her hand. "How come you left the Pickle so early that night? Didn't you move all this way up here to see me?"

"No," she said in a strained voice. "Besides, I'm working. You'll get me in trouble."

Louie made no move to find a seat. "Maybe the Pickle was a little too radical for you?" He leaned in as if he was going to whisper something in her ear. Helen jerked away, her elbow striking the seatback behind her. The fares sprung from her hand, scattering across the floorboards. Up front, unaware of the commotion, Irvine turned the crank and the car jolted forward. The nickels rolled under seats, skidded into the stairwell. Frantically, she fell to her knees, making a clumsy attempt to pluck one up, then ripped off her gloves and crawled after another that had rolled against someone's muddy brogue. Pumps and wingtips shuffled out of her way.

Louie crouched beside her, patting the floor beneath the seat of a stout matron who quickly drew in her skirts. All this time the streetcar swayed along the rails. Suddenly the brakes emitted a rusty squeal. The next stop! Not yet. Just let me find the rest. She lay on her belly to look under the seats. Nothing. Short at least seventy cents. Seventy cents that she had already rung in on the fare register, seventy cents that the cashier would be expecting to find in her cash bag. Seventy cents she didn't have. Conductors were fired for shortages of much less.

"Louie, could you loan—" she was whispering when a blunt finger tapped her shoulder.

"Get up, miss. You too, mister."

The voice came from a chesty middle-aged man with pale eyes and cheeks covered with whiskers.

"What's the problem?" Louie asked irritably.

"Both of you is the problem."

The car rolled the last few inches to the stop. Several passengers crowded around the door, impatiently waiting to get out. A handful of others wanted to board. "What's the hold-up?" someone shouted.

The man leaned close to Helen, saying in a low tone, "I'm from Chicago Surface Line. Go ahead and handle this stop. We don't want to make a scene."

"A scene about what?" Helen snapped. Her knees shook beneath the woolen skirt.

"About this little knock-down racket you and your boyfriend here got going. Just handle the stop like I said."

Helen blanched. "Knock-down? I just—"

"Go on." The beefy man waved.

"Come on, sister, open the doors!" someone yelled.

Helen pulled the lever and the bottleneck of passengers emptied onto the sidewalk. The new arrivals climbed up the iron steps. Helen's fingers shook so much she could hardly pull the register cord. All the while the unshaven man, who smelled of cigar smoke, peered over her shoulder. When at last the streetcar jolted forward and Helen had deposited the fares in the coin barrel, she turned angrily.

"Look, I dropped the coins. It was an accident. I'll make good."

Under his derby the man's wiry brows rose. "Miss Garland, your motorman reported awhiles ago that some things were not right with you. You seemed to be awfully friendly with a couple of your male passengers, among other things, and—"

"What? No!"

Several riders turned, listening to the exchange with eager faces. Helen stared them down until, reluctantly, they made a show of picking up their newspapers, staring out the windows. Meanwhile Louie examined his paint-splattered shoes.

"I was called in to investigate," the man said.

"You're a spotter!" Helen cried.

The spotter pulled a cigar out of his coat pocket.

Louie said, "I'm not her boyfriend."

The man glanced dismissively at him and then turned back to Helen. "Is he? He knows you. Knows your name."

Under the wrap collar of her uniform, the tendons in Helen's neck pulsed. "Yes, but he's not my boyfriend and I'm not stealing from the company."

"Not your boyfriend, huh?"

"No! Just someone I used to know. And he has absolutely nothing to do with my job or this . . . misunderstanding."

The man eyed Louie. After a moment he said, "Okay. The company's beef is with this lady, not you. Get off at the next stop." He turned to Helen. "You finish the run and then you and I will have a talk in the supervisor's office. I'll be sitting right over here, so don't try nothing."

By increments, the audience of businessmen and matrons again turned their attention her way and, when Helen glared, several stared back coldly. Already convicted, she thought.

At the intersection of Maxwell and Halsted, Louie hopped off the car without a backward glance. There were about twenty minutes until the end of the line. At each stop, Helen jerked open the doors, yanked the fare register cord with a vengeance. Yet all the time her legs were like water, her brain boiling. One thought that kept circling was Irvine's betrayal. She couldn't believe it. Nothing, absolutely nothing, had passed between them that could be interpreted as malicious, yet he must have been harboring resentment toward her all this time.

Ten, fifteen minutes crept by. It seemed as if the motorman was purposefully slowing to the point where the car was simply rolling from stop to stop. At last they passed into the depths of the car barn. Helen followed the spotter up the aisle. Irvine remained in his seat waiting, Helen guessed, for a replacement conductor to finish the shift. When she reached the front of the car he stared stonily ahead.

She stopped at the control box. "I don't know why you've done this. Reported me for things that you know I didn't do."

He didn't flinch.

"You can't even look me in the eye," Helen said with disgust.

"All right," Irvine turned, his flaccid face a mottled crimson, "I'll tell you what it is. A streetcar is not a fit place for a woman to work. Out at all hours, fraternizing with all sorts. Besides the jobs you're taking away from men. Dragging down the wages for fellows who have families to support. It's a disgrace. You women make me want to puke."

The blood drained from Helen's face. "What? All the men are going overseas. Or haven't you—"

"When this war is over, everything will be set to rights."

Adrenaline flooded her veins. "Nothing's going to be the same after the war. Women in this state already have the vote and soon *all* of us will."

"That'll be fixed too!" Irvine shouted.

"Come on," the spotter said. "Save your wind for the super." He roughly grabbed her arm and escorted her out. She looked back at Irvine, smugly observing her departure as if this was something he'd been looking forward to for a long time. I should have figured something like this would happen, she thought.

The superintendent's office was at the back, a one-story room built into a corner of the cavernous car barn. The inside was bleak—a battered desk tattooed with scratches, two wooden chairs, and a spittoon. The superintendent was operating an adding machine when the spotter and Helen entered. He held up a finger, indicating for them to wait, punched a final series of keys, pulled the lever, and jotted down the total after the dials stopped spinning. He raised his fleshy head and the spotter nodded. No discussion.

"All right, sister. You're out," the superintendent said, turning back to his machine.

"What! Now, wait a minute. This isn't—"

"You're lucky we're not pressing charges," the super

interrupted, not taking his eyes off the dials. "Get her out of here."

Five minutes later Helen was striding angrily up the alley, yanking her tam over her ears. She could barely see straight. The nerve of those men. Purposefully lying in wait for some small slip-up. Her boot heels clicked sharply as she passed onto the crowded sidewalks of Halsted. The warmish spring sun had brought out a glut of office workers looking for a breath of fresh air on their lunch break. A number of couples strolled arm-in-arm. Helen dodged them. Louie the Louse. Just standing there like a lump while that weasel accused me of stealing.

Back in her room, she rapidly stripped off her uniform, bundled it into a ball, and hurled it into the corner. I'll be damned if I return it to them clean and pressed. The bureau's warped drawers required several tugs. Helen yanked the top compartment with such force that it clattered to the floor, spilling out shirtwaists, shifts, and collars. Swearing, she kicked the fallen clothing aside and abruptly dropped into the desk chair. Her eyes grew moist but she refused to give in to tears. Sniffling, she pulled out several sheets of stationery, deciding to write Marian about the unfairness of it all. As the pen's nib touched the paper, however, she changed her mind and began composing an article for the league's newspaper.

Women workers, did you know that the common belief among your employers is that women are barely adequate fill-ins, to be used during the labor shortage on a temporary basis? That we are only barely tolerated as placeholders? That we are resented by our male colleagues? That has been my experience . . .

At dawn, Helen had a neatly written draft. She located the newspaper's address on the masthead of the edition, as yet unread, that she'd picked up two nights before.

The *Women's Weekly Gazette* occupied a ground-floor space in a respectable brick commercial building. The latest edition was taped to the glass. Helen examined the lead story. Under the headline *Women Workers Lauded* ran a lengthy article in very small type, illustrated with a smudged drawing of two women, one saying, *Ha ha*, in a speech bubble. Through narrowed eyes, she read the piece, larded with typos and poorly written. She scanned the remaining pages, her lips puckered as if she'd just smelled something rank.

The lights were on inside. One worker, whose skirt was smeared with grease, was indiscriminately jamming a crowbar in the sheetfed press. The other was bent over a type case, laboriously plucking out one letter at a time, then balancing each on a composing stick. When Helen shut the door, both women flinched. The typesetter dropped the stick. Lead bits skittered across the floor.

"We're closed," said the woman at the press. "If you want to take out an ad, you'll have to come back tomorrow." The woman turned back to press. The typesetter dropped to her hands and knees, and began picking up letters.

Helen set her mouth firmly. "I have an article I'd like to submit."

The press woman sighed loudly, strode toward the counter. "We're not accepting unsolicited pieces at this time."

Helen's glance took in the broken press, the scattered type. These women don't have the vaguest idea of how to run a newspaper. She pinched back her unkind thought. "My article is about women in the workplace. It would expand your readership beyond league members who are just focused on the vote. There are a lot of working women out there who are waging other battles."

The presswoman crossed her arms, refusing to be won over. "I don't know who you are—"

Helen broke in with her name, adding, "*And* I'm a member of the league."

The woman continued, "As I said, I don't know who you are but Mrs. McCormick, our patron, is quite satisfied with the editorial content. She should know, since her husband owns the *Chicago Tribune*. If you have a comment, I suggest you bring it up at the next general meeting."

Helen snatched up her handwritten pages and jammed them into her handbag. As she shut the door she saw the typesetter tearfully attempting to rebalance the bits of type on the composing stick.

At the *Tribune*'s central counter in the tiled lobby, she asked for Mrs. McCormick.

"She just left," said the switchboard operator. "In fact, you passed her." The operator gestured toward a robust middle-aged woman with a towering Gibson Girl hairstyle climbing into the backseat of a highly polished motorcar.

"Thanks," Helen said, hurrying toward the door.

A chauffeur was closing the passenger door when she reached the sidewalk.

"Could you wait just a moment? I'd like to talk with Mrs. McCormick."

The chauffeur was an elderly man with stooped shoulders and heavy bags under his eyes. "You'll have to move along, miss. She is on her way to an appointment."

"But this is important!" Helen glimpsed Mrs. McCormick nonchalantly surveying their exchange from behind the glass. Helen held up a finger and mouthed, *One minute.*

The publisher's wife rolled down the window. In the fruity tone of a patrician she asked, "Yes?"

Helen stepped up quickly. "I'd just like a moment of your time. It's about the league's weekly. It is only in its infancy, I understand that, but it could be so much better."

"And you are . . . ?"

"I'm Helen Garland." She extended her hand.

Mrs. McCormick shook it. The bones of her well-tended hands were large and strong.

Helen continued: "My stepfather owns a paper down in Emporia. I grew up in the newsroom. I know how to set type, how to run a press. And I was editor of my high school newspaper."

Mrs. McCormick unlatched the door and waved Helen inside. "I have a moment."

Helen ignored the butterflies in her stomach and slid across the mohair seat. She pulled the *Women's Weekly Gazette* from her purse. "First of all, the content. These articles are fluff and deadly boring." She paused.

"Go on," Mrs. McCormick said.

"The paper should be educating its readers. Giving them facts and figures about the vote, and so much more.

Women have gained positions once held only by men, but we're paid less. As a matter of fact, I've written an article about women in the labor force and was hoping the *Gazette* might print it."

"We definitely should," Mrs. McCormick said. She took the paper from Helen's hands and leafed through it. "I've had some board members also complain to me about the number of typos."

Helen nodded. "The typesetting needs work and so does the layout. If you hire me, I'll give you a paper our organization can be proud of."

Mrs. McCormick was silent for a moment. After a time she folded the issue and laid it aside. "You're absolutely right that the paper needs improvement. I'll give you a chance as editor with those other two working under you."

Helen had not even realized that she was holding her breath. Now she exhaled loudly, resisting the urge to hug the woman. "Thank you for your confidence. I won't let you down."

C

HAPTER TWENTY-ONE
NEW PLATFORM

It has been two months since your last letter.
Nothing since. I scan the papers every day for
news of the Picardy region and the aftermath of
the Spring Push and find only lists of casualties
and accounts of roads clogged with soldiers and
refugees. A lilac made a home in the alley behind
the print shop. As I lay awake late into the night,
the scent rescues me from gloomy thoughts.

HEAVY SUMMER RAINS HAD TURNED many of the roads in northern France into fast-flowing creeks. Marian was within two miles of the American military hospital in Compiègne when the Red Cross truck she was driving sputtered and died in a submerged crossroads. Swearing, she tucked up the hem of her skirt and slid out. Water immediately engulfed her legs up to the knee, saturating her boots and heavy stockings. She slogged to the radiator, steadying herself along the truck's body as her feet skidded on the mud below. The dark brown current swirled around her arm as she searched blindly for the crank. After a minute of fishing, her fingers gripped the familiar lever. She yanked. Nothing. She widened her stance. The flooded engine block refused to spark. She got in three more tries before her fingers were too cold to grip. She climbed behind the wheel, boots swamped, to wait for a ride. But no other vehicles emerged from the curtains of rain. After two hours she began the trudge toward town.

For the past three months, since the dismemberment of the unit and Nezzie's death, Marian had been hauling hospital supplies and visitors back and forth along the fifty miles between Paris and Compiègne. The city had once been a resort town, its graceful Pont Neuf arching over the River Oise attracting tourists. But that was before the bridge was dynamited by the Allies, to stop the German advance on Paris. While not as prone to breakdowns as old Lulu, the Red Cross truck brought its own set of headaches—primarily flabby belts that tended to fly off at a moment's notice. Most days, she was on the road for twelve, fifteen, sometimes eighteen hours, depending on the number of malfunctions. That was fine with Marian. When her mind and body weren't occupied with itineraries, inventories, and roadside repairs, she tended to dwell on Nezzie's death, sinking into melancholia as inescapable as Picardy's sucking, sticky mud. That had happened more than once and then she was no good for anything. Twice, four Red Cross nurses had resorted to lifting Marian from her bed and shoving her behind the wheel of the truck. She was learning to keep busy, so lately, when she wasn't driving, she forced herself to the typewriter in the nurses' lounge, tapping out her diary.

It was late afternoon when, soaked to the bone, Marian finally mounted the marble steps of the city's former library. Now it served as a hospital as well as a dormitory for nurses and Red Cross volunteers. The hem of her uniform, filmed with mud, flapped against her calves and her boots squished noisily as she crossed the reading room's parquet floor.

At the reception desk, a nurse in a starched pinafore took down the details of the truck's location and inventory. "You've got a visitor," she said.

Marian hadn't had a guest for weeks. Not since Links, who was stationed at a canteen fifteen miles away, had hitched a ride in a louse-infested ambulance heading back toward the front. Links's blue eyes were somber, and there was a hardness around the mouth that Marian hadn't remember from before.

Upon hearing she had a visitor on this day, the curtain rose on a fantasy that it was Nezzie. That somehow Links had got the information all wrong. That it had not been Nezzie who died in the crash but some other girl. Marian rushed through the maze of rooms that had once been the administrative offices of librarians, sublibrarians, and sub-sublibrarians. The Red Cross workers were housed in the basement, in what used to be the children's department. She descended the stairs as fast as she could. The ankle had never healed right since it had been reinjured during the evacuation, and she now had a slight limp that appeared to be permanent.

As Marian eagerly turned the corner from the stairs, she was not greeted with Nezzie's shining face. Rather, it was the director, with a dour expression embossed on her mouth. She was seated on one of the room's tiny, brightly painted chairs, her knees pressed uncomfortably against her chest.

"What happened to you?"

Marian couldn't answer at first, she was so crushed. Finally she managed, "Let me change. I'll be right back."

In the dormitory, Marian dejectedly peeled off the wet skirt, combinations, and stockings. She washed off the worst of the mud in the lavatory's low sink and pulled on clothes, not much cleaner but at least dry. She splashed water on her face, willing herself not to cry in front of the director.

When Marian returned, the woman was studying a framed watercolor of Jeanne d'Arc, sword raised and leading soldiers to victory.

"Here to check up on me?" Marian asked. She'd assumed that reports of her bouts with paralyzing melancholy had filtered through the ranks.

"No. But how are things going for you?"

"Doing my best."

"I'm here for another reason. A new assignment."

From upstairs came the clang of a school bell. It signaled that an ambulance of wounded had pulled up in the library's circular gravel drive. There was a clatter of heels from above: nurses and aides scurrying to unload the soldiers whose eyes were pain-glazed, whose bodies stank of sweat, shit, and the sweetish smell of rot.

Both women remained silent for a moment.

The director continued: "I have it on good authority, from an officer under Commander in Chief Philippe Pétain himself, that the war will be over by fall. Our boys are already pushing back hard. When that happens, our unit will resume work in Picardy. The task of rebuilding will be tremendous. I don't need to tell you that. We'll need thousands and thousands of dollars. Securing the goodwill of the American people, and their donations, will be vital." From her pocket, the director pulled a wrinkled Chautauqua program. "I have here—oh my, you've changed these last six months!"

She held out the leaflet which featured a full-length photograph of Marian, standing in profile, caftan draped across her statuesque frame. It was true. Marian had lost at least sixty pounds. Last week, when she'd thought to glance in a mirror, she was surprised by the gaunt face, the dull hair.

The director added, more kindly, "We all have." She fingered the ropy cords at her neck. "I have recommended to the Fielding College Board that you join the Chautauqua Circuit this summer to spread the word about the unit's work and collect contributions."

"Leave France? But I'm needed—"

The director held up a hand. "A *driver* is needed. I can find other drivers. You're uniquely qualified for this. It will mean returning to the States within the month. Fielding will make all the arrangements."

Marian froze. Leave France? Leave those fragile threads that connected her to the villages, the château, to Links, The Gish? And to Nezzie? Most importantly to Nezzie. She couldn't. It would be unbearable.

The director bent to remove her clipboard from a chair and sat down. Seeing the sheaf of neatly printed lists, Marian was reminded of all the precious goods with which the unit had stocked its households during the winter and spring. Iron bedsteads, library books, classroom slates, galoshes, cooking pots, sewing kits, bolsters, beet seeds. All those necessities that were now likely confiscated or smashed to pieces or ground into the mud by the soldiers of one side or the other. Everything that would need to be reprovisioned. And all that would take money.

Marian slowly nodded her assent. "But I'll rejoin the unit after the war?"

"Of course." The director stood. "I'll write the college trustees today. It'll take a couple of weeks for me to arrange your passage back."

After the director left, Marian paced around the little chairs and tables, her agitated mind jumping from one thing to another. There was the Packard to get out of storage. It would need a complete tune-up before she dared take it on the back roads. At the thought of driving those dusty miles her mind leaped to Emporia . . . and to Deuce. Would the town be on her itinerary? The Prairieland Agency tended to shift its performers around each season. Should she request it? Did she want to? In the end, she decided to leave it to fate. Some things were out of her control and she understood that now.

PART III

C HAPTER TWENTY-TWO
GOING DOWN THE LINE

MARIAN SHIPPED OUT FOR THE STATES in late June. In France, the German troops were in full retreat. Spirits were high among her fellow travelers, overriding the continued risk of attack by U-boats. Most of the passengers were wounded doughboys, riddled with shrapnel or taken down by mustard gas. Besides Marian, there were only three civilians on board. A Belgian couple of advanced age had miraculously appeared on the dock the morning of departure with tickets and passports but no luggage. They spent the entire crossing huddled together, speaking only to one another and sharing cigarettes; inhaling, then passing to the other. The third was an American businessman with the stern face of a New England preacher and an overstuffed valise he never let out of his sight, tucking it between his legs at the dinner table.

After an uneventful crossing, the ship anchored at the White Star Pier. There had been a bomb scare the night before and the dock was crawling with police. Two German sympathizers had been discovered planting an explosive against the wall of a Newark munitions plant across the Hudson River. Victory seemed imminent, but no one as yet felt fully safe.

The moment she stepped off the gangplank, Marian

was cast among dense knots of soldiers in khaki and brass buttons, some flowing in her direction but most heading toward the boats. Once inside the terminal, the crush grew worse as shouts and yells bounced off the tiled surfaces. She made her way quickly to the row of telephones on the far wall, only to be stopped short by the long lines in front of each booth. She took her place at the end, toeing her traveling satchel along as she advanced. Twenty minutes later, she closed the folding doors and asked to be connected with Chicago. Jim Zellner, her old contact at the Chautauqua Prairieland Agency, was no longer there, but a Mrs. Stanley could speak with her "in a tick."

Marian was obliged to deposit two more nickels in the phone before Mrs. Stanley's voice, accompanied by static that sounded as if a violin bow was being raked across the receiver, entered her ear. Once pleasantries were exchanged, Mrs. Stanley quickly got down to business.

"We're swapping you into a slot currently held by a chalk talker. He's not too happy about it but someone from Fielding College must have clout because you're in. You're scheduled for a town called Wapakoneta in western Ohio next week. That's your opener."

"Starting in a week doesn't give me much time to get my auto ready," Marian said. "I only just landed. In fact, I'm still at the terminal. The car's been on blocks for almost a year."

Mrs. Stanley's voice was clipped. "I understand this is a push, but the chalk talker was so angry to lose his place he walked out. We're filling in as best we can right now, but you must be in Ohio next week. From there, you cross over into Indiana, and . . ." A pause ensued. Marian imagined Mrs. Stanley running a finger across a map.

"And hit, oh, I'd say twelve bergs before crossing into Illinois. That brings you to early August. The remainder of your itinerary is pretty much a straight shot across Illinois."

Marian tried to jot down the dates and places in her notebook, balanced on a shallow wooden shelf mounted in the corner. Someone had carved *Nuts to You* on it.

"And you finish on September 4 in Hamilton, right on the Mississippi. Did you get all that?"

A youth in uniform, his round face suggesting he was not more than sixteen, tapped on the glass beside Marian's shoulder. She held up her index finger, indicating she needed another minute. She turned back to the receiver but hesitated. In her ear, Mrs. Stanley was repeating her question.

"Yes, I got it." She traced her pen along the *N* in *Nuts*. "And those towns in Illinois. Is Emporia one?"

"Um. Let me look." After a moment, Mrs. Stanley said, "Yes, toward the end of the month."

Fizzy water flooded Marian's veins. "Could you give me the exact date?"

"I'll be mailing the entire schedule to you later this week."

Marian clutched the pen with rigid fingers. "Yes, I understand. But I'd like to know now."

"The printing on this list is so small. It looks like the twenty-fourth. No, the twenty-eighth. It's the twenty-eighth."

Later that day, after she'd collected her trunk and gotten herself back to her apartment, Marian wrote a hurried letter to Deuce. She filled him in on her new assignment. She attempted four different endings. She wasn't sure how he felt about her. Would he be as anxious to see her as she was to see him? All his letters had been affectionate, but made the point that he didn't expect anything from her. She finally ended with, *I am very much looking forward to seeing you. Can we plan on a late supper after my talk?* She added, *So you can tell me all about your new venture and about Helen.*

The out-of-state mail service in Emporia had been sketchy since June when two of the three postal clerks were shipped out. Deuce did not receive Marian's letter until three days before she and her Packard were slated to arrive in Emporia. He quickly sent a telegram to Lewistown where, according to the schedule, she'd be speaking that night. When he penciled in his message on the Western Union form, it sounded clipped, as telegrams often did. *Supper fine. Stop. Looking forward. Stop. Much to talk about. Stop.* He hesitated. He wanted to sign off, *With deep affection*, but held back. The telegraph operator would read whatever he wrote. And Deuce was uncertain how Marian would take it. Would she feel threatened that he had invested too much in such a brief encounter? He settled for, *Most sincerely.*

The morning of the day she was to appear in Emporia, Marian woke up at three thirty and again at four twenty. When her eyelids flew open an hour later she gave up and got out of bed. The hotel room in Mattoon smelled strongly of turpentine. Someone had treated it for fleas, Marian thought, and not successfully. She scratched her ankle. But she knew the real reason she couldn't sleep.

That same morning, Tula, too, had suffered from lack of

sleep. She had spent the last week in Jasper's apartment over the photography studio helping him nurse his three children through successive bouts of scarlet fever. She only managed to get home for a few hours each night and today, the seventh in a row, she woke exhausted. Jasper's four-year-old, Min, was not out of the woods. The two older children had recovered quickly. But Min couldn't shake the fever despite Jasper's patient application of ice to her cracked lips and spoonfuls of Tula's broth. Every day her eyes sank deeper.

This morning, the last day of Chautauqua, dawned with temperatures already in the eighties. These long days are catching up with me, Tula thought groggily, as she fumbled around her kitchen, taking a cup and saucer from the cupboard and absently putting them back. Yesterday she'd gotten a letter from Clay, postmarked from Milwaukee, and that had contributed to her restless night. Since her brother had skipped town in January, after arguing with Deuce about paying off the loan, he'd written from Chicago, then from Minneapolis. Both times he sent a small amount of cash that, along with what Tula herself made from sewing, had been enough to keep the house running. He boasted about the money he was making as a traveling photographer for a growing concern based in Chicago. If it was true, she was glad for him, but there lurked the dread he would announce he was coming back to Emporia. She didn't know what she'd do if that happened.

From the rear porch came an insistent meowing. The cat stood on back legs, hooking his front claws into the screen door.

"Coming, coming."

She set the coffee pot to boil with yesterday's grounds and opened the door. The cat, braiding himself around Tula's ankles, almost tripped her up

"Poor, neglected Snowball." Tula scratched under the lifted chin. "I'll bet you're hungry."

She pulled a chicken carcass from the ice box, pinched off a bit of dark meat, and shredded it onto Snowball's dish. The slippery remains went into a soup pot filled with water. How many gallons of broth had she simmered this week? Tula settled at the kitchen table and sipped her coffee, waiting for the mental fog to lift. From the window over the sink, sunlight formed white squares on the linoleum.

When the pot began rocking noisily, she turned down the heat. Beyond the window, Mrs. Johnson marched past, pulling Samuel by the hand while the little boy concentrated on scuffing the sides of his shoes against the concrete. This Chautauqua he had won the coveted role of Jack-Be-Nimble in the Mother Goose Festival, due to his mother's energetic campaigning, according to Mrs. Sieve. Across the driveway, Deuce's house was silent. The army of painters and paper hangers hired by Vera Mummert to redecorate for her son and daughter-in-law had not yet started their day. It was sad to see Winnie's brocade draperies cast out on the lawn. But Winnie was gone, the heavy furnishings of that age had passed, and Deuce seemed quite content in his digs downtown. Tula had noticed the *Garland Weekly* showing up on the porches of her neighbors. More people than she'd first imagined seemed to like the controversy that Deuce's editorials stirred up.

* * *

Knowing Helen would want to catch Marian's talk, Deuce had sent her a telegram as soon as he'd learned the schedule. Helen had arrived on the early train, after promising Alma, the nervous typesetter, that she'd be back the next day. She and Deuce walked over to the Rainbow Grill for a breakfast of over-easy eggs and bacon. They passed Sy Camp, who was setting up sawhorses in front of Tender's Candies, his carpenter's apron slung low on his hips. A rotten cornice lay to one side. At Jasper's studio the blinds were drawn, a *Closed* sign dangling from the doorknob.

"I'm happy for her," Helen said.

"Tula?"

"Um huh."

"Me too."

Outside the feed store, Floyd was rolling a galvanized hog trough out the front door, adding to a line of farm equipment already displayed on the sidewalk.

"How have sales been?" Deuce asked after the three exchanged greetings.

"Fair to middling. More than usual, but then it's Chautauqua week and we sort of expect that," Floyd said.

"Susan's coming over later this morning, right?" Helen asked, bumping her shoe into a small implement of screens and spouts. "What's this thing?"

"It's a corn seed grader. And she'll be there as soon as she's finished stocking for me."

When Helen had found out how Deuce was struggling with the newspaper, she'd suggested he hire an apprentice. She had lobbied hard that the apprentice should be a young woman, given a chance at man's work the same as she had, but with a better outcome, of course. After several letters back and forth, they had settled on

Floyd's daughter Susan, and she had accepted.

A farm wife stopped to examine an assortment of seed packets Floyd had spread out on display. Deuce and Helen moved along, taking a shortcut down an alley. The door was open at the Bide-A-Wee, its dark interior exhaling the odor of spilled beer and cigar smoke.

"Did Marian tell you what time she thought she'd get into town?" Helen asked in a neutral tone. Deuce had let drop a couple of times that he and the dress reform advocate had exchanged letters during the past year, but otherwise he'd been pretty tight-lipped with Helen. By the way he flushed—like now—when her name was mentioned, Helen guessed he was smitten. She suppressed a smile.

"No. She's coming from Mattoon. I think. Or one of those towns out that way. I don't know," he said, then added quickly, "So, what's on the docket today?"

"I can't wait to see her," Helen said.

Deuce plowed on: "You're going to show Susan how to print that letterhead for the Lutheran Church, right?"

"Yes, yes."

At the Rainbow, Deuce paused with his hand on the knob to peruse the daily lunch menu taped on the door. Roast beef with mashed potatoes. Ham and cheese sandwich. He frowned. Pork and liberty cabbage? What the hell?

"Did you see this?"

"What?" Helen squinted where his finger pointed. "Is that supposed to be sauerkraut, do you think?"

"No doubt." Deuce exhaled heavily. "This patriotism has gotten way out of hand."

Ever since the doughboys had first touched French soil, Emporia had been as tense as an alley cat. There'd been some ugly incidents. Yellow paint was slapped on mailboxes of "slackers," people who weren't contributing their share to the loan drive. Willie Heiserman, the German-American who ran a corner grocery near the Flats, was hauled out of his house in the middle of the night by three men with blackened faces. They threatened to tar and feather him for not contributing groceries to a Liberty Loan bond-sellers dinner but settled for forcing him to march down Main Street singing the "The Star-Spangled Banner." The next day, they organized a boycott of his store. Even the Lutheran pastor had received a threatening letter.

Deuce had run articles about these incidents in the *Garland Weekly*. Since the sheriff's office would not verify these events, he'd had to report them as "rumors."

They glanced at one another. "Guess I've got to find another place for breakfast," Deuce said.

Two blocks over, Jasper stood at his second-floor window. Passing on the sidewalk below, he spotted Tula's short-brimmed hat, generous bosom, and a blur of kid pumps. He'd gazed on this image every morning for the last week and never tired of it. This morning he had good news. Min's fever had broken during the night.

He greeted her with a kiss, took the Mason jar of broth from her hands, and stored it in the apartment's small kitchen. Dorrie and her brother, recovered but still weak, were on their stomachs, heels clicking in the air, dominoes arranged between them on the front room's carpet. In Min's back bedroom, Tula sat on the far side of the bed, applying a warm palm to the girl's forehead and exclaiming, "You *have* turned the corner!"

"See, what I tell you?" Jasper asked, his mouth stretched wide.

A shadow of a smile crossed Min's face too, before her lids slowly closed. Jasper sat down on the other side of the bed.

"Her color looks much better," Tula said, laying her hand atop Min's curled fingers, warm and sticky to the touch.

"I couldn't have done this without you. You know that," Jasper murmured.

They sat quietly for some minutes by the sleeping child, watching the rhythmic rise and fall of her chest. Tula began to softly withdraw her hand when Jasper placed his over hers and Min's.

She thought to say something funny about their pile of hands but caught Jasper's solemn gaze and stopped.

"Tula, you know I love you. I loved you the first time I saw you sitting downstairs, trying to get your courage up to ask me to buy Clay's old equipment. You've done so much for me and the children. But even if I was a confirmed bachelor and you couldn't cook a lick, I'd be asking you this. Because you are kind and loyal and because I believe we are meant to be together. Tula, my love, will you do me the honor of marrying me?"

Tula's eyes widened. Blood rushed up her neck, into her face. She put her hands to her cheeks. She was smiling. Then laughing. Above the pounding of her heart, she heard herself say, "Yes, yes, I'll marry you. Of course, I'll marry you."

* * *

Marian reached the edge of Emporia in late afternoon.
She pulled off onto a grassy bluff to stretch her legs, shake
off some of the road dust. Below her, the town stretched
out in a palette of green, ochre, and brown. There was the
railroad depot, where they'd seen Helen off. The tracks
cut across town like a silvery zipper. Off to the right, the
pale yellow courthouse dominated a grid of commercial
buildings. Most were three or four stories, with shops on
the street level and offices above. From her vantage point,
Marian saw that many had false façades, giving the impression of added height. The true roofs, running below
these extensions, were considerably less ostentatious: flat
and covered with tar paper. In the past, she might have
disdained these illusions as pretentious. But now they
struck her as brave, an attempt to soften the harshness
of the prairie. Like the Canizy *grandmères* insisting on
examining the charity blankets handed out from the back
of Lulu, as if making purchases from a fine shop. A lump
grew in her throat. Beyond the businesses spread the
shingled roofs of Emporia's houses. Somewhere out there,
under the surfeit of trees, was Jeannette's. She thought of
her last night in town, when she'd walked to the edge of
the Chautauqua grounds and gazed at the Bellman house,
every window alight. Tears rolled down her cheeks. She
turned away from the view and hurriedly cranked up the
Packard.

When she pulled under the oak at the Bellmans', the
front door was shut despite the heat. Across the pasture,
hundreds of townsfolk poured from the tent flaps as the
afternoon session let out. A hum of voices, broken by the
toot of auto horns, could be heard in the distance. But
here, all was still. Not a breath of air stirred the leave

overhead. Marian mounted the steps and rang the bell.

Ted Bellman, in a spotless work shirt and dungarees, answered. "Afternoon."

"Mr. Bellman, I don't know if your wife will speak with me, but I'm Marian Elliot Adams. I was here last—"

His voice broke in gently. "I know who you are."

Marian tucked in her lips, feeling tears welling up again. "If I could have five minutes with her. That's all."

Under the oak, the thick air lay motionless.

"She won't talk to you."

Marian dropped her head. The floorboards liquefied.

From inside the house, a thin voice called, "Who is it, Ted?"

He turned, saying, "Someone needing some carpentry, Mother."

Marian met his eyes. "I just wanted her to know how sorry I am. But I understand, certainly, I understand why she wouldn't want to speak with me. Thank you for your time."

She turned and started down the steps.

"I'll speak with you." His long sun-leathered face was placid. He stepped outside, closed the door, and indicated two straight-back kitchen chairs. The chaise where Jeannette had spent the night a year ago was gone.

"Thank you." Marian's voice was almost a whisper.

She took the seat farther from the door. Ted sat with his knees open, resting his arms on his thighs. He appeared to be studying his clasped hands, mapped with veins as coarse as twine.

"My father was a farmer," he said, before she could get a word out. "And his before that. I grew up taking care of the animals. My brother works the homeplace now, but I'll always be a farmer. Hazel, my wife, she's from town. Her father was a carpenter. Before he passed the business on to me, we built this house together."

Marian's eyes fell across the plain clapboards, the utilitarian sills and railings. Nothing ornate, but sturdy.

"Those last weeks, I knew Jeannette was dying. I'd seen pigs, cattle go through it. Something like hoof-and-mouth spreads around and you lose a lot of animals. The eyes become unfocused. There is a restlessness. I saw that in my girl before the Chautauqua tent even went up, but Hazel didn't. Wouldn't. After she breathed her last, before Dr. Jack got there, I wanted to have things right. Sometimes, at the end, the body voids. Hazel didn't know that might happen. I lifted Jeannette's nightie. She'd soiled herself. Hazel began howling. I said, *Hazel, this is the natural course of things. Go get me a basin of warm water.* She brought the water but left right away. I cleaned my girl up."

He drew a hankie from his pants pocket and pressed it against his eyes. Tears coursed down Marian's face. After a moment he raised his head and stretched out his arms.

"Take my hands." His fingers gripped hers. "I'm saying to you what I said to Hazel. Sickness, death—they're part of the natural course of things. Do you understand what I'm telling you?"

Marian's voice was barely audible. "Yes."

"Good." He rose and pulled her up with his rough farmer's hands.

Marian cranked up the Packard and got behind the wheel. She looked back. The porch was empty, the door already shut. She drove slowly down the lane, back t the street. As soon as she was out of sight of the Bellman house, Marian pulled over and laid her head on the steering wheel.

Earlier that afternoon, Helen had lost her temper with Deuce. Susan, bent over the type case, had been frowning intently at the jumble of letters.

"Will you quit hovering? I can handle this!" Helen shouted. "Go back to your office. Write up some of those briefs or something."

She gestured to the partitioned space up near the front that had been her suggestion. *You can't be a publisher without a private office,* she'd written. *Even I've got one.*

Once the wall had been erected and he'd moved his desk, chair, and lamp in, Deuce was pleased with the result. Most days it felt cozy, but today it was confining.

Helen was continuing, "Or go make a sales call. You've been as wound up as a watch spring all day. She'll get here soon enough."

Deuce flushed. Helen made a show of adjusting her visor and bent back over the type case.

"You're right. Sorry." He picked up his hat. "I'll go follow up on that print job for Father Flynn."

Main Street was surprisingly deserted. Dozens of clerks and merchants should be filling the sidewalks, strolling toward the Rainbow or home for an early dinner before the evening program. But the two Jenkins girls, spinster sisters who ran Emporia Shoes, were the only passersby. The girls turned the corner. Now the street was completely empty. Something's not right, Deuce thought. He quickened his pace.

On Center Street, there was a steady trickle of pedestrians, all walking in the same direction. A familiar pair of dusty trousers and shirt back crisscrossed with brown braces strode halfway up the block. Deuce caught up with Floyd.

"Accident?" he asked, matching his stride to the feed store owner's.

"Oh, hey, Deuce. Something at Jasper's. Don't know what."

"Lord. Hope it's not Min."

Deuce broke into a trot. A crowd of ten or more, mostly men, were knotted under the photography studio's swinging sign. Even as Deuce approached, more onlookers attached themselves to the outer edges, necks craning. The *Closed* sign still hung in the studio's door.

Henry Wilson, the aged member of the Young Ragtags who had walked out on Marian's talk a year ago, stood near the front.

"What's happening?" Deuce asked.

The old man took the time to direct a stream of tobacco juice onto the sidewalk. "Making sure everyone does their part buying Liberty Bonds. We just got word from the Defense Committee that this here slacker's not doing his part."

"Jasper?"

"You're not one too, are you? A Jerry sympathizer?" He leaned in close, the damp chaw exuding the cloying smell of cherries, saying, "We already know how you love them niggers."

Deuce ignored the barb. Shouts of "Open up!" from someone in the crowd broke the tension. Deuce quickly stepped closer, in between two men wearing the blue pinstriped overalls of Mummert Power Shovel. From th position he had a clear view of the shop and the two men provoking the mob: Harp's mechanics, Wade and Merle.

"He's in there!" Wade shouted.

Merle pounded on the door with a closed fist. Deuce broke into a sweat. He had seen what those hands did to Emmett. This could get ugly fast, he thought. The crowd grew as the courthouse emptied out for the day.

"He's got a sick child!" Deuce yelled.

Heads turned. Merle froze in his boxing stance, then pivoted smoothly in Deuce's direction. "This don't concern you. This is between us and this slacker. So get out."

From the back someone shouted, "Garland, you're not wanted!"

Merle resumed pounding.

"Put some weight behind those knuckles!" Wade yelled. His cousin banged with both fists.

Wilson's reedy voice called, "He's up there. I seen a curtain move."

Deuce glimpsed Jasper's pinched face before the lace drape fell back into place. Across the street, the courthouse doors opened and the last of the legal secretaries stepped out, laughing loudly at some joke.

"What's this all about?" Jasper asked, emerging from the doorway with Tula hovering at his shoulder.

"Why didn't you come down right off? You must have heard us," Merle said, turning to the cluster of men for confirmation.

"I did. But I have a sick child. Couldn't imagine anything so urgent."

"Well, it *is*," Wilson said. "Everyone's gotta pull their weight, and you're not pulling yours."

Jasper's shoulder blades stiffened. "That's not true."

Alvin Harp pushed his way to the front. A *Buy Liberty Bonds* armband was tied above the garage owner's rolled shirtsleeves. "You missed the last installment. It was due last week. And on top of that, the next bond campaign you'll need to come up with a lot more than you did in April. There's talk that some aren't doing their part because they're German sympathizers. You wouldn't want people to think that about you, would you?"

"If I'm late on that last payment, it's only because of my children. I will make good on it."

"Jasper's done his part," Tula blurted out. "No one here is a sympathizer."

The men shouldered into the doorway, ignoring her. Someone she didn't recognize leaned toward Jasper. "What kind of name is Watts, anyway? Sounds Hun to me." The vitriol in the man's voice was scalding.

Tula jerked back, her fingers pulling on Jasper's sleeve, when Deuce called out, "Hold on, fellows." He had mounted the granite carriage block out by the curb, standing a head above the throng. Great half-moons of sweat waxed under his arms. In the past few minutes the crowd had grown. It now stretched into the street, creating a bottleneck of horse-drawn wagons, delivery trucks, and automobiles. A Packard nosed past the outermost fringe. Deuce surveyed the faces. Most he knew by name. First in the *Clarion* and now in the *Garland Weekly* he'd broadcast their weddings, the births of their children, the deaths of their grandparents; he'd boosted their fraternal clubs and church suppers; he'd promoted their businesses and charities; and in recent days, he'd composed eloquent send-offs for their sons leaving for war, grand enough t be clipped and saved in the family Bible. But at this n ment they looked like strangers—the men at the front with mouths twisted in anger, most others wearing the avid expressions of gawkers at a train wreck. He thought of how they might have looked differently to him a year ago. He thought of what he might have said. Then he thought of how far he'd traveled since. I'm not that person anymore.

Deuce shifted, the granite scraping beneath his soles. "Before this goes any further, it's time for cooler heads to prevail." He pointed at Wade and Merle. "These men are murderers. They killed a man and I'm not going to let them get away with it again."

Wade, his face purple with rage, his fists raised, began pushing through the crowd but was restrained by Alvin.

Deuce continued: "Jasper will do his part. I know the man."

Wilson broke in with a shout. "But that's how they work! Worm themselves in. He's Hun through and through. Can't shake off your origins just like that." He snapped his fingers. A chorus of muttering backed him up.

Deuce flushed. For a moment he was again the young boy stung by slurs. The crowd grew silent. From down the tracks, the Illinois Central announced its arrival with a deep wail. He studied the faces before him. At the farthest edge of the crowd was a woman in blue whose posture, whose set of the head reminded him of Marian. But no, he realized, he must be mistaken. Although tall, the woman didn't have Marian's generous figure. She was almost certainly over at the hotel, resting before the night's performance. But you are close, Deuce thought. You may hear my words, but you are close.

When he answered, his voice was strong. "Yes, some say blood will tell. It's an old expression. But I don't believe that. It's the easy way out. You may accuse Jasper Watts of not giving enough to the bonds, yet he's done more than his fair share. Accuse him of tending more to his children than his business, fair enough, but you can't convict him based on the legacy of his birth. These are flimsy rumors and you can't risk a man's reputation, his livelihood, on that."

Here and there, the listeners twitched like river weeds in a current as they shifted from one foot to the other.

"Deuce is right!" Dr. Jack shouted. Heads turned in recognition. "Sitting in a sickroom through the night, you get to know people. I've sat with Jasper these last few nights at his children's bedsides. He's upright."

Standing nearby, Floyd and Mr. Meyers, the butcher, called out in agreement. Deuce caught sight of the Reverend Baumgartner of the Lutheran Church and a couple of Irish factory workers nodding too. Floyd raised his hand as if in school. "I'm with the doc and Deuce on this." It was clear from the glances of the crowd that they expected him to elaborate. "That's all I've got to say."

"Thanks, fellows." Deuce pushed back a hank of hair that had flopped damply across his forehead. "All my life, I've boosted Emporia. It's the best place in the world. But these last couple of years I've come to believe that we can do even better. Belonging, fitting in—those qualities have been the cement that binds us together. I think of the old pioneers, our grandparents and great-grandparents, who settled here and needed to work together. Any dissent might cost them their lives. Frontier life was unforgiving. Survival was the name of the g

But things are different now. We've each got to be willing to think for ourselves. I'm not speaking from a high-and-mighty place. You all know that for most of my life, I've done nothing but boost the town. I was afraid to print anything negative in the newspaper. But now I no longer think that makes us stronger or better. It weakens us. We need to face our town's faults, our individual faults—I've got them in spades, we all do—and try our best to fix them. Or maybe just live with some of them."

For a moment, silence fell across the throng. No one called out. No trains announced their arrival. The courthouse clock did not sound. The iceman's horse stood patiently in its traces.

After a time, the county clerks standing at the fringes began drifting away. Others followed. It became clear that the majority of the crowd did not, at least on this evening, share in the fury of the men knotted around Jasper's door. Wade, Merle, and the others watched in silence until Alvin, who didn't want to lose paying garage customers over a dust-up, muttered, "Let's go get a drink, boys."

As Deuce stepped down from the carriage block, Tula shoved through the throng and swung her arms around his neck. "Thank you." She pulled back, her face wet with tears. Jasper pumped his hand. Floyd was there too, along with half a dozen others.

Dr. Jack approached, hand outstretched. "Beers on me," he said.

No one noticed the tall woman in blue starting to ꜱproach, hesitate as Dr. Jack and the others surrounded ꜱce with grins and backslaps, and then quickly head in ꜱpposite direction.

* * *

A half hour earlier, after she'd wiped the last of the tears from her cheeks and chin, Marian had driven back into town with the image of Ted Bellman's hands on hers. There was a jam-up on Center Street. A crowd clustered around a shop, spilled out into the street, and completely blocked traffic. A nervous flutter rose in her breast. What if I can't get to the hotel? I can't go on stage tear-stained and dusty. And Deuce will be in the audience. He can't see me like this.

A farm wagon had come to a halt behind the Packard, and the streetcar was just beyond her front bumper. She was completely hemmed in. Unable to move forward or backward, she yanked on the brake, grabbed her valise, and left the car in the middle of the street. Which way was the hotel? She'd find out from someone in the crowd. As soon as she saw the sign, *Watts's Studio*, she recognized the name of Tula's suitor. She asked a matron jiggling a baby carriage what was going on. "Someone not doing their part with the Liberty Bond," was the answer. Then Marian heard Deuce's voice, saw his thick wave of silver hair, his face and shoulders rise above the sea of hats.

As his words rolled across the crowd, tenderness bubbled up in her throat, filming her eyes, quickening her breath. When he had finished talking, stepping down into welcoming arms, she sprang forward. There was Tula's beaming face and the short man beside her must be Jasper. She wriggled around the baby carriage, was now close enough to see the pattern on Deuce's tie. But then came the earnest face of that doctor, the one who had banned her from Jeannette's house. The man was patting Deuce on the back, shepherding him up the sidewalk. Marian shrank back. Her frothy mood evaporated. The last thing she wanted was some kind of confrontation in front of all these people at what was Deuce's moment of triumph. Better to see him after the program. She reluctantly asked an onlooker for directions to the hotel.

Just as it was one year before, the air under the tent was very hot. The same superintendent in white duck trousers trotted terrier-like across the stage, promoting next year's program, while in the audience, palm fans fluttered like so many moths. Stationed behind a canvas flap, waiting to go on, Marian toed the ground, plucked the neckline of her dress. Minutes before leaving the hotel for the Chautauqua grounds, she'd impulsively changed from her uniform into a gown she'd reconstructed from an old caftan, its yards of intense peacock-blue silk too magnificent for the rag bag.

Now, hearing the audience moving restlessly, she regretted her change of clothes. She felt naked, exposed under the sheer fabric. Oh for the security of the uniform with its brass buttons!

Out front, the superintendent switched gears. "And now it is time to welcome an old friend from last season who is here tonight with a new message, illustrated with moving pictures, that I'm sure you will find both fascinating and edifying. Just recently returned from eastern France, this brave soul will share her firsthand observations of the war in all its devastation. Please join me in a warm Chautauqua welcome for Mrs. Elliot Adams!"

Marian's stomach tensed, but the response was polite. She mounted the steps on trembling legs, giving the exiting superintendent a rigid smile. Before her spread the entire populace, redolent with the scent of starch and talc. A constellation of garnet-tipped cigars glittered aromatically. Many of the faces she recognized and even those strange to her seemed familiar. A rush of affection for this place and these people overtook her. Hoarsely, she managed to say, "I'm so very glad to be back here among you."

A burst of clapping erupted from the front row; it was Helen. On her left sat Deuce. A great smile stretched across his generous mouth, his dark eyes shone. She broke into a grin. Abruptly, the stage lights dimmed and the houses and church of Canizy flickered across the screen.

Marian cleared her throat, found her voice. "Here we see the small village of Canizy . . . before the war not so different from Emporia. This is the devastation the Germans left after their withdrawal to the Hindenberg Line . . ."

As if on cue, as soon as her talk ended, the tongue of film flapping noisily against the sprockets, cool air blew through the tent. The applause continued for several minutes, and when the superintendent hustled out to remind everyone to come back next year, a smattering of clapping could still be heard. The usual gang of little boys crowded around the projector, peppering the stagehand with questions about lenses and wattage. Marian scanned the milling swarm. Where was Deuce?

As she had a year ago, Helen hurried to the foot of the stage.

"Oh, no, I'll come down to you," Marian said, smiling. She took the side stairs, gripping the railing.

Helen hugged her. "You were grand!"

"Thank you, dear."

"And what a gorgeous gown."

Marian blushed. "I usually wear my uniform but to-night was going to be special. It *is* special."

"Come sit," Helen said, dragging her toward a chair. "I've so much to tell you. About Chicago and my suffrage work."

"Of course, I want to hear every bit." Marian cleared her throat but her voice was strained. "Where's your father?"

Helen smiled. "He had to leave early to finish print-ing the *Weekly*. But he wants you to come by the office as soon as you're able to break away."

"Of course." Marian felt her cheeks redden. "Helen, can we talk on the way to town?"

The two women joined the crowd moving across the pasture. A long snake of automobiles bumped slowly out of the grounds.

"It'll be ages getting the Packard out of here," Marian said.

"Leave it. We can take the streetcar."

It was jammed too, but one of the riders pulled Mar-ian into the top spot in the stairwell and Helen claimed the outside step, gripping the handrail.

The car lurched into motion. Someone toward the back embarked on, "Mademoiselle from Armentières," with several voices joining in on the chorus, "Hinky-dinky parlez-vous." An elbow was lodged in Marian's rib cage and Helen's straw hat almost blew off. When the singers got to, "She got the palm and the croix de guerre, 'or washin' soldiers' underwear," both women burst out 'ghing.

After the choir was shushed by an outraged matriarch, Helen commented, "If it wasn't for you, I'd have been stuck in this town forever, probably married to that singer in the back."

Marian smiled. "I don't think so. But maybe I sped things up for you a little. I hope so."

The two women talked as the streetcar gradually emptied, gliding from pool to pool cast by the streetlamps, the old elms rustling overhead. They passed from the residential streets into the business district and got off. Helen walked Marian to the *Garland Weekly*.

"Here it is," she said. "I've got to catch the milk train back to Chicago in the morning, so I guess I'll see you the next time we're both in town." She leaned over and gave Marian a peck on the cheek. "He's in there. The door should be open."

Marian entered. A young woman was stooped over a press at the back. To the left was a closed office door with light shining under the crack. The knob was warm to the touch and turned easily. Shyness suddenly overtook her. She hesitated, then slowly walked in. Deuce was bent over a page proof.

"Hello, Deuce."

He jumped up, rounding the desk in one swift motion. Silver stubble scraped across her cheek. She inhaled shaving talc and printer's ink. Her knees buckled in relief, feeling all the miles she'd traveled.

"Here, sit, you must be exhausted."

Reluctant to step away, she allowed him to pull over a chair.

"I'm just finishing proofing this editorial, if you'll give me a minute. I've already held the press up for an hour."

"Of course." She smiled. "Do what you need to do."

He took up the proofs but put them right back down. "I can't believe you're here. After all these months."

"Your editorial. Is it about what happened at Jasper's?"

He nodded. Footsteps sounded from the newsroom and a young woman poked her head through the doorway. "Are you almost—" She stopped, then continued, "Oh, excuse me, ma'am, didn't see you."

Deuce sighed impatiently. "I'll be right back."

Left alone in the office, Marian got up. She examined the framed portrait of Lincoln hung alongside Deuce's high school diploma. She fingered his jacket on the coat rack, tried on his boater. Outside the window an elderly gentleman on a bicycle pedaled erectly past. Emporia's version of Canizy's ancient postman.

Deuce burst back in. "Sorry."

"Everything under control?"

"Yep." He joined her at the window, planting his hands on the sill and leaning out. "Everybody seems to have gotten home safe and sound."

"Deuce." Marian touched his shoulder. He turned. "I'm so glad to be here." Tears spilled down her cheeks. She stepped into his arms. He stroked her hair, smoothing the dark strands. His breath was warm against her ear.

"There's nothing I want more than for you to be here with me." He kissed her neck and she turned to meet his mouth.

After several minutes, she pulled back from his embrace, her brows drawn together. "But I have to go back to France after the war. To finish our work. I want to."

"I know. But you'll come back here and I'll be waiting."

"Are you sure?"

"Here, sit with me." He swiveled the desk chair toward the window and sat, pulling her into his lap. "This is my favorite spot. Lean against me and we'll put our feet up on the sill."

The chair tipped back and, for a moment, Marian had the sensation they were stepping into an unsteady boat. But everything soon righted itself, their legs and feet comfortably entwined. Deuce was talking in low tones about their life together. The vibrations of the words in his chest were like ripples in a pond. She floated on the current, her breath mingling with his, no longer the solitary stone tossed and forgotten.

On the other side of Emporia, the folding chairs had been stacked, the lights unstrung and neatly coiled, the potted palms and the lecterns packed and loaded. Only the tent remained. And when the center poles were struck, the canvas fell upon itself, exhaling words and music and bits of sawdust that the prairie winds swept away to the far ends of the continent.

Acknowledgments

I would like to offer thanks to a number of people for their support during the writing of *Unmentionables*. Foremost is Kaylie Jones, author, teacher, and friend, who has been by my side at every step, guiding me on the bumpy road from journalist to novelist. Her courage and heart are valued beyond measure. Ken Moyer patiently read, reread, and read yet again these pages in their many different permutations, and for that, I am deeply grateful. Other readers (and fellow writers) who gave me critical feedback were Taylor Polites, Nina Solomon, Theasa Tuohy, Barbara Taylor, Deirdre Sinnott, Kevin Heisler, and Tom Borthwick. Ellen Athas, Al Ferlo, Patricia Shores, and Bob Bell listened patiently to my angst over each revision and were early readers as well. Deb Hull, bibliophile par excellence, has guided me to many extraordinary books over the years, most noteworthy for this project being Helen Zenna Smith's *Not So Quiet* . . . . Finally, I am in debt to Wilkes University archivist and history professor emeritus Harold Cox, who not only shared his extensive knowledge of railroads and trolleys, but lugged a weighty fare register into his office to show me how it worked.

Select Bibliography

Boudreau, Frank G. "The Problem of Supervision of the Milk Supply in Ohio." *Ohio Public Health Journal* XI, no. 11 (1920): 168–170.

Braddan, William S. *Under Fire with the 370th (8th I.N.G.) A.E.F. Memoirs of the World War.* Self-published, 1920.

Bruns, Roger A. *The Damndest Radical: The Life and World of Ben Reitman, Chicago's Celebrated Social Reformer, Hobo King, and Whorehouse Physician.* University of Illinois Press, 1986.

Canning, Charlotte M. *The Most American Thing in America: Circuit Chautauqua as Performance.* University of Iowa Press, 2005.

Case, Victoria and Robert Ormand Case. *We Called It Culture: The Story of Chautauqua.* Doubleday & Company, Inc., 1948.

Chuppa-Cornell, Kimberly. "The U.S. Women's Motor Corps in France, 1914–1921." *The Historian* 57, no. 4 (1995): 465–576.

Conroy, Jack. "Beliefs Mid Customs—Occupational Lore?" American Memory, Library of Congress, Federal Writers' Project, 1936–1940.

Cunningham, Patricia A. *Reforming Women's Fashion, 1850–1920.* Kent State University Press, 2003.

Ebbets, Jan McCoy. "Despair in War-Torn France Eased

After Smith Women Arrived in 1917." *NewsSmith*, Spring 2008. http://www.smith.edu/newssmith/spring2008/france.php.

Fields, Jill. "Fighting the Corsetless Evil: Shaping Corsets and Culture, 1900–1930." In *Beauty and Business: Commerce, Gender, and Culture in Modern America*, edited by Philip Scranton, 109–136. Routledge, 2001.

Gaines, Ruth. *A Village in Picardy*. E.P. Dutton & Company, 1918.

Gavin, Lettie. *American Women in World War I: They Also Served*. University Press of Colorado, 1997.

Griffith, Sally Foreman. *Home Town News: William Allen White and the* Emporia Gazette. Oxford University Press, 1989.

Harrison, Harry P. *Culture Under Canvas: The Story of Tent Chautauqua*. Hastings House Publishers, 1958.

Heap, Chad. *Slumming: Sexual and Racial Encounters in American Nightlife, 1885–1940*. University of Chicago Press, 2009.

Israel, Betsy. *Bachelor Girl: 100 Years of Breaking the Rules—A Social History of Living Single*. Perennial, 2003.

Johnson, Russell L. "Dancing Mothers: The Chautauqua Movement in Twentieth-Century American Popular Culture," *American Studies International* XXXIX, no. 2 (June 2001).

Luebke, Frederick C. *Bonds of Loyalty: German-Americans and World War I*. Northern Illinois University Press, 1974.

Quillin, Frank U. *The Color Line in Ohio: A History of Race Prejudice in a Typical Northern State*. George Wahr, 1913.

Russell, Francis. *The Shadow of Blooming Grove: Warren G. Harding in His Times*. McGraw-Hill Book Company, 1968.

Saville, Deborah. "Dress and Culture in Greenwich Village." In *Twentieth-Century American Fashion* edited by Linda Werters and Patricia A Cunningham, 33–56. Berg, 2005.

Schultz, James R. *The Romance of Small-Town Chautauquas*. University of Missouri Press, 2002.

Smith, Helen Zenna. *Not So Quiet . . .* The Feminist Press at the City University of New York, 1989.

Stewart, Charles D. "Prussianizing Wisconsin," *Atlantic Monthly* 123 (January 1919): 101–102.

Also available from Akashic Books

SPEAK NOW
a novel by Kaylie Jones
308 pages, trade paperback, $14.95

"Perceptive, gritty, and compelling, this is an absorbing book that dives headfirst into issues facing recovering addicts . . . Beautifully written and richly detailed, it is highly recommended." —*Library Journal*

"*Speak Now* is written with extraordinary skill, and is compulsively readable . . . an excellent novel." —*Southampton Press*

A SOLDIER'S DAUGHTER NEVER CRIES
a novel by Kaylie Jones
200 pages, trade paperback, $15.95

"Although we've gotten used to second-generation actors equaling or surpassing the accomplishments of their parents, the same hasn't happened with second-generation novelists. Nonetheless there are a few . . . and added to their small number ought to be Kaylie Jones." —*New York Times*

"Jones's third book, a delightful account of Americans living in Paris, captures the essence of childhood . . . Jones, the daughter of James Jones, writes with sensitivity and compassion. Highly recommended." —*Library Journal*

LONG ISLAND NOIR
edited by Kaylie Jones
288 pages, trade paperback original, $15.95

Brand-new stories by: Jules Feiffer, Matthew McGevna, Nick Mamatas, Kaylie Jones, Qanta Ahmed, Charles Salzberg, Reed Farrel Coleman, Tim McLoughlin, Sarah Weinman, JZ Holden, Richie Narvaez, Sheila Kohler, Jane Ciabattari, Steven Wishnia, Kenneth Wishnia, Amani Scipio, and Tim Tomlinson.

"There is plenty of mayhem for fans of dark fiction in the pages of *Long Island Noir:* shootings, killings, all manner of brutality . . . Suburbia may be even meaner than the big city." —*New York Times*

"An eclectic and effective mix of seasoned pros and new voices . . . The seventeen contributors portray a wonderful diversity of people driven to extremes." —*Publishers Weekly*

THE ICE-CREAM HEADACHE AND OTHER STORIES
stories by James Jones
224 pages, trade paperback, $16.95

"We feel the impact of Jones's vitality. He is masculine, uninhibited, not abashed by whatever he uncovers of human weakness and sexuality."
—*Chicago Sun-Times*

"The thirteen stories are anything but dated . . . a compact social history of what it was like for Mr. Jones's generation to grow up, go to war, marry, and generally, to become people in America."
—*The Nation*

THE MERRY MONTH OF MAY
a novel by James Jones
300 pages, trade paperback, $15.95

"Many critics, including *LJ*'s, considered Jones's 1970 novel his best since *From Here to Eternity*." —*Library Journal*

"The only one of my contemporaries who I felt had more talent than myself was James Jones. And he has also been the one writer of any time for whom I felt any love." —Norman Mailer

CAPE COD NOIR
edited by David L. Ulin
224 pages, trade paperback original, $15.95

Brand-new stories by: Kaylie Jones, William Hastings, Elyssa East, Dana Cameron, Paul Tremblay, Seth Greenland, Lizzie Skurnick, David L. Ulin, Fred G. Leebron, Ben Greenman, Dave Zeltserman, and Jedediah Berry.

"[T]he stories sneak in the back screen door of those summer cottages after Labor Day, after all the tourists have gone home and Cape Codders of the authors' imagination drop their masks and their guards. It's a fun read, a little like tracing the shoreline of a not-quite-familiar coast." —*Boston Globe*